W9-CDY-761

Damn! Why him? Why now? **Deme thought as he headed straight for her.**

A familiar heat flashed over her, filling her chest and crawling up her neck into her cheeks. Worse still, the heat raged south into her belly and lower, sending searing liquid flames into places that hadn't been lit in a long time. Not since the last time she'd seen him.

As his boots ate the distance, a slight smile tipped the corners of his lips, as though he knew the secret and he was going to enjoy every bit of it.

When he stopped in front of her chair, he held out a hand.

Deme stared at it a moment, her mind refusing to engage, her voice choked in her throat. Without even thinking through it, she laid her hand in his.

Instead of shaking it, he yanked her to her feet and into his arms.

Books by Elle James

Harlequin Nocturne

Harlequin Intrigue

ELLE JAMES

A Golden Heart Award winner for Best Paranormal Romance in 2004, Elle James started writing when her sister issued a Y2K challenge to write a romance novel. She has managed a full-time job and raised three wonderful children, and she and her husband even tried their hands at ranching exotic birds (ostriches, emus and rheas) in the Texas Hill Country. Ask her, and she'll tell you what it's like to go toe-to-toe with an angry 350-pound bird! After leaving her successful career in information technology management, Elle is now pursuing her writing full-time. Elle loves to hear from fans. You can contact her at ellejames@earthlink.net or visit her website at www.ellejames.com.

THE WITCH'S INITIATION

ELLE JAMES

HARLEQUIN®

entertain, enrich, inspire™

If you purchased this book without a cover you should be aware
that this book is stolen property. It was reported as "unsold and
destroyed" to the publisher, and neither the author nor the
publisher has received any payment for this "stripped book."

Recycling programs
for this product may
not exist in your area.

ISBN-13: 978-0-373-88557-2

THE WITCH'S INITIATION

Copyright © 2012 by Mary Jernigan

All rights reserved. Except for use in any review, the reproduction or
utilization of this work in whole or in part in any form by any electronic,
mechanical or other means, now known or hereafter invented, including
xerography, photocopying and recording, or in any information storage
or retrieval system, is forbidden without the written permission of the
publisher, Harlequin Enterprises Limited, 225 Duncan Mill Road,
Don Mills, Ontario M3B 3K9, Canada.

This is a work of fiction. Names, characters, places and incidents are
either the product of the author's imagination or are used fictitiously,
and any resemblance to actual persons, living or dead, business
establishments, events or locales is entirely coincidental.

This edition published by arrangement with Harlequin Books S.A.

For questions and comments about the quality of this book
please contact us at CustomerService@Harlequin.com.

® and TM are trademarks of Harlequin Enterprises Limited or its
corporate affiliates. Trademarks indicated with ® are registered in the
United States Patent and Trademark Office, the Canadian Trade Marks
Office and in other countries.

www.Harlequin.com

Printed in U.S.A.

Dear Reader,

Five ordinary witches are drawn into an extraordinary struggle when they converge on a small college campus in the heart of old Chicago. The youngest sister has disappeared during her sorority initiation and it's up to the others to find her.

This story gave me chills as I wrote it, knowing my youngest was headed off to college. When she said she wanted to join a sorority, I bit my lip and gnashed my teeth, wanting to tell her no. After the wicked things my characters experienced in the book—even knowing everything I wrote was fictitious—it made me wonder what my daughter's initiation would be like. Would she find herself in a group of desperately vain girls? Or would she find a home with sisters to cheer her on and come to her rescue when the chips were down?

Luckily my little girl found a group of sisters who are sharing her joys and triumphs, and helping her through her troubles.

Join the Chattox sisters as they fight against evil, their own insecurities and their malfunctioning talents to save their sister from the lord of the underworld.

To find out more about my writing, visit my website at www.ellejames.com.

Elle James

To my sister, who is my greatest cheerleader, who always has my back and who challenged me to take the journey on this exciting road to publication. Sisters rule!

Chapter 1

Movement in the shadows caught her attention.

Aurai Chattox strained to see what lurked in the dark. It wasn't something or someone hiding, but wispy shapes growing and creeping steadily closer to the circle of girls gathered around the candles. Had someone lit a smoke bomb? Were there girls or guys hiding among the rosebushes producing the special effects for this weird show?

When she sniffed, all she smelled was the scent of pine and roses and something she couldn't quite define. A pungent, decayed smell, almost imperceptible, buried beneath that of the more powerful aromas of the roses and natural vegetation.

As the dark, shadowy tendrils drifted closer, goose bumps rose on Aurai's skin. She fingered the pentagram at her neck and closed her eyes, drawing on the forces within, the strength of her sisters, the knowledge of the light and her own inner connection with the air, the wind and atmospheric conditions.

She'd made a promise to herself not to use her craft. She wanted to stand on her own as a mortal, not a witch. But something stirred deep inside—call it premonition, call it a portent of evil. If she gave it a nudge, perhaps it would go away.

Aurai lifted her hands by her sides, just enough to stir the air around her. Just a little, not enough to scare the other sorority initiates standing in the circle, their eyes wide, bodies trembling. But maybe enough to dispel the shadowy mist creeping in around them.

A light breeze blew in from the west.

When the West wind blows o'er thee, departed spirits restless be.

A tremor shook Aurai from neck to knees as the breeze kicked up, lifting the tendrils of her hair around her face. Softly, at first, tickling her skin with the strands like the gentle touch of a lover's hand. The stroke was deceptively soothing, and Aurai opened her eyes. Her hood slipped backward, exposing her head to the night air.

Wind was her friend, her lover, her power, the one force within that always gave her comfort and foretold of change to come. Until now.

The gentle breeze intensified, mixing with the inky shadows to lift her hair away from her scalp, slapping it against her face. White-blond locks acted as whips stinging her open eyes.

She squinted against the onslaught and raised her hands to block the battering strands.

Tall pines, which a moment before had stood stately and stoic at the four corners of the garden, swayed like

erotic lovers in the throes of passion, twisting and undulating like naked bodies.

Something was terribly wrong.

Her gift of wind should have been a gentle influence to cleanse the air of the encroaching black shadows around the circle of pledges. Instead, it became a
force unto itself, gaining in power and magnitude until
the girls fought to remain standing.

Her roommate, Rachel, dropped to her knees, blocking her face against flying debris. "What's happening?"

"I don't know," Aurai called out. Branches broke
from the trees and pummeled the small gathering of
females, drawing blood, scraping and bruising delicate skin.

Thorny rose stems tore at her legs and battered her
face and neck. Aurai closed her eyes again, feeling for
the ornate pentagram at her neck. The solid piece of silver given to her by her mother. Each of her sisters had a
matching pendant, blessed with a protection spell. She
called on the spell now.

Unwanted spirits I call thee
I call thee into the light
Guardian spirits I call thee
I call thee to the fight

The spell had no effect on the wind raging around
her. The black, inky shadows swept in, twisting her
cape around her body until she couldn't move.

"Aurai!" Rachel reached out to her. "Aurai!"

Aurai tried to lift her hand to capture Rachel's, but
both arms were trapped at her sides, her cape plastered
to her limbs and body like a mummy's death shroud.

Her feet left the ground and her body twirled
through the air, faster and faster, caught in a funnel of

leaves, rose petals, thorny branches and black, shadowy fingers.

For a moment, Aurai thought she saw the face of a man in the swirling, black wind. The face transformed into a hideous creature with two heads, one with the teeth of a raging lion. Both heads had the soulless, black gaping eyes of a demon.

As the force lifted her above the girls' heads, she gripped her pentagram and cried out, "Sisters, come to me!"

The world spun in a vacuum, lifting her higher still. Then the bottom dropped out of the dark cloud, the earth opened and the wind sucked her down, into a black abyss deep below the surface of the mossy garden soil.

Chapter 2

Sisters, come to me!

Deme Chattox's hands shook as she held the paper cup of green tea, letting the warmth permeate her skin. She'd been chilled since arriving in Chicago. Having left her cushy private investigative business in the balmy breezes of St. Croix and flying overnight to get here, she hadn't had a chance to acclimate. Hell, she hadn't had a chance to breathe.

A nit in the scheme of things, considering her baby sister was missing. Deme could stand to be a little cold. She could only guess at the horrors Aurai faced. For her sister to reach out in the middle of the night and across great distances with enough force to knock Deme out of her bed, she had to be in serious trouble.

She downed the last of the tea and crushed the cup between her fingers. Deme and her sisters would find her if it was the last thing they did. She just hoped they found her before anything really bad happened to the youngest sister of the five of them. For now, her heart told her that her little sister was still alive.

Now where the hell was that detective?

She glanced around the student commons, searching every face for the one that looked most like an undercover cop. Her sister Brigid had given the detective a description of Deme, but she didn't have a name or description of him, and he was already ten minutes late.

The girls at the table next to her leaned close, their expressions nervous. "Did they find her yet?" one asked.

Deme blocked out the extraneous noises of the large cafeteria-style room in order to hear every word spoken by the college girls. That's why she'd come to this campus as a nontraditional student. Not because she wanted to improve her lot in life through a college degree. She already had a BS, an MS and a private investigator license. She'd enrolled as one of the students only to get inside and learn the truth about her sister's disappearance.

"No, they haven't found her," a blonde responded, her blue gaze darting around the nearby tables, briefly pausing on Deme.

Deme's attention remained on the entrance as she used her peripheral vision to study the girls beside her.

The blonde's glance moved on. "I bet the Gamma Omegas know what happened to her. Hell, they probably kidnapped her as part of the hazing."

A brunette snorted. "I don't think any of them are smart enough to get away with it."

The group of six giggled, their fingers pressed to their lips, their glances taking in the room.

The blonde sipped from her soda before asking, "Did the police interview you yesterday?"

"No," the brunette answered. "What about you?"

"No. They seem to be concentrating on the staff and the sorority. I hear the G.O.s were performing their initiation ceremony in the garden when the girl disappeared. I mean, like really, how can you lose a fully grown college student in a garden? That's just random, if you ask me."

Deme wondered the same, and then her attention was distracted by a gray-haired man stepping through the glass entrance doors. He could be a college professor… or maybe an undercover detective.

With the patience of a Yorkshire terrier dying to be unleashed, Deme tapped her plastic spoon on the laminate tabletop. The man stopped at the coffee urn, filled a cup, paid and weaved his way through the tables. He didn't stop until he came to a table in the far corner by the floor-to-ceiling windows overlooking a garden. He never once looked her way.

Damn. Either he wasn't her detective or he was playing hard to get. A man like that would fit right in. No one would ever suspect a guy who looked the image of a college professor of being an undercover cop.

For several long moments, Deme stared at the man by the window. She cleared her mind and focused on him, trying to read into his thoughts. Her sister Selene was much better at reading minds than she was. It wasn't Deme's talent. Give her dirt and plants, and she could whip up a tempting spell with her knack for all things relating to the goddess of earth. Reading minds? Nah. Not her bailiwick. Still, who was he and what was he doing here? Did he have anything to do with her sister?

The man stopped sipping his coffee, a frown pressing his silvery-gray brows together. Was he feeling her probe?

Excited that maybe for once her mind probing might work, Deme concentrated harder. *Who are you? Did you take my sister? Who are you?*

A thin, bookish, young man carrying a tray with coffee and a Danish passed by, stopped and spoke to the professor. At first it all looked like any student stopping to say a word to his instructor. Until the gray-haired man lurched to his feet and shoved the younger man's tray into his chest, toppling the coffee cup. The boy yelled and dropped the tray, pulling his sweater away from his chest, cursing as scalding liquid burned his skin.

The older man hurried from the room, pushing people out of his way as he went.

Deme half stood, torn between helping the guy with the soaked sweater and chasing after the man who'd blown a gasket. A student commons worker beat her to the younger man with a handful of napkins. Meanwhile, the gray-haired gentleman had already left.

She sank into her chair and stared through the glass doors at the back of the retreating professor. What the hell was that all about?

The young man walked by her table talking to the employee, his brow wrinkled in a frown. "I don't know what set him off. All I said was 'How's it going?' Then he yelled, 'No, I didn't, and none of your effing business' and slammed my tray into me." He lifted his sweater away from his skin and flapped it. "That coffee was hot."

"Wonder what came over Professor Dane. He's never blown up like that before."

"It's like he was possessed or something. Did you see his face? Even his eyes didn't look right."

They moved out of range and Deme sat back in her seat. Was the gray-haired Professor Dane feeling the pressure of a missing student? Was he responsible for Aurai's disappearance? Had Deme's probing pushed him over the edge?

She'd never been successful at probing before, so why should it work now? And why in such a way as to cause a violent reaction?

Her chest tightened. Not known for her patience, Deme could feel the blood boiling inside her. She wanted to follow the professor and shake the truth out of him. If Brigid hadn't insisted on this detective, who came highly recommended by the Chicago police as the best undercover operative on the force, Deme wouldn't have waited ten minutes past their scheduled time for him. She could have conducted her own search and interviews. She had shoved her chair back and leaned forward to stand when the glass doors opened again.

Deme sat back in her chair, her mouth falling open. *No way.*

He strode in as if he owned the place. Every female gaze riveted on his incredibly broad shoulders encased in a black leather jacket. Black jeans caressed his thick, muscled thighs and tight ass, moving with him like a second skin.

His black hair hung to his shoulders in loose waves, and he carried a helmet in one hand. Pausing for a moment, he removed sunglasses and stared around the room.

Deme held her breath. When rich, brown eyes collided with hers, her heart skipped several beats then made up for the loss by hammering a staccato against her ribs. She'd never reacted to a man so instantly or with such impact. For a moment she couldn't breathe, and then every nerve ending lit up like the Fourth of July.

No way.

No way this biker bad boy could play an undercover role at a school. The Chicago police might as well have hung a red flag on him, announcing him as the superhero who would magically reveal the location of their missing sister by waving his incredible magnetism around a room full of women.

He set out across the floor headed straight for her.

A familiar heat flashed over her, filling her chest and crawling up her neck into her cheeks. Worse still, the heat raged south into her belly and lower, sending searing liquid flames into places that hadn't been lit in a long time. Not since the last time she'd seen him.

Damn! Why him? Why now?

As his boots ate the distance, a slight smile tipped the corner of his lips, as though he knew the secret and he was going to enjoy every bit of it.

When he stopped in front of her chair, he held out a hand.

Deme stared at it a moment, her mind refusing to engage, her voice completely choked in her throat. She'd never been this off balance in the presence of a man, no matter how good-looking, except this one. The intensity consumed her. Without even thinking it through, she dropped the mutilated cup on the table and laid her hand in his.

Instead of shaking it, he yanked her to her feet and into his arms.

As her chest crashed into his, shock and the whoosh of air escaping her lungs kept her from crying out. Her lips parted in a gasp just in time for his to descend and claim them.

One hand cupped her ass and pulled her pelvis against the natural bulge behind his zipper. The other circled her neck and threaded through her long, auburn hair.

Firm, sensuous lips plundered her startled ones, his tongue delving deep, pushing past her teeth to taste her and drink his fill.

Where their bodies touched, her skin was on fire. Deme squirmed, constrained by the clothing she wore, longing for her naked skin to melt into his.

Long, loud sighs from the young girls at the table beside her brought Deme out of the trance the man's sheer allure had thrown her into. She pulled back, fighting to mask the shock in her eyes. How could she have fallen into his arms—his kiss—without so much as a mew of protest? What had come over her? She never acted so mindlessly. She'd fallen for this macho bullshit before, and what had it bought her?

Heartburn and heartache.

The blue-eyed blonde coed sighed again. "I wish someone would kiss me like that."

"Hi, sweetheart." The man caressed the back of Deme's neck again before he dragged his fingers over her shoulder and downward to capture her hand in his.

Deme tried to pull free, struggling to come up with words to voice her anger at his flagrant attack on her senses. Anger at herself for responding so willingly. By the goddess, she was here to save her sister, not to crawl into a man's skin.

"Want to find a quieter spot?" His look was like liquid chocolate, melting into her pores. With a flick of his eyes, he indicated the girls drooling at the table next to them. More sighs rose from the hormonal young ladies.

"The table by the window." Deme cringed. Was that her voice, that reedy squeak?

Without releasing her hand, he led her to the table at the far corner of the student commons with a lovely view of a rose garden. A table near to where the professor had exploded in a fit of rage.

As she walked like a docile dog behind him, Deme let the anger build. Righteous anger beat mindless lust any day of the week. She'd been in one too many relationships where a man had tried to take charge of her life. Okay, so only one doomed relationship—the relationship she'd had with this man. Besides, her purpose for being at Colyer-Fenton was to find her missing sister, not get all weak in the knees over a cop too sexy to blend in.

With his empty hand, he pulled out a seat and dragged her into it.

Deme sat down hard, her lips drawn into a tight line.

He leaned over her, pressing his lips to her ear. "Try to look a little less like you swallowed a lemon." Then he slid his mouth down her jawline and claimed hers in a brief kiss.

Rendered speechless yet again, Deme sat with her mouth open and nothing coming out. *How'd he do that*?

He pulled out a chair, flipped it around and straddled it like a Harley, his brows hiked into the hair dangling like temptation over his forehead. "Deme Chattox. You never did tell me what Deme means. We can talk about that later. We have business to discuss." He lifted one of her hands and threaded his fingers through hers.

With her lips still tingling from his kiss and the warmth of his fingers on hers stirring up those old feelings of lust all over again, Deme finally pulled herself together. Yanking her hand free, she hid it in her lap.

She leaned forward, her head turned away from the others in the union still watching them. "Is this a joke?" She stared around the room, hoping she'd find some sadistic huckster ready to spring out and tell her she'd been punked. When no one did, she sat on her hands to keep them from shaking in front of him…Cal Black, her former fiancé, lover and her own personal nemesis. "How the hell did you end up on this case?"

He smiled, the act an unaffected thing of beauty. His dark chocolate eyes twinkled and his full, kissable lips stretched over straight, white teeth, a stark contrast to his coal-black hair. She'd fallen for that look once before. "You're my cover, sweetheart." He ran his fingers down her cheek and touched a finger to her swollen lips. "To you, I'm the detective the Chicago police assigned to this case. But to everyone else, I'm your boyfriend until we find your sister."

Cal almost laughed out loud as Deme Chattox's mouth opened then closed before she gathered enough steam to blast him. He had his cover as a maintenance man nailed shut, having spent the past half hour with the Human Resources Department of the small college, charming everyone from the secretary to the woman who ultimately hired him. She'd explained it was only a temporary position until they could find another, more permanent replacement for their previous maintenance man.

He'd asked what happened to the man, but no one knew. He didn't show up for work three weeks ago and hadn't been back. No call, no resignation. Just disappeared. Unfortunately, he didn't have a worried family calling to report him missing.

Cal didn't like that. That made two disappearances in the past three weeks from the same campus. He didn't believe in coincidence and placed a call to Martin Warner, the detective in charge of the case back at headquarters. Was the missing maintenance man responsible for Aurai Chattox's disappearance? If not, was the same perp responsible for both the missing persons?

Now, sitting across the table from Deme Chattox, he drank his fill of the woman who'd managed to turn his world upside down in just the four short weeks they'd known each other. He hadn't even realized she had sisters. She'd never told him. Apparently Deme was the oldest of the Chattox sisters. He wondered if Aurai was anywhere near as beautiful. It was hard to tell from the photograph he'd been given.

Deme's long, auburn hair fell in loose waves around her shoulders and all the way down to her waist. A man could get lost in all that glorious hair. Her deep green eyes sparkled in the fluorescent lights. Lights that normally made everyone else look ill made her pale skin seem only more ethereal. Beautiful women were natural targets for demented kidnappers and killers. "You don't look anything like your sister, do you?"

"Not even close." She pushed her hair behind her ear and sat up straighter. "I'm the redheaded Amazon of the family. Aurai's the pale blonde, petite sister." Her brows furrowed. "Now what's this about being my boyfriend? I don't need a boyfriend."

His lips pressed together in a thin line. "Maybe not to you and me, but for everyone else on campus we need to be convincing." He tipped his head up. "Come here and give me a kiss."

Deme shook her head. "I can't work with you. I work alone." She leaned over the table toward him, the swell of her breasts visible above the figure-hugging, low-cut sweater she wore.

As if a hand had reached out and cranked up the thermostat, the air in the room heated. Cal resisted the urge to tug at his black T-shirt or shrug out of his jacket. As perspiration eased from his skin and his pants tightened uncomfortably, he frowned. He was *not* getting bothered by this woman with enough attitude to overwhelm most men, no matter how sexy she was in that skin-tight sweater.

He made it a strict habit to separate business from pleasure. No matter how pleasurable he had found her in the past. Despite the warnings going off in his head to refuse the assignment and run the other direction, Cal couldn't stop his body's reaction to her nearness. Certain parts refused to forget what it felt like to lie naked against her, to bury himself deep inside her warmth. "I need a cover so that we can talk and not raise suspicion. If you want my help finding your sister, you're stuck with me as a boyfriend."

She opened her mouth and closed it before words could spew forth. Then she leaned across the wooden tabletop and rested her hand on his, squeezing harder than typical for a lover's affectionate grip. "Understand this. I'm only tolerating you because I want to find my sister. So, don't get in my way." She tipped her head to the side and gave him a saccharine-sweet smile. "Am I clear?"

"Crystal." He turned his hand over and captured hers before she could withdraw. "I'm here to do my job. Either help me or go home. Understood, sweetheart?" His words were spoken in a deep, rich timbre, the tone soft and modulated like a caress. But the steely strength between the lines could not be missed.

Her luscious lips thinned. "Look, you're too pretty. Working undercover requires a detective who can blend in. Sorry, you don't blend. Do they have any other agents they can send?"

"No, I'm it. Besides, I'm the best." He grinned, knowing it would set her off and added another jab, "So you really think I'm pretty?"

Deme sighed and resigned herself to having biker boy as her connection to the police force. "Look, if we're stuck with each other, let's just keep in mind what we're after. We're here to find my sister."

"Naturally. Now, are you going to play nice and be my cover, or not?"

That frown was back, crinkling the bridge of her nose. "Okay, but don't get any ideas. You're not my type."

"You made that abundantly clear last time we met." With her hand still in his, he stood, bringing her to her feet. Then he tugged her hard enough to throw her off balance. The only place she could go was smack against his chest, again. "Besides, you're not my type, either." He pushed her hair behind her ear, thumbing her earlobe in a tender caress. "At least do a better job of faking that you like me."

The rigid line of Deme's spine slowly relaxed until she melted against him, her hands clutching the fabric of his shirt instead of pushing him away. One hand slid around his backside, where it found its way into the pocket of his jeans. Using a surprising amount of strength, she slammed him hard against her, his cock nudging firmly against her pelvis. At the same time, she reached up with the other hand and slipped it around the back of his neck, tangling in his hair. Steady pressure brought his mouth closer to her lips until they were only a breath away.

She leaned close to his ear. "As your girlfriend, do I make you hot?"

Did she make him hot? At the warmth of her breath in his ear, Cal's cock jerked beneath his zipper and his hands clenched around her arms. He wanted her. Wanted to plunge his tongue into her mouth. He wanted to get naked and have hot, juicy sex with her. His body remembered hers in ways that would make a virgin squirm.

Her lips dragged along his jawline until they reached his. For a moment she hovered over him, and then she pressed in for the finale, slanting her mouth over his, thrusting her tongue deep inside to slide across his. Her hips ground against his, teasing his engorged member, converting it to granite.

As quickly as it began, it ended and she stepped out of his arms and reach. Her brows rose and she smiled. "I can fake it with the best of them."

For a moment, Cal breathed in and out. The teasing look in her eyes was enough to bring Cal back to his senses and stir him up all at once. Forcing a light tone into a voice he was sure would crack, he said, "That's more like it. I'll see you tonight. Your room." With that, he left, inwardly cursing his momentary loss of control. Deme Chattox was a prop to get his job done. A prop, damn it. Anything they might have had in the past was just that…in the past. He was in charge of the inside investigation.

Once outdoors, he slipped his helmet over his head and fastened the buckle. As he slid onto the seat of his Harley, he could imagine sliding into Deme. He kicked the starter and the engine roared to life, rumbling beneath his still-hard cock. Oh, yeah, Deme Chattox was a hell of a ride. But that wasn't the point.

From the moment he'd stepped into the student commons, he'd been drawn to her. Irresistibly. He'd had no intention of making her agree to be his girlfriend in order to provide himself additional cover for his investigation. Hell, he'd half convinced himself he could do the job without her help altogether. She could go home for all he cared.

Then what the hell had come over him? The idea was for Deme to help his investigation by infiltrating the Gamma Omegas, but at this point, Cal feared her presence would only distract him, in more ways than one.

He'd better get his mind in the game instead of on the sexy redhead he'd wanted to toss across the nearest table and make love to in front of God and everybody.

Chapter 3

Deme dumped her backpack on the narrow bed tucked against the wall in the tiny dorm room, the echo of her sister's cry reverberating through her. Having met with Detective Cal Black hadn't set her mind at ease, not when her lips still burned from his kiss. If anything, her meeting with the cop had left her more shaken than she cared to admit. Her overwhelming attraction to him couldn't be natural. Not after their breakup over a year ago. Something wasn't right.

Her aversion to the man had a basis. Every time she was near Cal, she couldn't think straight, couldn't focus, couldn't even claim every thought coming from her head was her own. He infiltrated her mind, body and life in a way that left her off balance, her world in a perpetual tilt. She'd kept her relationship with Cal separate from her sisters, and her special "talents" secret from

Cal. How would he react if he'd known about her pro-pensity for magic? Would he think her a freak or crazy?

Torn between the rampant lust raging through her body and her sacred duty to protect her family, Deme avoided his questions, dodging his desire to know more about her personal life. When he'd pushed to know more, she dumped his ass and moved as far away from Chicago as possible to avoid him and his overpowering magnetism. Once bitten by the lust bug, twice hesitant to make a repeat performance.

From the start of their relationship, he'd been clear… He was dedicated to his job protecting the good citizens of Chicago. Nothing and no one would get in the way of his work. He took his responsibilities seriously. He demanded as much passion in his work. And he demanded full disclosure from the people he let into his world. Namely her.

Cal Black was exactly the kind of man Deme didn't need in her life, even if he was there to help her find Aurai.

She crossed to the one small, dingy window and set the ceramic pot containing her beloved angelica root in the meager sun, distorted by the aging glass. The plant drooped, the colors appearing dull in the dreary environment. Deme empathized with how the plant felt. She, too, needed the light to flourish and chase away the emptiness. She touched the fragile stems and they seemed to brighten and reach upward. A ghost of a smile curved Deme's lips.

"The girls are usually pretty good about obeying curfew. I'm sure you'll have no troubles keeping tabs on them." Dr. Diane Masterson entered the room behind her and gave the space an appraising glance. "It's not much, but I hope you'll be comfortable."

"Thank you." Deme faced the college president. "I'm sure I will."

"I'm so glad you chose our school to complete your degree. We needed an older student as a resident assistant. If nothing else, the girls will have a mentor, someone to look up to. You should have no troubles catching up with the coursework." She paused, her eyes narrowing slightly. "Miss Jones, tell me again why it was you decided on Colyer-Fenton College and to start three weeks into the semester."

"I was out of the country visiting a sick relative. I chose Colyer-Fenton because the campus suits me. Quaint and quiet."

"Oh, yes, yes, of course. And that's what we are, quaint and quiet." Dr. Masterson glanced back over her shoulder as if to search the hallway for anyone who could refute her lie.

Deme found it odd that the college president personally escorted her to her room instead of one of the administrative employees in charge of housing.

"If you need anything, just ask one of the girls. They can show you where things are. I'd better go. I have a meeting with my staff in five minutes." The older woman backed out of the room, closing the door behind her.

A meeting, ha! The Chicago police detective in charge of finding Aurai had interviews with the staff scheduled throughout the afternoon. Her Harley-riding sister, Brigid, had met the officer in charge of the case and he'd informed her of the steps they were taking to find their sister, including a thorough interrogation of each campus employee and a number of the over six thousand students.

As far as Deme was concerned, it wasn't enough.

She stared around the stark confines of the room deemed the resident assistant's quarters for the Gamma Omega sorority dorm. She'd had to pull some major strings to land in this one. But this is where she needed to be in order to discover the whereabouts of her youngest sister.

Deme unlocked the window and pushed it upward. A cool blast of fall air blew in, stirring the stale air. She had the best view of all the rooms in the dorm. Maybe it was a perk for being R.A. Located on the shortest side of the building, the room overlooked a fenced courtyard garden. The majority of the dorm rooms stretched out and away from the courtyard.

Deme inhaled the scent of the pines growing close to her window and the sweet fragrance of roses. Ivy clung to the brick walls just below her window, the leafy green vines filling Deme with a sense of calm. The roses in the garden below were in the full bloom of late summer, early fall. Before long, frost would claim the plants and lay them dormant for the chilly winter months.

They would find Aurai before then. She was their sister, the fifth point of the pentagram. They were a unit. Together they were as one. Deme's fingers wrapped around the ornate silver pentagram hanging by a delicate silver chain at her throat. They couldn't fail.

Water dripped from the faucet in the single sink against the wall. Deme moved across the room and twisted the handle to make it quit, but no amount of tightening the handle stopped the slow, steady dripping. She'd have to get maintenance to fix it or she'd be up all night counting each drop.

A light knock at the door echoed against the plain white walls. Before Deme could call out for the person to come in, the familiar willowy, sandy blonde with bright sea-green eyes slipped through the door.

Deme hurriedly closed the gap between them and hugged her sister tightly against her chest. "Oh, Gina. I can't believe this is happening."

Aegina Chattox squeezed her around her middle and then pushed her far enough away to look her in the eye. "Me, either. I'm just glad you and I got in without anyone knowing who we really are."

"Did you have any troubles selling yourself as the aquarium cleaner?"

"None whatsoever. And the aquariums are in atrocious condition in the central library. I should have several days' work on my hands and lots of opportunities to snoop around."

"Let's hope it doesn't take long to find Aurai."

Gina hugged her again. "I'm glad you're home."

Deme nodded. "Me, too."

Without so much as a knock, the door burst open and another one of her sisters entered. Selene, wearing a flowing white skirt, with her long, rich, chocolate-brown hair tied up in a bright colored scarf, entered, stepping into Deme's arms. Tears trembled on her thick lashes, blurring her deep brown eyes. "Where could she be?"

Deme fought the lump in her throat. "I don't know, but between the four of us, we will find her." She patted her second-youngest sister on her back and set her away. "What do you know so far?"

"We met with Brigid off campus and she filled us in."

Gina drifted toward the window and peered down into the garden. "Supposedly, she disappeared during a sorority hazing ceremony. None of the girls know what happened. Or at least they're not talking." She wrapped her arms around her stomach. "How could someone vanish in a crowd of people and no one see it?" She turned back, a frown marring her smooth, tanned forehead. "They know something."

Footsteps in the hallway made the three women fall silent. When the steps continued on, Deme relaxed but she spoke in quiet tones. "No one knows we're related. Brigid was the only one of us to openly meet with the detectives in charge of the investigation and the school officials as Aurai's sister. She can continue to be our contact with the external investigation. I met with the undercover detective. He'll pretend to be my boyfriend so that we can pass information."

Both Gina's and Selene's brows rose. "Boyfriend?"

"His idea, definitely not mine."

"I'm impressed already," Selene said.

Deme glared at her sisters. "Don't get any ideas."

Gina touched her sister's arm. "You can't let that last guy you dated affect every relationship, Deme. What was his name, anyway? You never did tell any of us."

"Yeah, why all the secrecy?" Selene added.

Deme shrugged. "No reason. Besides, it didn't last."

Gina slid a glance sideways at Selene. "Still evading the question."

"No kidding." Selene addressed Deme. "Well, you shouldn't let him taint your feelings for the other men in the world. There are some nice ones out there to choose from."

Deme closed her eyes and drew in a deep breath, guilt pressuring her. She really should fess up to her sisters. She'd never kept secrets from them, with the exception of her relationship with Cal.

For the first time in the year she'd been away from

him, she could actually think of him without choking up. Leaving him had been about the hardest thing she'd ever done. She couldn't begin to contemplate how she'd feel after leaving him a second time. As best she could, she would remain aloof...an overwhelming challenge in the presence of the man's alpha-male sex appeal and bad-boy biker persona. "The undercover detective's name is Cal."

"Nice, strong name. What does he look like?" Gina's eyebrows disappeared into her sandy-blond bangs.

"Does it matter?"

"Of course!" both sisters agreed as one.

"He's your typical eye candy with dark hair and dark eyes." And muscular legs and arms that could wrap around her and carry her to places she'd never been. That flash of heat she'd experienced in the cafeteria returned in force. "Not my type," she lied.

Selene's brows drew together. "Since you're not interested, perhaps I could provide his cover."

Deme held up a hand. "We've already established our so-called relationship in public. Otherwise I'd let you."

"Point made." Gina grinned. "In the meantime, loosen up, sis."

"I'm not here to find a man. I'm here to find Aurai."

Selene wrapped her arm around Deme and hugged her tight. "That dude you dated really did a number on you, didn't he?"

"Let me at him," Gina said. "Any man who makes my oldest sister a basket case for a year deserves to be infested with the fleas of a thousand camels." She pulled a pen and notebook from her hobo bag and jotted down a note to herself. "I'll come up with a potion that'll give him webbed feet."

Deme's lips twitched. "Although I like the image, you can't do that. Cursing someone is delving into dark powers."

Gina's lips twisted. "I'd only do it once. And it would be well worth the risk if it makes the man as miserable as he made you."

Deme turned away. The image of Cal with webbed feet almost brought a smile to her face. Not that her sister could conjure webbed feet. Their powers didn't work like that. But wait until her sisters saw Cal Black. They'd never give her a moment's rest with their sisterly teasing. Even the thought of the tall, dark cop made Deme's body burn. "We all have our covers established. We need to maintain our anonymity in order to gain the trust of the other girls. We want answers, and the sooner the better."

"All I know is that it's been two days. Two days too long." Selene winced and pressed fingers to the bridge of her nose.

Deme laid a hand on her shoulder. "Are you all right?"

She breathed in and out for a moment before answering. "There's a dark aura surrounding this campus. I sensed it as soon as I came through the gates. It feels like someone trying to push into my mind."

"Do you think you should let that someone in? Maybe he or she can tell you what happened."

"I tried, but so far there's like this wall blocking them."

"Them? As in more than one?" Deme asked.

Selene's fingers moved from the bridge of her nose to her temples, where she massaged the skin, her eyes squeezed shut. "I think so."

Still staring out the window, Gina asked, "Think it

would help if we get together tonight to cast a circle and call them forth?"

Deme had sensed the darkness, too, but Selene had a better connection with the metaphysical world than any of them. She'd even had conversations with the dead. On more than one occasion, her ability to sense trouble had saved their butts. When Selene perceived a disturbance in the spiritual balance, invariably she was right. It was her gift, as knowledge and connection to the earth was Deme's and Selene's was water. Brigid connected with fire, and Aurai, sweet Aurai's gift was her ability to influence and communicate with the wind and air currents.

"Let's wait and see what happens and what we can learn from the students and staff on campus," Deme said.

"Brigid said the Gamma Omegas' sorority initiation ceremony was conducted in a garden." Gina turned back to the others. "Do you suppose it was this one?"

Selene walked toward the window, her face paling as she neared the opening. When she reached the windowsill, she wavered, her body swaying. She clutched the raised window and pulled it down, pressing her forehead against the glass. "Something happened here. I can't tell exactly what, but it wasn't good."

Deme's lips tightened. "Then that's where we start our search. Gina, see if you can find any history on the college in the library. Past students, old newspaper articles, anything. Selene, you'll be a member of the faculty. Check out the other professors and staff for anything concerning Aurai's disappearance, the garden and the sorority. I'll work on the girls in the sorority."

"We need to maintain our distance in front of others." Gina looped an arm around Selene and led her away from the window. "Hanging out together will blow our cover. If there is a kidnapper lurking on campus, we can't let him know we're sisters. When we meet again, it needs to be away from campus."

Deme nodded. "Agreed. I'll get close to Aurai's roommate. I think she's in this building." Deme flipped through the roster Dr. Masterson had given her of students living in the dormitory. "There she is—Rachel Taylor. Brigid said she was one of the girls initiated into the sorority that night."

Selene gripped her arm, her clutch pinching Deme's skin. "You aren't going to try to pledge the sorority, are you?"

"I don't think it's possible." Deme loosened Selene's grip and patted her hand. "Don't worry. I can take care of myself."

"I know you can. But promise me you won't join the sorority. It's too dangerous." How she just seemed to know things was a mystery to all the sisters, but they didn't ignore her when she gave them warnings.

"I promise. Pledge week is over and they've done their initiation. New members have already been inducted. I'll be on the periphery since I'm the R.A." Deme glanced at Selene. "Are you sure you're going to be all right?"

She smiled, her dull, green eyes brightening. "With my sisters around me, I'll be fine. Speaking of which, where's Brigid now?"

"She's working with the detective on the police investigation." Gina closed the window and twisted the latch before she crossed to the others. "We'll see her around campus as they conduct their interviews. However, everyone will know she's Aurai's sister. They won't know who we are, if we're careful."

"Then come on, we need to part ways and get this investigation under way." Deme held out her hands. Gina took one and Selene the other until their hands closed the ring.

Without her other two sisters, Deme sensed how incomplete the circle was. She closed her eyes and began, her sisters joining in.

"Feel the power
Free our hearts
Find our way
Be the one
With the strength of the earth
With the rising of the wind
With the calm of the water
With the intensity of fire
With the freedom of spirit
The goddess is within us
She is power
We are her
We are one
Blessed Be."

As each word passed their lips, the air in the room grew thicker until breathing became more difficult. A funny odor filled the room, similar to the scent of decaying vegetation. A scratching sound penetrated Deme's concentration. Selene's hand squeezed hers in a death grip.

"Do you feel them?" Selene asked. "They're screaming. Can you hear them?"

Deme opened her eyes and stared around the room. The lights seemed dimmer, and the sunlight that had a moment before shone through the window had disappeared behind a cloud. The scratching sound she'd heard was English ivy rubbing against the window.

She didn't remember it being that high before. Had she missed it?

The water dripping in the sink had become a thin, steady flow. Gina dropped Selene's and Deme's hands and reached for the handle on the sink. "What's with this faucet?" She twisted the handle and nothing happened.

"I can hear them, but I can't understand what they're saying." Selene clutched her head between her hands and swayed. "They're so loud. I can't shut them out." Her hands dropped to her sides and her troubled gaze searched the room until she found the door. "I have to leave."

Deme wrapped her arm around Selene's waist. "Go. Get off campus."

"I'll go for now, but we need to meet tonight. I want to know who they are and why they're fighting to get in my head."

"This damned faucet isn't working." Gina slammed her hand against the handle.

"Leave it." Deme herded her brown-haired sister toward the door. "Selene needs to get out of here."

Gina jiggled the handle again. "Give me a second. I think I can get this thing—" The handle flew off and water gushed from where it had been, shooting in a four-foot radius around the room.

"Damn, what the hell's wrong with this place?" Gina slipped on the floor and dropped to her knees, reaching beneath the sink for the shutoff valve.

"I have to go." Selene staggered toward the door, her eyes squinting and her forehead lined with pain.

Deme opened the door and glanced out into the hallway. "You can go now. The hallway's clear." When

Selene passed her, she gave her sister's arm a squeeze. "Be careful."

As she closed the door behind Selene, Deme turned to the scratching at the window. The vines now choked out the little bit of light. A chill that had nothing to do with being wet or cold shivered across Deme's skin.

Gina turned the shutoff valve, and the geyser of water slowed to a trickle and finally stopped. She straightened, soaked to the skin, and shook some of the water from her arms. "What just happened?"

"I don't know, but you'd better go before the Gamma Omega girls come looking for all the commotion." Deme checked the hallway and held the door for her sister. "See you tonight. Be safe."

Once her sisters were gone, Deme closed the door and leaned her back against it, staring at the wreck of her room.

She wasn't Selene, but she'd felt it, too. As they'd stood in the circle, the air in the room changed as if drawing on their power.

Standing in a puddle of water, the lights dim and the window blocked by ivy, Deme knew with certainty they were dealing with more than just a kidnapper. Aurai was in a lot more trouble than they'd originally thought.

Chapter 4

After Cal left campus, he returned to the Chicago Police Special Investigations Division. Lead investigator Lieutenant Martin Warner had requested his presence. Cal hoped he'd fill him in on the rest of the details he'd left out in the hurried initial briefing that morning.

Cal passed the front desk, waving at the sergeant who manned the telephone. He wove his way through the office cubicles to the rear of the building, where the Special Investigations Team had set up a war room.

Having been on the team all of four hours and twenty-seven minutes, Cal didn't know anyone but the lieutenant who'd briefed him earlier that morning.

When Cal entered the war room, Marty had his back to the door. He stood with his feet braced wide and his chin resting in his hand, staring at a white board with a thick black horizontal line stretched across the surface. Taped in one corner was a preprinted map of the

Colyer-Fenton College campus. Beside the lieutenant, a woman dressed in black leather with long, ink-black hair hanging down to her waist leaned against the edge of the table, her arms crossed over her chest. "Has to be connected," she said, her voice husky, yet smooth, like milk chocolate-covered gravel.

Marty, as he'd asked Cal to call him, nodded. "Every one of the incidents occurred either on campus or were performed by people who are related to Colyer-Fenton."

Cal cleared his throat.

Marty spun and faced him. The woman beside him turned more slowly. When she saw who was standing there, her lips curled up on the sides in a devilish smile. "Ah, our detective has arrived."

Cal's eyes narrowed. He couldn't remember meeting this woman, but there was something familiar about her. "I'm sorry, I haven't had the pleasure." He stuck out his hand. "Cal Black."

When she took his hand, an odd burst of heat streamed from her hand to his, shooting like an adrenaline burst up his arm and into his chest.

He pulled his hand back quicker than normal, his palm still tingling. "And you are?"

"Brigid." Her smile grew wider.

Marty clapped Brigid on the back. "Brigid is one of the team."

"How long have you been on the force?"

"Counting today?" She checked her watch. "Approximately four hours."

Cal's gaze shot from her to Marty.

Marty sighed. "It's a long story, but suffice it to say, she's been working with the Chicago Police Department for almost a year and demonstrated her...uh...expertise.

Mostly with arson investigations, but we have reason to believe she could be of assistance on this team."

Cal frowned. "Does she understand the risks of working on the Chicago police force?"

Brigid crossed her arms over her chest, her black leather vest creaking, the black nail polish on her fingertips shining. "I can take care of myself, if that's what you're asking."

"Do you have a license to carry a weapon?"

"No."

"Do you even know how to shoot?"

"No." She glanced at Marty.

"She's not a trained police officer, Cal." Marty grinned. "But she has talents that could come in handy on this case and others we've seen like it."

Not until she stared up at him, forcing him to look directly into her eyes, did he realize how intensely blue hers were.

Cal nodded, not entirely sold on Brigid's so-called talents, but willing to give the lieutenant the benefit of the doubt. "Maybe you can explain to me what exactly the Special Investigations Team does?"

"Yeah." Brigid sat on the conference table and crossed her legs Indian fashion. "Tell him what we're up against."

"That's just it." Marty shook his head. "We don't know what we're up against. We've taken a select few of Chicago's finest from the police force and a couple detectives like you and a few trusted civilians we've worked with in the past…"

Brigid shot a frown at the lieutenant.

The man's lips twisted. "Okay, one trusted civilian… to form this team."

Brigid's frown smoothed.

The lieutenant stared hard into Cal's eyes. "We get all the cases no one knows what to do with, the ones that don't make sense, and we try to make sense out of them."

Brigid snorted in a very unladylike manner, yet in keeping with the black leather, bad-ass persona she'd adopted. "What the lieutenant is trying to say, but isn't quite nailing, is that we will be investigating the cases involving paranormal activities. Incidents that defy the norm. The quirky, weird, bizarre, uncanny and down-right strange occurrences that usually get shoved under the radar because they make people feel too uncomfortable to address."

"What are you talking about? I thought I was investigating the disappearance of a girl." Cal reminded himself this girl wasn't just any girl. She was his ex-girlfriend's sister.

"And you are," Marty assured him. "First and foremost, we want to retrieve the missing girl and reunite her with her family." The lieutenant stared over at Brigid. "While I have both of you here alone, I need to know something."

"Know what?" Cal demanded.

"I need to know that your connections with the victim's family members will not get in your way of performing a thorough investigation."

"What connection?" Cal's heart beat faster, but he played dumb to the lieutenant's question. What did Marty know about his relationship with Deme Chattox?

The lieutenant shook his head. "We conduct a thorough investigation of all our team members, security check, background check down to what vet you take your dog to."

"I don't have a dog," Cal stated flatly.

"Well, we knew you had a thing going with Deme Chattox, the victim's oldest sister."

Brigid's eyes narrowed. "Were you doing my sister? Tsk, tsk. And here I thought we'd have a shot at making things happen."

"Sister?" Cal glanced from Brigid back to Marty. "What do you mean, *sister*?"

"Our missing girl, Aurai Chattox, has four sisters."

Brigid gave him a little wave with the tips of her fingers. "Brigid Chattox, Deme's younger sister. She didn't tell you about us, did she?" She tapped her chin with her fingertip. "I wonder why."

Cal wondered, too. Seems like when you're sleeping with someone, they'd tell you all their secrets. Family shouldn't be a secret. But not Deme. From the get-go, their passion singed any other thoughts from his head. When he finally got around to asking, she'd gone. Completely out of his life. There one day, gone the next.

"One of the reasons I brought you in on this case was because I knew you had dealings with Deme Chattox and probably knew a little about her and her family. When Brigid told me what the Chattox sisters had planned, I knew I needed one of Chicago's best detectives on the inside."

Brigid shook her head, her lips twisting. "He didn't trust us to do it on our own."

"Damn it, Brigid!" Marty pounded his fist on the conference table so hard, even the ubercalm Brigid bounced, her eyes widening.

Marty's lips pressed into a thin line, his face beet-red and getting redder by the second. "We've already lost one young woman to whoever or whatever kidnapped her. I don't want to lose four more."

Brigid uncurled her legs and pushed off the table, standing tall. "She's not gone for good. We just can't find her." Her jaw tightened. "But we will, I have no doubt. I only told you because I wasn't going to refuse a little help."

"And rightfully so. A missing girl on a campus is not something to take lightly. The police need to be just as involved in returning the girl to her family as bringing the perpetrator to justice." He aimed the remarks at Brigid, then he turned to face Cal. "Back to my original question. Is your relationship with Deme Chattox going to cause you any difficulties?"

"I don't have a problem keeping on track." Heat rose in Cal's belly as he recalled the feeling of Deme's lips on his. She could be a major distraction, but he refused to let her. Their "thing" had ended a year ago.

Brigid's hand brushed his, ever so lightly and briefly, the heat burning a path across his nerve endings. "Yeah, and you didn't want to kiss her, but you did," she whispered to him, low enough only he could hear.

"Huh?" Cal jerked away from the woman. How'd she know?

Brigid's lips twitched. "You heard me. Play nice with my sister. She had a nasty time of it with a man almost a year ago and hasn't dated since. If I'd known who it was, I might have been tempted to inflict some bodily harm on him."

Cal almost laughed out loud. The petite woman with the long, black hair didn't look as if she could harm a fly, much less a full-grown man. Besides, she had her facts all wrong.

A year ago placed Deme with him. He had to be the man Brigid was talking about. But Deme hadn't had a nasty time of it. More like she'd given *him* a nasty time. As soon as he'd asked her to marry him, she'd left. Talk about cold feet.

It wasn't as if he'd meant it—he'd blurted it out immediately following the most mind-blowing sex he'd ever had. Hell, they'd spent every night for a month in his bed, in his apartment. It must have seemed like a natural progression for her to marry him and move in permanently.

He'd waited two days, thinking maybe she'd been thrown off balance by his proposal.

Those two days had been the longest he'd ever experienced. When he'd gone by her apartment in downtown Chicago, she'd moved out. Nothing left but an empty roll of box tape.

Apparently Deme hadn't told her sisters any more about him than she had told him about them. Why all the secrecy? If she didn't want to be a part of his life, all she had to do was say so. Moving away had been extreme.

When Marty had told him about Deme's involvement in the case, his first instinct was to walk away. Getting answers to why she left was one of the reasons he'd agreed.

In the back of his mind, the need for a little payback had spurred him into action. Thus his kiss in the student commons. And if he wasn't mistaken, Deme Chattox was not immune to him…unfortunately, not any more than he was immune to her.

"Very well, then." Marty turned toward the white board hanging on the wall. "Let me fill you in on what's been happening on or around campus. Maybe you'll understand why the Special Investigations Team is working this case."

Brigid shot a narrow-eyed glance at Cal before turning her attention to the board as if to say, *I'm watching you.*

Cal could have laughed out loud, but the lieutenant was talking.

He pointed to a time line on the board with a tick mark near the start of the line. "Two weeks ago, a male student attacked a female student while she was walking through the campus. She'd never talked to him, he'd never expressed any interest in her. Up until the attack, he'd been a model student, making good grades, working toward a prelaw undergrad degree. Clean record, no criminal history. Nothing. Out of the blue, he attacks a girl."

"So? Doesn't it happen every day?"

Marty nodded. "You'd think. But when questioned, he broke down in tears claiming it was as if he had no control over his actions. One minute he was worried about his economics test, the next he'd jumped a girl and practically raped her before a member of the faculty came along and pulled him off."

"Again…so?" Cal had seen rapists claim temporary insanity too many times to believe. If a man could rape a woman, he had to have something wrong with him and needed to be taken off the streets.

"At first, it looked like a cut-and-dried case of attempted rape…but then it happened again." Marty shot a glance over his shoulder at Cal and Brigid before he pointed at the second hash mark. "Two days after the first incident, another boy attempted rape."

"Same one?"

"No, a different boy. Same thing. He was a model student, premed degree. On his way to the library when he lost it and tried to rape a girl."

"Power of suggestion?" Cal offered.

"You mean because news got around the other boy wanted to get in on the action?" Marty shook his head. "That's what I thought at first. The university didn't let the information out about the previous attempted rape for fear the parents would yank their kids midsemester. That and we had their rapist."

"Is there any connection between the two guys? Are they in the same fraternity? Do they live in the same dorm? Involved in a hazing event or something?" Cal asked.

Marty shook his head. "We checked into all that. Again, one of the students is prelaw, the other premed. Neither has joined a frat house. One lives on campus and the other in an apartment nearby. As far as both are concerned, they didn't even know each other existed until these events occurred."

"Where did the attempted rapes happen?" Brigid stared at the campus map, her gaze so intense her blue eyes appeared steel-gray.

Sweat popped out on Cal's forehead. "Is it me, or is it getting hot in here?"

The lieutenant tugged at the tie around his neck, loosening it, a bead of perspiration sliding down the side of his head. "It's getting hot." He stared across at Brigid. "Do you mind?"

She flushed, a weak smile crossing her lips. "Sorry." Then her smile disappeared, she clasped the medallion hanging around her neck and closed her eyes.

Within a few seconds, the room temperature dropped enough that Cal could tell a marked difference. He looked around for who might have adjusted the room's temperature. When he located the thermostat, nobody stood near it. The only occupants of the room were the three of them.

His gaze returned to Brigid, who clutched at the medallion, her eyes blinking open. She met his gaze with quirked lips and raised eyebrows.

"The Chattox girl disappeared here." Marty poked the time line, smearing the black hash mark identified with a date and the letters *AC* for Aurai Chattox.

Cal lifted the dry erase marker and added a dark slash before all the hash marks three weeks prior to the girl's disappearance.

The lieutenant's brow rose. "What's that for?"

"One missing maintenance man. I spoke with HR this morning. I'm their new maintenance man as of today. The prior guy never showed up for work three weeks ago. Since he had only been on the job for a couple of months, they assumed he'd just quit. They didn't have any emergency numbers to contact next of kin, and he didn't return their calls."

Marty's brows pulled together into a V. "And they didn't file a missing persons report?"

"No family to miss him." Cal shrugged. "Think he might be our kidnapper?"

Brigid shook her head, her gaze fixed on the board though she appeared lost in thought. "I don't think so, but we should add him to our list of people to find."

"Two other incidents happened off campus involving a professor and a student," Marty continued. "Both separate, but somewhat the same. A female student who'd been part of the sorority Aurai was pledging tried to commit suicide by slashing her wrists," Marty said.

Cal sucked in a breath. "How is she?"

"She'll live, but she's in the hospital, recovering from blood loss and she's under psychiatric observation."

"The professor?"

"Ran her car into the Chicago River."

"Accident?"

"No, she'd left a suicide note at her apartment. Her sister found it."

"And her prognosis?"

"Dead." Marty pointed at the time line where two more marks broke the line, one before Aurai's disappearance, one after. "Her car was found this morning by a bicyclist."

Marty faced Cal. "Your job is to work the school staff, ask questions, get answers. Your connection to the sorority will be Deme Chattox. I expect you to pass information to her and gather it from her on a regular basis. Brigid will be working with the rest of the team on the outside of campus, questioning other victims' families and acquaintances."

"When will I meet the other team members?" Cal asked.

Marty smiled. "Soon enough. For now, get inside the campus and find out what the hell's going on."

"Will do." Cal stood tall, all but saluting his superior. "And thanks for your confidence in my abilities."

"Don't thank me. Prove you deserve it." Marty started to turn away but stopped. His voice lowered, and he pinned Cal with an intense stare. "And Cal, be open-minded about the strange and unexplainable. There's been some really weird stuff going on you probably aren't aware of."

Cal's gut tightened at the tone of Marty's voice, a chill rippling across his skin. "Yes, sir." As he turned to leave, he caught a glimpse of Brigid fingering the medallion she wore around her neck. The metal was shaped into a star with five points inside a circle. He'd seen a similar one, but where?

As Cal left the war room, Brigid fell in step beside him, her fingers still wrapped around the metal.

An image of Deme lying nude in his bed flashed through his mind. When they made love, she'd taken off everything but the medallion—a pentagram just like the one Brigid wore. She'd said it was a gift from her mother and she never removed it.

When Cal stopped to face Brigid, she looked up at him, her brows rising up into her black hair.

Cal reached out and touched the pentagram at Brigid's neck. "Does your medallion have meaning?"

Brigid's lips curled upward. "Deme didn't tell you?"

"Tell me what?" He had a feeling Deme had kept a lot more than her family from him, and the anger at being kept in the dark rose to the surface and boiled there.

"It's a pentagram. The sign associated with the Wiccan."

He had an open mind when it came to people of different religious persuasions. To each his own as long as it didn't interfere with others' beliefs.

But he also believed that everything had a logical explanation. Magic and what some would call woo-woo was just superstitious bullshit some people used to scare and control others. The lieutenant had said the Special Investigations Team, or SPIT, as Cal had shortened it, was responsible for taking on the cases that didn't have an obvious explanation. It was up to them to find it. But logic could be found in every situation.

He nodded toward the pendant. "Does it represent your religion? Your faith?"

"Most definitely." Brigid held the pentagram out in front of her to the end of the chain. "You see, our mother was a witch."

Chapter 5

After Deme cleaned the water from her dorm room floor, she set out to find Rachel, Aurai's roommate. She'd scanned the roster she'd been given as the resident assistant and found her listed on the same floor several doors down from where Deme's room was located.

Girls ducked in and out of rooms, wafts of perfume or hair spray filling the air with each passing. The cloying scents overwhelmed Deme. She didn't use scented candles in her apartment or in her rituals, preferring the natural odors the earth gave off. The sharp aroma of pine sap, the earthiness of decaying leaves or the extravagant natural fragrance of roses blooming, in her mind, could not be duplicated.

On every door she passed, the Greek letters for gamma and omega hung. Some of the rooms had the girls' names hanging on cute signs. The more young women she saw, the more surreal the experience became. Each girl seemed perfect. Thick, beautiful hair, perfectly coifed, figures a model would die for and skin as smooth and blemish-free as a newborn babe's.

Where were the late teens with acne scars? What happened to bad hair days and the few extra pounds the sedentary life of a college coed generated?

Perhaps Rachel was a thorn among the roses of the sorority sisters. Deme had received text messages from her sister describing her first impressions of her dorm room and her roommate. Aurai had given Deme the impression that Rachel was a plump young woman with frizzy hair and thick glasses, her face riddled with pockmarks from a bad case of acne.

After all the Barbie look-alikes, Deme could appreciate a real girl with curves and flaws. She'd be more human, more approachable than the other residents of the Gamma Omega dormitory.

Deme paused in front of the room her sister had occupied up until forty-eight hours ago. Her chest tightened, her hand shaking as she reached out to knock. Deep in the back of her mind, Deme desperately hoped Aurai would open the door and hug her, telling her the cry for help was all in her imagination and that everything was fine.

Her eyes stinging, Deme blinked. And if wishes were horses… She tapped her knuckles on the hard wooden door and waited, refusing to hold her breath. No matter what she told herself about wishing things better, she couldn't slow her heartbeat. As she waited, her blood slammed through her veins, pounding against her eardrums.

"Just a minute!" a voice called out from inside.

After what seemed a very long time, but in fact had been only a matter of seconds, the door swung open.

A dark-haired beauty peered out, her eyes widening when she saw Deme. "Oh." Her gaze darted to each side of where Deme stood. "Can I help you?"

"Hi, I'm Deme Jones, the new R.A. for the dorm." She stuck out her hand. "Are you Rachel?"

Rachel nodded, taking Deme's hand in a limp grip, her dark, shiny hair falling into her smooth-skinned face. She had her purse slung over her shoulder and appeared to be on her way out.

Deme frowned. This girl was not what she'd expected. From Aurai's texts, she'd conjured an image of a shy girl with self-esteem issues because of a less than perfect body and face.

This young woman was like so many others in the building, beautiful and too perfect for her comfort. Deme touched her own chin, conscious of the scar there from the time she dove into a creek as a preteen and hit the bottom. The mouthful of rocks had been the least of her worries at the time—the scar a constant reminder to look before you dive into unknown waters.

Deme swallowed hard to keep from choking on her next words. Words she fought hard to keep natural. "I hear your roommate bailed on you."

Rachel's elegantly arched brows drew downward into a frown. "What did you hear?"

"Only that she bailed. Do you want me to find another girl to share your room?" It cost Deme to offer. More than anything she wanted to find her sister, but she didn't want the girls of the dorm to know that was her real reason for being there.

"No!" Rachel reached out to touch Deme, her hand shaking, a pained twist in dark brows. "Aurai will be back. I just know it. She probably just got homesick or something and went home for a few days. She'll be back, I tell you." Her hand fell to her side, her voice fading. "She has to come back."

"Rachel?" A male voice called out behind Deme. "Is that you?" The voice belonged to a tall, gangly young man, more typical of what Deme expected from a college student. His hair hung too long around his ears, the excess flesh around his cheeks and middle gave him a big teddy-bear look.

Rachel's smile widened and her chin dipped. "Hi, Mike."

For a beautiful girl, she lacked the confidence that came with a perfect complexion and figure. No, Rachel didn't resemble the outward picture Aurai had painted. Not in the slightest sense. But the way she acted around the boy displayed a hint of the crippling shyness Deme had expected.

"Um…can we talk later?" Rachel looked up at Deme, who stood at least a head taller than the girl. Rachel's expression begged for release.

"Sure. Just wanted to introduce myself and get to know some of the girls in the dorm."

"I promise I'll come by later. It's just…" She blushed and shot a shy glance at the boy. "I have to go."

The young man stood as though transfixed, his jaw drooping. "Rachel?" He didn't seem to recognize the girl in front of him.

"Yeah, Mike, it's me." She hooked his arm and led him away from Deme.

"What happened to you?" Mike was saying as Rachel dragged him down the hall.

"Sorority science project?" she quipped, laughing shakily, her voice fading as she stepped through the door leading to the stairwell.

Sorority science project? Deme shook her head and

took out the ring of keys she'd been entrusted with as the resident assistant. She waited until the hallway emptied and jammed the key into the lock. She unlocked and opened the door, darting in as one of the doors on the floor squeaked open.

Her heart racing, Deme shut the door and stood with her back to it.

The room was nothing to write home about. Two twin-size beds, two utility dressers and two closets comprised the major assets. The dormitory was old enough that the bathroom was down the hall and shared by the entire floor. Deme had passed it on the way to Aurai's room. A cleaning schedule had been worked out and posted on the bulletin board beside the entrance.

One bed had a soft pink comforter with a giant black-and-white-dots pattern spread across its surface. Leaning against the wall were three pillows in the black, pink and white of the coverlet. Not something Aurai would have chosen in a million years. It had to be Rachel's bed.

As Deme glanced around the room, her stomach knotted. The other bed had a midnight-blue coverlet with gold stars, silver moons and white clouds sprinkled across it. So typical of Aurai. Always the dramatic one, playing up her heritage as a witch in subtle ways without actually confessing to those around her. While she'd dreamed of blending in with regular people, she was drawn to the mystical and magical in ways only her sisters understood.

Her eyes blurring, Deme continued her perusal, her gaze landing on a picture frame perched on the dresser beside the pink bed. A dark-haired, nondescript girl stood between two adults, equally nondescript, presumably her parents.

Deme lifted the frame and stared down at the photograph. Scrawled in flowing cursive were the words *We love you, Rachel. Mom and Dad.* Upon closer inspection, the girl in the picture was everything Aurai had described, chubby, pockmarked, frizzy-haired and slumping like a shy girl.

How could a person change so much in so short a time? As if she'd transformed overnight. Deme removed her cell phone from her back pocket and snapped a picture of the photograph. She'd show her sisters and get their opinion. No amount of makeup could cover pockmarks that deep. And the Rachel she'd met in the hallway didn't have a single blemish. Could there be two Rachels with the same last name?

Deme replaced the picture frame and examined the contents of the dresser. Beside the frame was an ornate blue bottle with a very small amount of liquid inside.

Careful so as not to spill it, Deme pulled the glass stopper out of the top and sniffed. An acrid aroma wafted up in her face and stung the insides of her nostrils. She quickly jammed the stopper back on the bottle, snorting to get the stench out of her system.

She held the bottle up, looking for a label where it had none. What the heck was it? Was it medicine? It had to be something strong. Even now, her sinuses pinched in protest, her head aching from the residual stench. She shook her head to clear a sudden dizzy feeling then set the bottle on the dresser and continued her search. For what, she wasn't certain. Any clue as to her sister's whereabouts would be nice. She wasn't so sure it could be found in her roommate's belongings.

The first drawer inside Rachel's dresser contained a myriad of hair accessories, facial cleansers, acne medication and perfume bottles. Typical toiletries for a female exiting her teens. The acne creams were in keeping with the girl in the picture.

The remaining drawers contained clothing befitting the conservative lifestyle of a shy, withdrawn girl of larger proportions than the Rachel who'd left the room a few minutes earlier.

Books, a backpack and more clothing were the contents of Rachel's little closet. Nothing that gave a hint to her part in Aurai's disappearance, except perhaps the black robe hanging as far to the back as possible, almost hidden by a pale blue formal. Deme snapped a picture of the robe, unsure of its purpose in a coed's closet. Especially a freshman so far from potential graduation. And the robe had a hood. Not typical of graduation gowns.

Having avoided her sister's belongings, Deme finally turned to her side of the small room. Throughout her investigation of Rachel's things, she'd felt her sister's presence in her belongings. Everything Aurai touched left a residual aura of the youngest Chattox sibling.

The photograph on her dresser was a picture taken several years ago when all five sisters had been home at the same time. Her mother had been alive and snapped the picture, capturing the essence of each girl in one still image. Deme stood tallest in the center, her red hair glinting copper in the sunshine, loose and wavy around her shoulders, her face serious, as befitting the oldest daughter.

Selene stood on one side of Deme, her dark brown hair piled high on her head, her brown-black eyes fathomless, a secret smile playing on her lips. On Deme's other side, Gina had her arm around Deme and Brigid, her willowy body clothed in light blues and greens, her sandy-blond hair a sharp contrast to Brigid's coal-black mane and bold, black, Goth attire. Gina's smile was gentle, like a day at the beaches she loved. Brigid, on the other hand, stood with a cocky tilt to her head, her eyebrows arched as if to challenge anyone to say anything even slightly offbeat.

Beside Selene, Aurai stood with a happy, innocent grin, her pale blond hair lifted by her blessed wind. She couldn't have been more than twelve in the picture, her body lean and boyish. She hadn't yet blossomed into the beautiful young woman who'd gone off to college full of dreams of the future. She hadn't come into her talents, verging on puberty and all the responsibility of the adult Chattox women.

A simpler time for Aurai.

Deme squeezed her eyes shut and pressed the picture to her chest, fighting back the tears. She hadn't cried since her mother died right after Aurai's high school graduation.

On the island of St. Croix, Deme hadn't been there to say goodbye to her dear mother. She'd run away from her life in Chicago, away from her feelings for Cal Black. Deme had spent the better part of a year trying to forget that, because she was who she was, she couldn't have a normal relationship with a man. Especially a man like Cal who saw only the black and white, the good and bad. Shades of gray would disturb him. Hell, her shades of gray would disturb most men. Why bother trying?

Fiona Chattox had been their rock. Deme hadn't known her father long when he'd disappeared from their lives. She'd been the tender age of six. Her mother told the girls he'd died, but Deme never believed it, certain that her father would return some day and tell them he'd been spirited away by some unknown force and held captive all those years. Why else would he leave his beautiful wife and five daughters?

Deme opened her eyes and stared around the room Aurai had made her second home. She might not have her parents to fend for her, but Deme would be damned if her youngest sibling disappeared forever like her father. She'd find her. And when she did, she'd make whoever had taken her pay.

She couldn't bring herself to let go of the picture. Instead she slipped it from its frame and tucked it beneath her shirt, sticking the frame inside the dresser drawer.

With one quick last look, she opened the door and stepped out into the hallway. When she turned toward the R.A.'s room, she came face-to-face with a girl with golden-blond hair and pale blue eyes, her complexion so perfect she could have been a model for a cosmetics company.

The blonde's eyes narrowed. "Who are you and what were you doing in Rachel's room?"

Taken aback and feeling like a thief, Deme clutched her middle to keep the picture from falling from beneath her shirt. She forced a smile and straightened, throwing her shoulders back. She still had to look up at the young woman, who was just a bit taller than Deme's five feet nine inches. "I'm Deme Jones, the new R.A. And you are?"

"Zoe Adams. President of the Gamma Omegas." Her eyes narrowed into slits. "When did we get a new R.A.? Why wasn't I informed?"

Deme's fingers tightened into fists as she struggled to resist the urge to punch this princess right in the face and make a mess of her perfectly upturned nose. "Perhaps the college president didn't feel it necessary to consult you before hiring me."

"We'll see about that." She crossed her arms over her chest. "You didn't answer my question. What were you doing in Rachel's room?"

"If I'm not mistaken, which I rarely am, you are rude and the room is not only Rachel's but Aurai Chattox's, as well. I was inside looking to see if our missing girl has returned. Since she hasn't, I was looking for her emergency data."

"And you don't have that on file?"

Caught. Deme didn't let the Amazon flap her. Instead she smiled. "I have emergency data for everyone but her. As president of the Gamma Omegas, you don't happen to have her emergency data, do you?" Deme tipped her head, allowing a smug smile to turn up the corners of her lips.

Zoe's lips remained firmly pressed, her eyes narrowing even more. "She's not a Gamma Omega. She just lives here. And don't unpack your bags. Things are likely to change."

Deme met her stare for stare. "Count on it." Before Zoe could come up with a retort, Deme spun on her heels and left the younger girl standing there, her mouth open.

As she rounded the corner, a hand reached out and snagged her arm, pulling her through an open doorway.

Once she was inside the dorm room, the door closed behind her.

Deme rounded on the girl, and gasped. This new girl was almost a clone of Zoe. The same tall stature, golden-blond hair and model-perfect figure. If not for the eye color, Deme might not have recognized a difference.

When Deme opened her mouth to demand an explanation for her pulling her inside her room, she stopped.

The blonde pressed a finger to her lips and leaned her ear against the door.

Deme let her fingers rest against the wall, feeling every vibration down to those of footsteps resounding in the corridor.

When the vibrations faded, she focused her attention on the girl, whose gray eyes were wide, her hands shaking. "You can't let Zoe know we talked."

"I don't even know your name."

"Shelby. Shelby Cramer."

"Why all the secrecy? Why didn't you just talk to me in the corridor?"

Shelby shook her head, her face pale. "Zoe can't know."

"Why? Will she boot you out of the sorority?"

The girl nodded slowly, her eyes narrowing. "Something like that."

"So, spill. What's so important you can't say it in front of the sorority prez?"

Shelby's hands twisted together and she couldn't meet Deme's eyes. "It's just…well…" She sighed and let her hands fall to her sides. "Just be careful, will you? Zoe can be a real force to be reckoned with when she decides she doesn't like you."

Deme smiled. "I can handle Zoe. Question is, can you?"

Shelby's eyes swam with unshed tears. "No."

A knock sounded on Shelby's door and her eyes rounded. "You have to hide," she whispered, grabbing Deme's arm and hauling her with surprising strength toward the closet.

Because the girl was obviously petrified of being discovered harboring the new R.A., Deme allowed her to shove her into the closet and close the door.

The door to the room squeaked open.

"Shelby, have you seen the new R.A.?" Zoe asked.

"No," Shelby's voice quavered.

"Just remember, part of initiation into the Gamma Omegas is your vow of silence."

"I remember," Shelby said, her voice so soft Deme wouldn't have heard if sounds didn't echo so well off the linoleum tiles.

"Now that you're one of us, you don't want to go back, do you?"

For a second, Shelby hesitated, then she answered, "No, of course not. Who would?"

"Exactly. No one wants to go back. Nobody can."

Silence followed.

"Well, if you see the R.A., let me know what she says and does."

"I will," Shelby responded.

The door squeaked open and closed again. The room was silent except for the soft vibrations Deme could feel through her shoes, vibrations caused by bare feet on hard floors. The closet door opened.

Deme blinked as she stepped from the dark closet into the brightly lit room. "What was all that about?" she added softly.

Shelby shook her head. "Nothing. It was a mistake to bring you in here."

"No, it wasn't. You obviously had something you wanted to tell me."

"No. It's not important. You have to go now." She gathered her toothbrush and a hand towel and opened the door, peering out into the hall.

"Shelby, you can trust me. I'd never tell Zoe anything you told me in confidence."

"I have nothing to say." She held the door and motioned for Deme to leave. Once Deme stepped out into the corridor, Shelby followed and closed the door behind them, then hurried toward the bathroom.

Deme retraced her footsteps to the R.A.'s room, wondering what had just happened, determined to get a background check on Zoe Adams. If anyone was crazy enough to make off with a coed, Zoe would be top of her list.

Back at the campus, Cal parked his motorcycle outside the Gamma Omega dorm. Despite his determination to remain focused on the case, he couldn't help the way his pulse raced at the thought of seeing Deme again. He called himself all kinds of fool for letting her influence him in any way.

She was like an accident. A hit-and-run ready for a repeat performance where he was concerned. Only this time he'd be ready. He wouldn't let her leave him scratching his head, wondering what the heck he'd said or done wrong.

He took the steps in the stairwell two at a time to the second floor, where Brigid said Deme's room was. He'd told her he'd be there at six o'clock to fill her in on what he'd learned that day and vice versa.

Question was, would she be there? Now that she knew she'd be working this case with him, would she bother to show up?

Since the missing person was her sister, Cal figured she would. Deme struck him as someone dedicated to her family, even if she wasn't dedicated to her lover.

Outside the door marked R.A., he raised his fist to knock.

"Don't bother, I'm here." Deme's voice caught him off guard, sending a wave of heat through his body.

When he turned, he couldn't stop the way his groin tightened at the way she looked.

Her red hair fell in loose waves around her shoulders, and the V of her button-down cotton blouse exposed the rounded swells of her breasts. Breasts he'd tasted, massaged and caressed long into the nights they'd shared.

Damn, this assignment was going to be a lot harder than he'd anticipated. Tamping down his libido, he stepped to the side as she pulled a ring of keys from her pocket and opened the door.

She walked in without looking back, holding the door just long enough for him to step through.

Once inside, she shut the door and walked several steps away, putting as much distance between them as the tiny room allowed. She leaned against the windowsill overlooking a garden and asked, "What have you found out?"

In the hallway, she'd been a turn-on. Inside the tight confines of the R.A.'s small room, her nearness sparked a lot more flames than even Cal could predict. He tugged the zipper of his leather jacket down, opening it to let in cooler air. Anything to lessen the heat rising inside. "There have been more incidents than just your sister's disappearance."

Deme's eyebrows rose. Her gaze captured his. "What kind of incidents?"

"Two cases of attempted rape, two cases of attempted suicide and one other missing person besides your sister." He glanced around the room. "Could you turn the thermostat down? It's hellacious hot in here." He stripped his jacket from his shoulders and slung it over a chair.

Her gaze shifted from his eyes downward over his shoulders and chest, the heat in the room rising the lower she went. "I haven't touched the thermostat. It was on seventy when I left the room a while ago." She crossed to the device on the wall beside him and studied the box. "Still seventy. Must be you." Her eyes slid sideways.

"No, I think it's you." Cal didn't know what came over him. All he knew was that he had to have his hands on her. He grabbed Deme and pulled her into his arms, crushing her against his chest.

"What do you think you're doing?" Her hands rested flat against his chest, barely applying any pressure as though she was torn between dragging him close or pushing him away. "We don't have to pretend in here. There's no one watching."

"Who's pretending?" His hands slipped lower, circling her hips, slamming her against the hard ridge of his erection. "Can't you feel it?"

She nodded, her eyes glazed, her tongue sweeping across her lips. Her hands slipped up his back, beneath his shirt, her fingernails digging into his skin.

The sharp pricks of pain only flamed his desire, flushing his senses with a need so powerful he couldn't hold back.

His fingers found the hem of her shirt. Instead of working the buttons loose or slipping it up over her head, he ripped it up the front, buttons flying everywhere.

"That'll cost you." Deme pulled his shirt up over his head and flung it to the corner. She bent to take one of his hard, brown nipples between her teeth and nipped, hard.

Cal jerked back and slapped her bottom. "Two can play rough."

In a flurry of motion, they stripped each other bare,

hands roaming over naked skin. Cal lifted her, wrapping her legs around his waist, walking her backward until her naked back pressed against the window choked on the outside in ivy. "Miss me much?" he murmured as he trailed kisses and nips along her jawline and down the length of her throat. He tongued the pulse beating frantically at the base of her neck.

"No." Her fingernails dug into his back, piercing skin, drawing blood. "I can't miss you. We have no future together." Her head leaned back against the glass, her breasts pressing against him.

"Who said I want a future with you now?" He shoved her up high enough to take a nipple into his mouth, biting down hard enough to elicit a gasp. Wicked satisfaction spread through him with the flame of desire. He wanted to cause her pain. Wanted to see her suffer as she'd made him suffer with her disappearance. "Is that why you left? You couldn't picture a future with me?"

"I had good reasons to leave." She sucked in a deep breath, her head lifting, her green-eyed gaze capturing his as her hands slid up to cup his face. "For the life of me I can't remember one of them now." She kissed him, her tongue thrusting into his mouth, taking his in a desperate tangle.

He lowered her over his cock, penetrating her in a hard, punishing thrust. Anger and desire merged to become a living, breathing entity within him, taking over his actions, destroying his self-control. He couldn't stop himself from taking her, even if she'd said no.

His thrusts increased, until the glass in the window rattled.

Deme's legs clamped hard around his waist, her body arching against his, taking him in as deeply as he could go until she cried out loud. Her body tensed around him as he slammed into her once more.

Just as he climaxed, he had enough sense to lift her off him at the last minute before he shot his seed into her womb.

Anger and desire still burned in his veins, but he didn't have the strength to act on them. He let Deme slide down him until her feet touched the floor. His arms remained around her waist, his palms cupping her buttocks. Guilt flowed through him as he realized he couldn't have stopped himself. If Deme had said no, he'd have raped her anyway. "What the hell just happened?"

Chapter 6

Deme stood with her back to the window, the thoughts in her head spinning like so much debris in an F5 tornado. The air in the room was thick, hard to breathe. "I don't know. Just don't let it happen again." She pushed away from Cal and gathered her clothes.

Cal shoved a hand through his hair, standing it on end. "You weren't fighting me."

"Fine. *I* won't let it happen again," she reassured him, her lips firmly pressed into a line, even as her body tingled with awareness of his nakedness standing within reach. Inside, her blood raced through every organ, vein and the furthest reaches of her body, burning a path downward to her core. She ached with need and she still wanted him. Damn him! She turned away, gathering her clothing. "This isn't about you and me."

"I know. It's about finding your sister."

Deme faced him, pressing her jeans to her chest.

"That's right. This is about finding Aurai. It can only be about finding Aurai."

"Message heard. It's not as if I'm asking you to marry me. I learned my lesson. So don't feel like you have to disappear again."

That barb hit dead center and guilt burned in her gut. She drew herself up to her full five feet nine inches and faced him. "I had to leave. There are things you don't know about me. Things you wouldn't understand."

"You didn't give me a chance to understand. You didn't give me a chance to get to know you." Cal grabbed his jeans and slipped his legs into them, dragging them up his body. "I didn't even know you had sisters. Seems like something a lover should know about the woman he's sleeping with. The woman he proposes to."

Deme couldn't respond. She wanted to stop him getting dressed—wanted to drag his jeans down and take him into her again. Wave upon wave of desire slammed into her like a freight train.

Her mouth watered with the need to taste every inch of his body, to lick, bite and rake her fingers over him in penalizing thoroughness. Her tongue swept across her lips to moisten their sudden dryness.

Scratching at the window penetrated the fog of desire encroaching on her ability to think.

She turned to discover that what she'd originally thought was English ivy growing outside her window was a dark brown tangle of vines whose thorns scratched against the glass, tapping…tapping…as if to gain entrance.

"What's with the vine?" Cal walked to the window and shoved it open. When he reached out to push the vine away, he yelped, pulling his hand back. A drop of blood oozed from where a thorn had gouged his thumb.

Deme grabbed a box of tissues and hurried to his side. "Let me see."

He held out his hand. "It's nothing, just a prick."

"You're bleeding." She pressed a tissue to the wound, absorbing the blood. As she stood so close, inhaling the musky scent of their lovemaking, she made a decision. "Maybe it's time you know a little more about me." Deme let go of his hand and took a step back. She closed her eyes, gathering her inner strength, summoning her ability to feel nature, to influence it. She breathed in and out, the air unusually thick.

She entered a fog of internal awareness, blocking out the room she stood in, the man she'd made love to and the desperation with which she sought her sister, only for a moment.

"Goddess of earth
I call to thee
Guide me now
Set me free
We are one
You with me
Grant me power
Blessed Be."

With her senses she reached out to the thorny vine, wrapping her mind around it, sending soothing thoughts, pushing it toward the ground, away from her window on the second story of the dormitory. A strange tension filled the room, as though her calming influence had run up against a wall, blocking her attempt to communicate with the vine.

Deme pushed against the wall, gently at first. The more it pushed back, the harder she concentrated. So wrapped was she in the inner battle, she lost track of time, forgot where she was until a voice penetrated her consciousness.

"Deme!" Strong arms scooped beneath her knees, lifting her up off her feet.

Her eyes opened and she stared into Cal's anxious face. "Why did you stop me?"

He raced for the door. "I don't know what's happening, or what you were doing, but you aren't safe in here."

Dragged from the fog of her connection to the goddess, Deme struggled to focus on the dorm room. A sickly aroma of decay filled her nostrils, gagging her with its intensity.

As her vision cleared, she saw what Cal was talking about. The thorny vine that a moment ago had been outside her window had draped itself down over the sill and slithered across the floor like a deadly serpent aiming for the two of them.

She shook her head, her arms circling his neck, her pulse racing. "But that can't be."

"I don't get it either, but we have to get out of here."

"No!" She stopped him, forcing him to drop her to her feet. "I can't go out into the hall like this." She motioned to her nakedness.

He hesitated only a moment, then pushed her behind him. "Stand back." Cal grabbed the comforter from the bed beside him and advanced on the vine.

Deme watched in horror as the vine lashed out, the thorns raking across Cal's legs, penetrating the denim, ripping into his skin.

"Cal!" She rushed toward him.

"Stay back!" With the blanket wrapped around his hands, he grabbed the thorny vine and wrestled it toward the window. He twisted and grunted, attempting to keep the vine from wrapping around his legs and arms.

As he neared the window, he shoved the vine, comforter and all, through and slammed the window down.

A bend in the vine stopped the window from closing completely, allowing the leaves to slip through the crack.

Cal leaned his weight into pressing the window downward. "Get something to shove it through!" he yelled.

Deme's gaze searched the room for something to use to poke the vine through the narrow slit. She grabbed a number two pencil and raced toward Cal.

Without thinking, she shoved the pencil at the vine, pushing it back through the opening. The window slammed down on the sill, the leaves retreating at the last moment to the other side.

Cal twisted the lock and leaned his back against the wall, breathing hard. Then his gaze captured Deme's. "I think you have some explaining to do."

Cal slipped his shirt over his head and tugged it down across his chest. What had just happened completely defied explanation. Never in his life had he had a vine attack him. It was as if the plant had come alive, intent on causing them harm. Surely he had imagined it.

The pain in his shin and thumb where jagged thorns had torn his skin reminded him it wasn't in his mind. He wasn't going crazy. And the sudden urge to ravage Deme's body that had taken him over was beyond any anger he might have felt at being ditched. He truly couldn't have stopped if she'd said no.

As Deme pulled on her jeans and a T-shirt, her gaze never left the window and the vine tapping against it. "I don't understand."

Residual anger simmered beneath the surface as he waited for her to finish dressing. He fought to remain in control, refusing to give in to baser instincts of a moment ago. "I don't know what's happening, but we can't talk in here."

"I agree." She straightened from slipping on her shoes, tugged the strap of her purse over her shoulder and met him at the door. "We need to get out of here." A chill chose that moment to track down her spine. She shivered as he opened the door for her, casting one last glance at the thorny vine pressing against the glass.

In the hallway, Zoe Adams stood with her back to the wall, her arms crossed over her chest. "Having troubles?"

Blood rushed into Deme's face as she thought of the violent sex she and Cal had just experienced behind the R.A. room door, probably breaking a few dozen rules. Despite her guilt, Deme managed to frown at the girl. "No troubles. Can I help you?"

"You can help by leaving." Zoe's lips twitched at the corners and she stared so hard at Deme, it was if a shaft of heat burned into her head.

"You're not scaring me, Zoe." Despite her tough words, Deme's hand raised to press against the bridge of her nose, applying pressure to the sudden headache.

Zoe flipped her hair over her shoulder and pushed off the wall. Without another word, she strode down the hall, her feet crossing over each other like a runway model's, her hips swaying perfectly.

"Did you feel that?" Deme shook her head, the pain easing slowly.

"Feel what?"

Maybe she was imagining it. Deme shrugged.

"Nothing. Let's go to the student commons. Maybe we can talk there."

Deme couldn't leave the dorm fast enough. The farther away from her room she got, the better she felt. When she stepped out into the cool evening air, she stopped just outside the dorm entrance and breathed in, absorbing the scents and aura of the surrounding trees.

Cal stood silently beside her, his brows set in what appeared to be a permanent V.

"By the goddess…this is better." She stood for a long time sucking in light, fresh air, filling her lungs, cleansing her aura of the darkness that had invaded her in her room. When she felt closer to normal again she turned to Cal. "Something is not right about that room."

"You're telling me." Cal hooked her arm and steered her toward the student commons. "Now that we're out of there, we have some catching up to do. I want to know everything you haven't told me." He squeezed her arm tight enough it got her attention. "Everything."

Being hurried along like an errant child on her way to the principal's office didn't make Deme happy, but nothing could erase the level of pure lust she'd experienced in her room only a few minutes ago. Knowing she was in control of her own emotions once again felt almost like freedom.

As they passed the administration building, the offices closed and dark, a scream ripped through the air.

Cal let go of Deme's arm and ran toward the sound.

Deme followed. In good shape, she still had trouble keeping up with Cal, his stride leaving her far behind.

Deme neared the garden fence at the center of the campus, her chest heaving, the air growing as thick as it had been in her dorm room. She struggled to fill her lungs, the darkness more menacing with each step closer to the wrought-iron gate.

Cal stood with his feet apart, his fists up in the fighting position. Behind him on the ground was Rachel, her face in the shadows, her shoulders shuddering with muffled sobs.

"What's going on?" Deme stepped up beside Cal.

Standing in front of him was Mike Hubbs, Rachel's date, his shirt torn, hanging out of his waistband, his hair mussed, his eyes wide, glazed and wild. "She's mine," he said, his shy voice low and guttural, unrecognizable from the young man Deme had met in the hallway of the dorm.

"Don't let him touch me. Please." Rachel huddled on the ground, her knees drawn up to her chin, her arms wrapped around her legs. "Please." Another sob shook her body and she whimpered.

Deme dropped to her haunches beside Rachel. "What happened?"

"I don't know…" She took a shuddering breath and wiped her arm across her eyes. "One minute we were walking, the next he…he…tried to…rape me." She sobbed, burying her face in her hands.

Mike lunged for Rachel.

Cal stepped in front of him, landing a punch to the young man's jaw that sent him flying backward. He landed with a thud on the ground and lay still for several seconds.

Rachel cried out, attempting to rise.

Deme's hand on her shoulder kept her in place.

Mike pushed himself to a sitting position and gazed at the people staring at him, his eyes wide, the glaze gone, confusion taking its place. "What are you doing here? Where's Rachel?" He struggled to stand.

Cal stepped in front of him, blocking his access to the troubled girl on the ground. "I suggest you leave Rachel alone."

"But we have a date."

"Date's over." Cal held his fists at the ready for round two.

"I don't understand."

"I bet you don't." Deme snorted and stood, adding her body as a barrier between Mike and Rachel. "For your information, most girls don't like to be raped."

"Rape?" He shook his head. "What are you talking about?" He leaned to the right, peering around Deme. "Rachel? Are you all right?"

"No thanks to you." Cal grabbed Mike's arm when he tried to step around Deme. "You aren't getting near her. I'm calling the police."

"No." Rachel lurched to her feet, streaks of mascara making dark tracks on her face. "Don't call the police. It may have been my fault. I never should have done it."

"Done what?" Deme asked.

"I never should have changed."

"No man has the right to rape a woman."

"But he didn't mean to, did you, Mike?" Rachel tried to push Deme aside, but she refused to let her by.

"I would never rape Rachel. Hell, I'm still a virgin." He clapped a big hand over his mouth, his face turning so red that even in the shadows Deme could see the glow. He removed his hand and said softly, "I wouldn't know how." He shoved his hands through his hair. "I swear I didn't rape her. I wouldn't try. I respect her too much."

As much as Deme tried not to, she couldn't help but believe that Mike meant what he said as the truth. "Then explain why you attacked her."

He shook his head. "I don't remember attacking her. I must have blacked out. I swear, Rachel, I would never hurt you."

"But you did." Her voice hiccuped on a sob.

Mike backed away a step, tears glistening in his eyes. "I'm sorry. I don't remember." He took another step. "I wouldn't…" Mike turned and ran.

Cal started to follow, but Rachel's voice stopped him. "Please, don't." She laid her hand on his arm. "Let him go. He wasn't himself."

"He can't get away with this," Cal said. "What if he tries it again?"

"He won't." Rachel stared into the darkness where Mike had disappeared.

"How can you be sure? You have to turn him over to the police." Deme took Rachel by the arms. "What if he tries to rape someone else?"

Rachel shook her head side to side and jerked out of Deme's hold. "It's not him. It's me."

"What do you mean, it's you?"

"It happened that night."

"What night?" Deme grabbed the girl's arms again. "The night Aurai disappeared?"

"Yes." Rachel's head hung down, her eyes shadowed, unreadable. "Everything happened, everything changed."

"Tell me." Deme shook her gently.

"I can't." Rachel broke free, backing away much as Mike had done. "They'll kill me."

"Who will kill you?" Cal asked.

"Leave me alone," Rachel pleaded. "Please."

"What happened that night, Rachel?" Deme demanded. This girl knew something, and she'd shake it out of her if she had to. "Where is Aurai?"

She shook her head, tears streaming down her face. Rachel turned toward the Gamma Omega dormitory.

Deme captured her arm and spun her around. "At least tell me where it happened."

The younger girl looked into Deme's eyes and whispered, "In the garden." She glanced over Deme's shoulder and gasped, her eyes round. Before Deme could stop her, she'd knocked aside the hand holding her and ran away from the dorm and into the darkness.

Deme glanced behind her.

A group of five girls emerged from the shadows near the gate to the wrought-iron fence surrounding the central garden. A garden Deme had been told was strictly off-limits to all students and faculty.

At the point was Zoe Adams, her blond hair shining in the light from the windows of the Gamma Omega dormitory.

She didn't advance on Deme and Cal. She stood with the others fanning out to each side of her. Five girls in all, each as beautiful as the next.

"There's something not right about them," Cal muttered.

"You're telling me." Not in the mood for another confrontation with the Stepford sisters, Deme hooked Cal's arm and led him toward the parking lot. "Come on. Let's get away from campus. I'm supposed to meet my sisters at Burger Barn at nine o'clock. You might as well meet the rest of the Chattoxes."

Cal took the lead, guiding Deme to where he'd parked his motorcycle. He slung his foot over the seat and jerked his head. "Get on."

Without hesitation, Deme climbed on the back, wrapped her arms around his waist and held on. The danger of falling in love with Cal all over again seemed minor compared with the sinister darkness of a face-off with the leader of the Gamma Omega sorority.

Chapter 7

"Who is this Zoe Adams, anyway?" Brigid tapped her fingernails on the table to the same rhythm as her petite foot encased in black leather boots. "She doesn't scare me. I'll rip every hair out of her head and make her beg for mercy."

Cal suppressed a grin. He'd already gotten a taste of Brigid's brand of finesse at the police station earlier that day.

Sitting among the four sisters, it struck him how different they all were. As though they came from completely diverse families. Not one looked like the other, and each had unique characteristics and personalities. But they all wore the silver pentagram and they all cared about their missing youngest sister. That they turned to Deme's strength and maturity to bring order to the group seemed natural since Deme was the oldest.

"No matter how much the girls disturb us, we can't

go in like a bunch of ninjas kicking ass." Deme's gaze moved from one sister to the next. "We have to find out what's going on by blending in, getting to know them or at least some of them. Not everyone is Zoe Adams. Rachel might come clean given enough time."

Gina nodded. "Or that Shelby chick."

Brigid slammed a palm on the table. "We don't have time. While you're out playing college coed, our sister is missing. She could be in danger."

"She is," Selene said, her voice quiet, intense.

Deme sighed. "I know and we'll get to her. In the meantime, the girls of Gamma Omega are afraid of something. I want to know what it is. I think it has to do with Aurai's disappearance."

"Not Zoe Adams." Cal's words were spoken in a low, calm tone, but every feminine eye turned toward him. "Zoe isn't afraid of anything."

"It's as though she has power over them," Deme agreed.

"You think she'd kill them if they leak information?" Gina asked.

Deme's gaze met Cal's. "You know...I wouldn't put it past her. She's trouble."

That she'd looked to him warmed his insides more than Cal cared to admit. On the outside of this band of sisters looking in, he could use an ally, even if Deme didn't have the best reputation for sticking around.

Deme tore her gaze from Cal's and aimed it at her sister Gina. "You start cleaning the aquariums in the library tomorrow, right?"

Gina nodded. "They're a mess."

"Good. You can use that opportunity to dig through any information you can find on the history of Colyer-Fenton, the Gamma Omegas and especially the central garden. I want to know why it's off-limits. Did something happen there that could have an impact on the aura?"

"You felt it, too, didn't you?" Selene asked, her brown eyes glazing over. "The garden has a dark aura, a sense of anger and frustration...and ultimate doom." She stared across the table at Cal, but he could tell she wasn't looking at him so much as through him.

A tingling sensation rippled down the back of his neck as though Selene's fingers trailed across his spine. Which was ridiculous. Cal looked around the room for an air vent, something that would cause him to shiver.

"What else can you sense? Earlier you said there were voices calling to you. Back when you were in my room. Who did they belong to?" Deme asked.

Voices? Cal frowned.

Selene continued to stare, her brow knitting into a pained frown. "I can't...quite...see them."

"Them? More than one. Male or female?" Deme shot out.

Cal stared at Deme. The line of questions she shot at her sister made less and less sense.

"Female," Selene responded with conviction.

"Alive or dead?"

Okay, that bordered on downright weird. Cal started to rise and thought better of it, remaining seated to see this conversation through, no matter how bizarre.

Selene closed her eyes. "Screaming. Pain. Horror. Must leave." She opened her eyes and stared around at her sisters. "What?"

Cal could swear she'd been in some sort of trance, like the one Deme had been in when the vine went berserk in her room. What was with the Chattox women? Were they all a little...off?

"Go on." Brigid leaned forward. "What else can you tell us about these females?"

Selene cocked her brow. "What females?"

"The ones you said were warning us off in Deme's room. Don't you remember?"

Selene squinted. "Vaguely. In your room?" She shifted her gaze to her oldest sister.

"My room. The one that overlooks the central garden," Deme affirmed. She turned to Cal, her eyes narrowing.

He could almost see the gears in her mind turning. Off balance by all the talk of hearing voices and sensing dead people, Cal worked hard to maintain his outward appearance of stoic understanding, when all he wanted was to shout, "What the hell?"

"Rachel was walking with Mike just outside the gates of the garden when he attacked her. I'd like to know where the other girls were when they were attacked. Is something about the garden causing people to act out of character?" Deme's gaze shifted from Cal's, her cheeks stained in a subtle flush.

His eyes widened as he made the connection she was referring to. Had something influenced his and her behavior when they'd been in her room? Cal wanted Deme to look at him, to acknowledge him and the violent desire that had transpired between them. "Are you suggesting the garden is influencing behavior?"

As much as he would like to think he wasn't responsible for his actions earlier, he didn't buy in to the forces of nature or the spirit world making people perform unthinkable acts.

Still…he had never been more out of control than he had been for those passion-filled minutes with Deme. What scared him was the intensity, the violence of the sex. His back still stung from where her fingernails scraped his skin.

The shame and horror on Mike's face echoed in Cal's mind. A guy like Mike didn't force himself on a girl. In his gut, Cal knew that. But then Jeffrey Dahmer had appeared to be such a normal kind of guy to most of his acquaintances.

Deme turned to Selene. "Do you have any of the Gamma Omega girls in your drama workshop?"

"I checked my list of students and addresses. Seems like one Shelby Cramer had an address of the Gamma Omega dorm."

Deme nodded. "That's the one who tried to pull me aside earlier. Zoe scared her silent. See if you can gain her confidence. Maybe she'll tell you something when she's not surrounded by sorority sisters or Zoe."

"I'll do that." Selene sighed. "I wish we had something to go on. I'm really worried about Aurai."

"As we all are." Deme reached out to the sisters on each side of her. They joined hands with each other, forming a circle Cal didn't try to be a part of. Each closed her eyes and they chanted softly in unison.

"Feel the power
Free our hearts
Find our way
Be the one
With the strength of the earth
With the rising of the wind
With the calm of the water
With the intensity of fire
With the freedom of spirit
The goddess is within us
She is power
We are her

We are one
Blessed Be."

As the last word was uttered, a breeze shifted through the café.

Cal glanced toward the door. No one had gone out or stepped in.

"Did you feel her?" Selene opened her eyes.

The other three nodded, their eyes glassy with unshed tears.

Deme whispered, "She's still alive."

Brigid followed with another heartfelt, "Blessed Be." Then she stood. "We have our work cut out for us. Let's get to it."

The sisters stood and filed out of the café, leaving Deme alone with Cal.

Brigid was the last one out, glancing behind her at Cal. She tipped an imaginary hat and grinned.

"What was that about?" Deme frowned at Brigid's back.

"I could ask the same." Cal captured Deme's hand as she rose to leave. "Uh-uh. We've only just begun."

She sank into her seat and sighed. "Where to begin?" Her fingers curled around the medallion with the pentagram hanging around her neck. The one just like those each of her sisters wore.

"Start there." Cal reached out, his fingers touching hers and the medallion. A brief shock of electricity reminded him of how she'd felt in his arms earlier.

Deme glanced down at the necklace. "Oh, this." She smiled. "Our mother gave each of us one. It's a pentagram." She pointed to the top point of the pentagram. "This point represents Spirit. That's Selene. She senses the feelings and emotions of others, both live, dead and otherworld." She held up her hand. "Let the otherworld comment go for now and let me finish."

Cal nodded.

She touched the point to the left of Spirit. "This point represents Water—that's Gina. She can see, smell, taste and influence all things water, from the smallest drop of perspiration to the grandest ocean."

Despite his disbelief, Cal couldn't help but be mesmerized by Deme's voice. Clear, calm and completely convinced. The love for her sisters shone through above it all, making his own convictions of what was true and logical waver.

"The bottom left point is Earth." She smiled up at him. A brief smile, one that told him she didn't expect him to understand or believe what she was saying, though she did so absolutely. "That's me. I can feel the vibrations of the planet, tell you when someone is coming and influence the flora. If I really get cranked up, I've been known to shake a few rocks." She chuckled, the sound more self-deprecating than humorous.

She touched the point to the right of Earth. "This point represents Fire."

Cal frowned. "Brigid?"

Deme tipped her head to the side and stared across at him. "Yes. How did you know?"

"Gut feel." His palm still tingled where Brigid touched him earlier. That and the heat in the war room made him think of her.

Cal stopped there. If he didn't watch out, he'd start believing all this garbage.

"The final point is Air." Deme smiled softly, the look on her face one of such sadness, it made Cal want to reach out and pull her into his arms.

"Aurai?"

She nodded. "The youngest of the five of us." Deme looked up, her eyes glistening. "She just wanted to live a normal life. That's all any of us ever wanted."

Cal pressed his lips together. "You *are* normal."

"No." Deme shook her head, her smile fading, her jaw tightening. "We're not."

"What exactly are you telling me?"

She inhaled and let out a long, steadying breath. "We're witches."

"Brigid said the same thing." Cal leaned back, his arms crossing over his chest. "Is this the secret you couldn't tell me? The reason you left without saying goodbye, good luck or get lost?"

Deme nodded. "You're a cop. You live by a book of rules. Everything is either black or white. There's nothing in between to you. How could you understand?"

"You're right on one count. I don't understand. But you could have had the decency to give me a chance." He heaved a huge sigh. "Look, I can't say that I believe in witches. I can't say that I believe in magic, but I'll tell you this—something strange happened back in your room tonight."

"Strange things like that happen a lot around us."

"Maybe so, but they don't happen to me. I like to think there's still a logical explanation for the vine." His fingers curled around his coffee mug, the sting of the puncture wound he'd received bringing back the struggle.

"What about what happened between us in my room?" She raised her eyebrows. "You felt it, didn't you? The anger, the rage, the overwhelming desire, didn't you? Everything dark intensified."

He hesitated, a residual heat pooling in his loins. "I think that can be explained. I was mad."

Deme shook her head. "You never lose control."

"Really mad." His argument sounded lame even to his own ears.

Deme reached out and touched his arm. "Do you really think you could have stopped?"

He wanted to say yes. Being in control was who he was. He hated to admit it, but she was right. "No."

"It wasn't you. I felt it, too. I think it has something to do with the garden."

"Why? We had passion in our relationship before."

"Not that much. Not that violent."

Cal's jaw tightened. "I still don't believe in magic."

"Think about it...Mike attacked Rachel. Did he look like someone who could hurt a girl?"

"What do we know about the things a man is capable of? We don't know Mike well enough to make that call."

"Maybe not." Deme's gaze circled the restaurant before landing on him. "What about the two attempted rapes by model students? Think they were acting on their own?"

He shrugged. "It happens."

"Is everything a coincidence? I thought you didn't believe in coincidence?"

Cal didn't have an argument for that. "Let's agree to disagree on the magic thing. I'll investigate the students involved in the hazing, get some information from the staff and leave the woo-woo to you."

"Fair enough." Deme stood. "I need to get back to the dorm. Duty calls and I'm still the R.A." She hooked her handbag over her shoulder. "Besides, I need to check on Rachel."

Cal lifted his jacket and slipped it over his shoulders. "I'll check with the lieutenant and get him to run a background check on Zoe and Mike."

Deme rode on the back of Cal's motorcycle, her arms wrapped around his waist, glad he couldn't see her expression. He'd recognize the hunger in her eyes, the need for physical contact with him. Her body ached for this man, but she couldn't commit to him or any other.

What had happened to Aurai could happen again to any one of her sisters and herself. One minute there, another being dragged into some unknown hell. Being witches, having certain powers, made them targets. What kind of normal life could she live with a mortal?

She almost laughed out loud. Even to her own ears, using the words *witches* and *mortals* sounded so farfetched. She and her sisters had played down their abilities, refusing to live up to their full potential. Their mother had told them they could live whatever lives they wished, if they wanted it badly enough. Unfortunately, normal wasn't one of the choices.

As the motorcycle came to a stop in front of the dorm, Deme peered up. She wished this would all go away. But it wouldn't until she found her sister.

She swung her leg over and straightened.

Cal dismounted, pulled off his helmet and grabbed her arm as she turned to leave. "Deme—"

"Look, Cal." She faced him, her face set, her lips firm. She hadn't wanted to confront him, not when her emotions were still raw from their earlier encounter, but she had to set him straight. "What happened earlier shouldn't have. I don't intend to start where we left off a year ago. Once this case is solved, once Aurai is home and safe, we go our separate ways."

His lips twisted. "Who said I wanted it any other way? I was just going to say, be careful."

"Oh." She frowned. "Well, then, good night."

Before she could turn, his hand lifted to cup her cheek.

"Sweet dreams, little witch." He bent and pressed his lips to hers.

Fire shot through every nerve in her body. Deme knew she should pull away, should put a stop to something that couldn't be, but she didn't.

She leaned into him, her lips parting.

His tongue delved deep, wrapping around hers as his arms circled her waist, dragging her closer.

The hard ridge behind his fly pressed into her belly, making her exceedingly aware of her effect on him. The power of bringing a man to this surged through her, blasting her blood through her veins. She squeezed the apex of her thighs, the ache so prominent she wanted to crawl all over him, make love in the moonlight, discard all reservations and inhibitions to be naked with this man. All this without the added push she'd gotten in her room.

"Get a room, will ya."

Deme broke away from Cal, her breathing heavy, her heart racing.

Zoe Adams stood in the entrance to the dormitory, her hand on her hip, a sneer marring her perfection. She didn't repeat her comment, only stared.

Fighting the urge to squirm, Deme straightened her shirt and touched Cal's face. "That's one for the cover story," she said quietly enough only he could hear.

As she turned toward the dorm, squaring her shoulders, she caught a flash of pain winging across Cal's features. But when she looked back, his jaw was tight, his brown eyes expressionless.

Deme couldn't sense the vibration of his movement, so he must be waiting for her to get safely inside. She could feel his gaze following her as she neared the entrance to the Gamma Omega dormitory and Zoe Adams as the younger woman stood guard over her domain.

Zoe's smile was anything but welcoming. She didn't say anything as Deme stepped around her, the college coed's concentration fixed on Cal.

Deme's fists clenched as a flash of unexpected jealousy painted her vision green. Not that Cal would go for a college coed. He was more mature, had more class.

Still, Zoe was gorgeous, perfect in every way. Why wouldn't a man like Cal be attracted to her? He wasn't committed to any other female. Deme had seen to it that he wasn't tied to her. She had her reasons. But those reasons were beginning to wear on her.

As Deme opened the glass entry door, Zoe tossed over her shoulder, "Don't think you're going to change anything, R.A. We like things the way they are."

Deme froze, her fingers poised on the metal handle. "What makes you think I'll change things?"

Zoe didn't respond, her shoulder rising in a hint of a shrug.

"Are you afraid I'll get in your way of the games you play with the sorority?"

"I'm not afraid." She shot a glance at Deme before she fixed her gaze on Cal again. "I just wouldn't want to see anyone get hurt."

Deme let go of the handle and marched back down the steps to face Zoe. "Is that a threat?"

Zoe's mouth curled in a smile that didn't reach her eyes. "Do you feel threatened?"

Deme fought her desire to throttle this prima donna. "Not in the least. You don't scare me, Zoe. As the R.A., I determine who lives in this dormitory and who should be booted. Give me just one reason, and your ass is out of here."

Zoe's pale blue eyes narrowed. "I wouldn't do that if I were you."

"But then, you aren't me." Deme stared at her a little longer. She could almost see the steam rise from Zoe's reddening face. She could feel the heat in the air. The steps beneath her feet hummed with something she couldn't quite place. When the other girl didn't respond, Deme left her standing there and entered the dormitory.

Out of Zoe's sight, Deme's body shook. Something about Zoe Adams wasn't right. Her aura was dark, the air around her hung heavy, oppressive. Even the earth beneath her feet seemed thick with antagonism.

As she climbed the steps, her vision wavered. Or was it the steps shifting? Either way, she clung to the railing until she reached the second floor. For once the corridor was empty. Not a single girl ventured out to the sound of the stairwell door closing behind Deme.

The silence was eerie, unnerving. The closer Deme moved toward the R.A.'s room, the less she looked forward to sleeping there. What had happened between her and Cal still hung in the air. Her body thrummed with desire. She wanted to run back down to him and spend the night in his arms, preferably in his apartment.

She held true to her course, entering her room with the key. Her first glance shot to the window. The vine that only a few hours ago had attacked Cal was safely outside the window, the thorns appearing less intimidating, the leaves a lighter shade of green.

Was it her imagination? She checked the lock on the window and leaned over the angelica root plant. It looked normal, if a little more green since she'd brought it into the room. She moved it to the counter by the sink, away from the window.

Moonlight shone through the glass, drawing Deme back to overlook the garden. Tall pine trees framed the garden, and dark blobs of shadows indicated the locations of rosebushes. Nothing appeared sinister, yet Deme couldn't help how her chest tightened as though a hand squeezed her ribs, making it more difficult to breathe.

"Where are you, little sister?"

A whisper of air stirred the hair around her neck, as if a gentle hand settled on her shoulder, a silent voice calling out, *I am here.*

Restless, Deme couldn't imagine laying her head down to sleep. So much had happened in one day and they still hadn't found Aurai.

A glance at her bed, neatly made and untouched even after the violent sex she'd had with Cal, made her think of Rachel and Mike's attack. Was the girl okay? Would she feel more like talking if Zoe wasn't around to scare her silent?

Deme left her room and hurried down the hall to Rachel's room. Again, the hallways were deserted. At eleven o'clock at night on a weekend in a dorm, it wasn't right. She recalled staying up all hours. If not her, then others ran the hallways, giggling and making noise until the wee hours.

When she reached the room Rachel had shared with

Aurai, she knocked softly, hesitant to make any noise, the silence in the dorm so complete it gave her chills. There were girls behind the doors. Deme could feel them shuffling quietly.

No response.

Deme knocked again. "Rachel, let me in?"

The floor vibrated, feet moving toward her. "Go away." Her muffled voice barely carried through the solid door. Deme had her ear pressed to it and could feel the girl's sobs. Her lingering fear, regret and thoughts of self-inflicted harm flowed through the barrier, filling Deme with Rachel's frame of mind.

Deme had to get in. If Rachel was having thoughts of suicide, she had to talk to her. Get her some help. "Please, Rachel."

"Go away." The feet moved away, the door remaining locked, Rachel's aura drifting away from where Deme stood pressed to the door.

Deme straightened, pulling the keys from her jeans pocket. It took only a moment to find the master key and insert it into the lock. She turned the handle and, with a quick glance at the empty corridor, ducked inside, closing the door behind her.

"Rachel?"

The girl lay wrapped in a fuzzy pink robe, curled in the fetal position on her bed, her back to Deme. "What do you want? I told you to go away."

"I can't. I'm worried about you. About what happened."

"Don't. I'm fine. Mike didn't do anything wrong. It was my fault."

"It wasn't your fault. No man has the right to attack you like that." Deme crossed the small room and sat on the edge of the bed. When she reached out to touch the back of Rachel's neck, the girl flinched and groaned.

"Rachel?" Deme brushed the girl's dark hair aside, exposing the column of her neck and the angry bruise marring her smooth white skin. The bruise resembled the shape of teeth marks. Human teeth.

"Did Mike do this to you?" The edge of another bruise was barely covered by the robe.

Deme pulled the lapel farther down. She had two more bite marks, equally purplish-red.

"He didn't mean to." Rachel tugged the edges of the robe up to her neck. "He wasn't himself."

"That's not an excuse for what he did." Deme pulled the girl up and into her arms. "No one should do this to another human."

"You can't turn him in, unless you turn me in, too."

"Why?"

"I bit him, too."

She pushed Rachel to arm's length. "You bit him?"

"Yes. I don't know why. I've never done anything like that ever. He made me do it."

"Mike made you do it?"

"No, not Mike."

"Then who?"

"I don't know. It sounds crazy, but he got in my head and made me act like an animal. I didn't want to, but I couldn't stop."

She stared at Deme, her eyes widening. "He got to you, too, didn't he?" She pointed at Deme's neck.

"What do you mean?"

"There." She pointed again.

Deme left the girl on the bed and walked to the mirror on the wall between the closets. She pushed her hair aside and there on her neck just below her ear was a bite mark, just like the one Rachel had.

Cold washed over her, her stomach clenching, her skin clammy. Deme's world grayed around the edges as she realized just how out of control Cal's actions had been.

Chapter 8

Cal lay in his bed in the apartment he'd had for the past five years, wishing he'd stayed with Deme. Instinct told him she wasn't safe on that campus, in that dorm, with the craziness infecting people right and left. Someone was playing with them. With all the students and faculty at Colyer-Fenton College. The sooner he found out who, the sooner he could put a stop to it.

In the meantime he lay awake waiting for dawn and the start of another day of investigation.

He must have drifted off because the next thing he knew his alarm clock buzzed. He rolled over and hit snooze, but the alarm kept ringing. Then he realized it wasn't his alarm but his cell phone.

After fumbling on the nightstand, he found it, flipped it open and answered, "Black."

"Cal, I need you at the hospital."

Cal sat up straight, all vestiges of sleep wiped from his mind. "Who?"

"A young man, a college student from Colyer-Fenton, was just brought in comatose."

"What happened?"

"Attempted suicide." The lieutenant hesitated. "He might just have succeeded."

"Has he been ID'd?" Cal balanced the cell phone between his shoulder and his ear while he pulled on his jeans.

"Mike Hubbs."

"Damn." The phone slipped from Cal's ear. He barely caught it before it hit the floor. He jammed it against his ear to hear the lieutenant as he continued.

"I take it you know him," Marty said.

"Ran into him earlier. He'd attempted to rape his date, Rachel Taylor, on campus."

"No one turned him in?"

"The girl didn't want to press charges."

"I'm not liking this, Cal." The lieutenant sighed. "Get here, will ya?"

"On my way." Cal clicked the off button and zipped his jeans, slipping the cell phone into his pocket.

He tugged a black T-shirt over his head and was pulling it down when his phone vibrated in his pocket.

Without looking at the caller ID, he answered, "Black."

"Cal?"

Deme's voice brought him to a standstill.

"What's wrong?"

"I just left Rachel in her room."

"Funny you should mention her."

"She's in bad shape." Deme didn't sound in such good shape herself. Her voice was tired.

"Tell me."

"She's covered in bite marks."

"From Mike?"

"Yeah." She paused. "And Cal?"

"You mean it gets worse?"

"Yeah." Deme sighed.

Cal's gut clenched, his hand tightening around the phone.

"I have a few myself."

Cal's stomach took a freefall and he sat hard on the bed. "I did that?"

"Yeah."

"I don't remember doing it." He shoved a hand through his hair, bile rising in his throat.

"It's like I said earlier, it wasn't you."

"The hell it wasn't." He stood, rage flowing through him.

"There's something else."

"As if this isn't bad enough," he muttered.

"She said *it* made Mike do it. *It* made *her* bite Mike, too. Do me a favor will you?"

"Anything," he said, feeling like the lowest form of life on the planet.

"Go to the mirror and check yourself."

He stood and crossed to the mirror over the dresser. "Hold on." Cal set the phone on the dresser and tore off the shirt he'd just put on. There on his collarbone and again on his right shoulder were teeth marks. He touched them, pain an affirmation of the bruising.

He lifted the phone, his gaze pinned to the marks. "I'll be damned."

"You, too, huh?" she asked softly. "I'm sorry, Cal. I don't know what came over me."

"Same here."

Her voice got stronger. "But know this. It wasn't us. Something else is at work here."

"You know I don't believe in all that magic stuff." He blew out a frustrated breath. "I'd love to blame something or someone else, but I can't. I did that to you."

"And I did it to you. Think, Cal," Deme said, her voice tense. "In our past relationship, we never got that violent. Never."

"But how could something or someone else cause this?"

"What Rachel said made sense."

"What is this *it* she's talking about?"

"I don't know. But it's having an impact on more and more people. We have to find its source."

"Let's assume I believe there's some supernatural force at work here. How do we find it?"

"Again, I don't know. But I bet it has everything to do with Zoe's attitude, the attempts at rape…and Aurai's disappearance."

"I'm headed to the hospital now."

"Why?"

"Mike Hubbs was admitted. He attempted suicide last night."

Deme gasped. "Is he all right?"

"I'll know more once I swing by. Want to meet me there?"

"No, I get the feeling I'm needed around here. In case something happens. Let me know how it goes."

"Will do." He started to hang up and thought again. "Be careful, Deme. Even if you don't want me in your life, I care."

"Thanks." She clicked off.

Silence surrounded him and with it guilt so overwhelming he wanted to throw himself out the window.

Is this what had happened to Mike? Was there another being making them act this way?

If so, everything Cal believed to be true and logical teetered on the edge of crashing in around him.

He shoved his feet into his boots and ran out the door. Answers. He needed answers and fast, before someone else got hurt.

After a thorough look around the dormitory to verify all was quiet and no one wandered the halls, Deme returned to her room.

As soon as she walked through the door, she felt watched, which was ridiculous. No one else was in the room, and being on the second story of the building, no one could be hovering outside her window. Still the feeling persisted, even as she dressed for bed in conservative pajamas.

The skimpy baby-doll nightgown she normally slept in would have to wait for a night she didn't think she might have to risk running out of the building.

Deme didn't think she'd fall to sleep as keyed up as she'd been after her talk with Rachel. But as soon as her head hit the pillow, exhaustion claimed her.

Suddenly she was being lifted and spun in the air, her cries being sucked into a vortex along with her body and soul. Dragged down, down, down, she entered a dark world where light barely penetrated and slithery things skittered through the shadows.

"Deme?" a voice called.

"Aurai?" she answered, moving toward the sound, her eyes open but seeing nothing but black. With her hands out in front of her to keep her from bumping into things, she continued moving in the direction she'd first heard her sister's voice. "Aurai? Where are you?"

"Here," she said. "I'm right here."

"But I can't see you. Come into the light."

"I can't. I'm trapped."

"Where, Aurai? Where are you trapped?"

"I don't knoooowwww." Her voice faded into an abyss, swallowed like everything good and bright.

The darkness ebbed around her, undulating like a seductive lover, pressing closer until she backed against a wall. Feathery black tendrils stroked her skin, swirled around her face and into her mouth.

She couldn't breathe, couldn't cry out. Her fingers clawed at her throat trying to dislodge the evil. She had to get out before it consumed her, too.

"Go, Deme! Leave before he takes you, too!" Aurai cried out.

No. Deme didn't want to leave her sister. She had to get her out with her.

"You can't. He's too powerful. Let me go…"

Deme jerked awake, gasping for air, her heart thundering against her chest. She sat up, her gaze darting around the interior of the dorm room, pushing back the panic that threatened to take over.

Light from the hallway edged underneath the doorway.

As the panic receded, tapping increased on the window.

Almost afraid to look, Deme glanced across at the glass and almost screamed.

An image of her sister's face wavered against the inky blackness of night. Ghostly pale hair whipped in the wind and her eyes rounded in terror.

"Aurai!" Deme leaped from the bed and raced for the window. As she reached for the latch, her sister's face disappeared and in its place the vines formed a gaping maw, thorns pressing against the window like teeth, slashing at the glass.

Deme jumped back, her hand releasing the clasp, the lock remaining tight. For a long time she stood with her hand pressed to her chest. Then she heard it.

Chanting. Soft at first, rising in waves with the wind. It was coming from outside…in the garden.

Afraid to trust her own senses, and still shaking from her last encounter, Deme leaned toward the window, peering through the choking vines distorting her view.

Below in the open area between the towering pines, a circle of people stood in black robes, candle flames flickering in front of each one.

What the hell? The garden was forbidden. After Aurai had disappeared, Deme would think no one would venture into the deadly paradise.

The floor beneath her feet trembled as if warning of danger.

Dressed in her pajamas, her feet bare, Deme shot out of the room.

Cal arrived at the hospital in time to catch an ambulance preparing to leave.

"Crazy shift." A blond EMT shook his head as he closed and latched the outside door at the rear of the ambulance.

Cal paused beside one of the techs and flipped out his badge. "Did you guys deliver a Mike Hubbs here a little while ago?"

"The guy who attempted suicide?" The EMT, perched on the running board, about to climb into the driver's seat, nodded. "Yeah. That's what I'm talking about. Crazy."

"Who reported it?"

"His roommate found him. The guy slit his wrists and would have bled out if his roommate had gotten in a few minutes later. I think the kid was high on something."

"Hubbs?"

"Yeah, he was delirious, talking about a beast trying to come out of his chest."

The EMT at the rear of the vehicle joined them. "Yeah, he kept ripping at his shirt and disturbing the pressure bandages on his wrist. He slipped into a coma before we got to the hospital."

"Probably just as well. He was losing blood fast and all that jerking around only made it worse."

"The doc thinks they might save him, though." The radio inside the truck chirped static, a call going out to a unit.

"That's us. You need anything else, catch us at the end of our shift. We've been hopping tonight. Must be a full moon."

The EMTs climbed into the ambulance and drove out of the emergency entrance.

Cal looked up at the sky. Clouds obliterated the moon. He entered the hospital, immediately hit by the scent of disinfectant. His first instinct was to turn and leave, hating the sterile environment, the injuries and traumas that passed through the doors, but he had to see Mike for himself.

His hand went to the bite mark on his collarbone. Had Deme really bitten him? He couldn't remember any of that, only the hot sex and the need to do it again and again.

Even now his jeans tightened, his groin filling, pulsing to life.

As he entered the elevator, he adjusted, chastising himself for his continued lack of control. How could this be happening to him? He respected Deme more than that. Another wave of guilt plagued him, pressing down on him like a heavy weight. If he was a weak man, he'd be tempted to punish himself.

Cal's breath lodged in his throat, refusing to move any farther. The urge to punish himself grew, and he realized what Mike had felt and why he'd attempted suicide.

The logical side of his brain tried to reason with the side that piled more and more guilt on top of him. By the time the door slid open on the floor where Mike was being kept in ICU, Cal was sagging against the handrail.

"Black?" Marty hurried over from the nurses' station and helped Cal out of the elevator. "What's wrong?"

"I don't know." Cal staggered to the counter and leaned on it, breathing hard. "I can't seem to pull myself out of it."

"Of what?"

"That's just it, I don't know. It's as though I'm on drugs or something. Everything seems too much to handle. I can't fight it." Cal crumpled to the floor, the world going dark.

"Mr. Black? Cal?" A woman in blue scrubs waved something under his nose.

The pungent smell stung his senses and pulled him back to consciousness. Cal sat up, running a hand through his hair. "What happened?"

"You passed out." Marty squatted on his other side.

"Passed out?" Cal never passed out. But then he'd

done a lot of strange things he never thought he would in the past twenty-four hours. He pushed to his feet.

"Whoa, steady there." Marty rose beside him, a hand on his elbow.

The nurse had his other arm.

"I'm fine." He straightened, shaking off their hands. "Really."

"Still, you should see a doctor."

"Not necessary. I came to see Mike."

"Look, we don't need another patient in ICU. Let us help you." The nurse grabbed his arm again.

"I said I'm fine." Cal glared at her until she let go.

"Have it your way, but I'm not picking you up off the floor."

Cal turned to Marty. "Where's Hubbs?"

"Second door on the right."

Cal crossed the corridor and entered the room to find the big undergraduate covered in white, tubes running into his arm and down his throat, his arms wrapped in bandages.

"He's still in a coma. They'll try to bring him out in the morning when the doctor makes his rounds. He's not much help as he is."

Cal only half listened. He strode to the young man's bedside, pulled the sheet back and tugged the collar of the hospital gown down.

Just like Deme predicted, the man had bite marks on his chest.

"Human, aren't they?"

"Yes," Cal responded.

"Know who did it?"

"His girlfriend."

"Jeez. What's with kids nowadays?"

"I'm beginning to wonder that myself, but I'm thinking it's not the kids."

"Drugs?"

"No." He pulled the gown up, covering Mike's chest, and tucked the sheet around him. "Make sure they take good care of him."

The lieutenant's brow furrowed. "After what he did to that girl, you care?"

"I don't think he knew what was happening."

"Care to explain?"

"Not now." Cal turned and left the room.

Marty jogged to keep up. "What's going on?"

"I don't know, but I get the feeling Deme Chattox is in over her head."

"Well, hell." Marty stopped in the middle of the hall-way. "Keep me informed, Black."

Cal passed the elevator, opting for the staircase. He took the stairs two at a time, leaping past the last four to land on the street level. He burst into the open, breathing for what felt like the first time in days.

Worry had a way of making your vision sharper, your hearing more penetrating and your focus dead-on. Without a doubt, he knew he needed to get back to the campus. The sooner the better.

Deme entered through the garden gate. The lock and chain lay on the ground nearby. Who had the key? Who would be stupid enough to let these people in when they could be banned from campus if caught?

Keeping to the shadows of the buildings surrounding the garden, Deme eased closer to the circle. For the first time since she came to Colyer-Fenton, Deme realized the garden was in the shape of a pentagon, a building at each side, one of which was the Gamma Omega dormitory. She recognized the student commons building as another and the administration building as a third. The other two she couldn't identify but made a mental note to check into it when she got back to her room and could locate them on the campus map.

As she neared the circle, the chanting grew louder. All the voices were pitched high and soft. Girls. Probably the Gamma Omegas doing some hazing ritual.

The robes they wore looked much like the one she'd found in Rachel's closet—black with a full hood to hide their faces.

When she got close enough, Deme could make out the words, and she gasped. They were calling on the spirit of the dark lord of the underworld.

Deme couldn't feel power emanating from any one girl, but she knew you didn't mess with dark spirits, witch or not. Dark magic was unstable, hard to control and even harder to cleanse from your aura once it invaded.

Was that what had happened? Had dark magic invaded this campus, disturbing those who got too close to its center?

One girl stepped forward and pulled back her hood, exposing her face to the candlelight.

Zoe Adams.

She set a blue vial in the center of the ring of candles. With a flick of a match, she lit a sandalwood incense wand and jabbed it into the earth beside the bottle. Then she stood and, instead of lifting her face to the moon as a good witch would, she stared at the ground.

"God of love and beauteous might
Come unto us this moonless night
We cast this circle to ask thy boon
Bless beauty on us, bless us soon

We cast this circle one more time
Upon us let your splendor shine
Lord of Darkness great and wise
Let others see us through your eyes
We cast this circle one two three
We pray you bless us for all who see
So mote it be."

From a velvet bag tied to her waist, she tossed rose petals around the ring of candles and stepped back to the outer circle of robe-clad girls.

The members who'd obviously done this before bowed their heads and chanted.

"Night cloaks all with beauty
Shadows grow with power
Darkness, we embrace thee."

They continued chanting, repeating the words over and over until all the girls joined in.

Deme stood transfixed, dread pressing into her chest like an iron fist. These girls played at black magic. Didn't they understand? Dark spells like this one were dangerous.

Zoe knelt to retrieve the blue vial from the center of the circle and poured a single drop onto her lips. She passed it to the next girl in the circle, who repeated the performance and handed it to the next.

As the vial made its way around the circle, a cry rose up from one of the robe-clad girls. "No! I can't do this!"

Rachel Taylor collapsed to the ground, her hood flung back, exposing thick brown hair and pale, translucent, smooth skin. Her body shook with the force of her sobs, the earth vibrating beneath Deme's feet, sharing her sadness and something else.

Deme had to stop this ritual before it went too far.

She was afraid she was already too late, but she couldn't stand by and do nothing.

Calling on all the power of the earth she could muster, Deme pressed her bare toes into the grass, feeling the cool earth beneath. She closed her eyes and drew in a deep breath, her concentration nearly shattered by the amount of effort even a breath of air required in this cloistered garden.

"Mother of earth
Goddess of beauty
strength of spirit
I call upon thee
Ancient the stone
stalwart the tree
Your gifts of safe harbor
impart upon thee
Embrace these children
let peace once more reign
Bring moonlight to shadows
and ease to their pain
Mother of earth
Oh, radiant one
With prayers I beseech thee
Let darkness be gone."

Deme opened her eyes, her prayers echoing in her mind, hope rising inside her as she hid among the shadows. The earth beneath her bare feet quivered. Moonlight peeked out from a cloud, casting light upon the circle of girls.

A tentative smile curled the corners of Deme's lips. The goddess would shine down on the garden and protect the girls from the dark forces at work here.

The cloud slipped back over the moon, choking out all light but for the candle flames. A dark wisp of air whipped through the clearing, snuffing out every flame, leaving the garden in shadows except for the few lights shining from windows of the buildings surrounding them.

The hooded girls gasped.

"I can't see," a voice called out, quavering in the gloom.

"Anyone have a flashlight?"

"I do." A light flickered on, spreading a narrow ray through the ranks of the girls. The circle collapsed inward, the girls moving closer to one another, gathering around the beam of the flashlight.

"What's that?" a girl cried out. Then a scream ripped through the air.

The beam of light swerved toward the scream.

The ground parted, roots pushing up from beneath.

Girls screamed and ran in all directions, but the roots tripped them, wrapping around their ankles, bringing them crashing to the earth.

What was happening?

Deme watched in horror as more roots exploded from the ground, grasping at those girls racing for the open gate.

The gate swung shut, trapping all within the garden.

One by one, the girls were dragged to the earth, the roots weaving back and forth over their bodies.

Deme threw herself toward the nearest girl, clawing at the relentless root that twined and circled the girl's neck. The hood fell back, revealing the pale blond hair and gray eyes of Shelby Cramer. She reached for Deme, her eyes wide, fearful.

"Help me," she cried, then the root tightened.

Shelby clutched at the root strangling her.

Deme grabbed the root, pulling to free the girl.

Beside her the ground parted and darkness in the form of a bare black vine snaked up, twisting around her legs, dragging her to the ground and away from Shelby.

Deme dug her fingernails into the earth, reaching for the girl, her hand grazing the robe, but not for long.

The earth shook, the ground trembling as more and more roots sprang from below, slithering along the surface, attaching themselves to all those who occupied the garden.

"Deme!" From the second floor of the dormitory, Cal pushed aside the thorn vine blocking Deme's window and cursed. "Deme!"

Hope filled her chest and made her fight harder at the roots that bound her, dragging her deeper into the earth. "Cal! Help us!"

He disappeared, and with him all hope faded.

The roots around her arms swept up to her neck, cutting off her air. Deme couldn't draw a breath, the darkness more and more pronounced as her head grew light and fuzzy. Images of Cal flitted across her memories. Why had she run from him? From the potential for happiness. If she lived, she'd tell him how she felt. *Please, I have to live.* She closed her eyes and prayed, *Goddess of the earth, please let me live.* The more she prayed, the tighter the roots became, pressing her body into the earth, the dirt parting to let her slip beneath.

"Deme, hold on!" Suddenly Cal appeared wielding a big knife, slashing at the roots clinging to his feet. He cut and hacked his way across the garden until he reached Deme.

In two great swings, he severed the roots pulling Deme deeper into the earth. Air filled her lungs and she sprang to her feet, refusing to give in to the peace of death.

With Cal hacking and Deme pulling, they freed one girl after the next, shoving them through the gate and out of the forbidden garden. Bushes and vines reached for them as they exited the garden, the last to escape.

Cal slammed the gate behind himself and wrapped the chain around, bolting the lock in place.

Deme fell to the ground, breathing hard, her arms and legs laced with scratches and bruises.

"We can't stay here." Cal lifted her in his arms and carried her to the edge of the building farthest away from the seething garden.

There he stopped and crushed her to his chest. "Deme." He buried his face in her neck, his body shaking. "I thought I'd lost you."

"You and me both." Her arms wrapped around him and she held him close, tears wetting her cheek and his. "I tried to help them."

"Shh…it's okay now."

"But everything I did made it worse. My spell turned against the girls." The tears came faster and sobs rose in her throat. "They almost died."

"Deme." Cal set her on her feet and gathered her face between his palms. "*You* almost died."

"I'm okay, thanks to you." She pulled away, her gaze panning the yard surrounding the dorm. Not a single girl remained. Only Deme and Cal occupied the area. "Where are the girls?"

"They must have gone in."

"Let's check on them. I hate to think they went back into the garden."

"Surely not."

"Come on." She led the way into the dorm and

knocked on the first door with a Gamma Omega symbol on it.

A pretty girl with dark brown hair opened it, blinking at the light in the hallway. She yawned. "You're the new R.A., right? What's going on?"

"Random check," Deme said. "Were you outside earlier?"

"I got in from my waitress job around nine. Why?"

Deme shook her head. "No reason. Go back to bed."

As the brunette closed the door, Deme shot a narrowed glance at Cal. "I swear I saw her out there in one of the robes."

He nodded. "Did you see the dirt on her bare feet?"

"No, but I'll be looking next time." She walked to the next door with the Gamma Omega Greek letters and knocked.

It took longer this time for the girl to answer. When she did, the scratches on her ankles and calves and the dirt on her feet were all too obvious. "What's happening?"

"Maybe you can tell us." Deme crossed her arms over her chest. "Were you just in the forbidden garden?"

The girl shook her head, her eyes glassy. "I don't know what you're talking about. I've been in bed since ten o'clock. Got an exam tomorrow."

"How do you explain the dirt on your feet and the scratches?" Cal pointed to her feet and ankles.

The girl looked down and blinked, her eyes widening. "What the hell? How did those get there? Oh, my God." She looked up, tears welling. "I should call the campus nurse."

Deme frowned. "You don't remember getting them?"

"No. I swear I've been in my room all night. Ask my roommate."

Another girl lay in bed, completely out, her arm hanging over the edge, displaying cuts and bruises.

"Oh, God, she's been hurt, as well." The girl ran to her roommate and shook her. "Wake up, Abby."

Deme held her breath until the girl stirred and her eyes opened. "Lissa? Whadya want?" she asked, her words slurred.

"What happened to us? Why do we have cuts and bruises?" Tears poured down Lissa's face and she collapsed on the floor beside her roommate. "I don't know what happened."

Deme stepped into the room, pulling Cal in behind her to keep from waking the entire dorm with Lissa's sobs. "Mind if we look around?"

"No." Lissa scrubbed the tears from her face and held on to her roommate's hand. "Please do." She pulled her knees up under her chin and watched as Deme and Cal checked beneath beds. As Deme opened one closet, Cal opened the other. There hanging inside each were the black robes used in the ceremony.

Deme pulled one out on the hanger. "Do you remember wearing this in the garden earlier?"

Both girls shook their heads. "We only wear those when the Gamma Omegas have a sorority meeting."

"And you don't remember having one of those tonight?"

Both girls looked up at Deme, shaking their heads. "No," they stated in unison.

Lissa climbed up on the bed beside Abby and hugged the girl close. "We'd remember something like that."

Deme stared hard at both, but her gut told her that these girls thought they were telling the absolute truth. Obviously they didn't remember being attacked by roots in the garden and almost killed.

"What's happening?" Abby asked.

"I don't know." Deme replaced the robe in the closet even though she wanted to take it out and burn it. "But I'm going to find out. Use a clean washrag and soap to clean your scratches. I'll bring ointment and bandages by in a few minutes."

Deme and Cal left the girls, closing the door behind them.

"What do you make of that?"

"You were there. You saw what happened." Deme faced Cal. "It happened."

He nodded, stroking his hand down the side of her cheek. "It happened."

"Right before I cast my spell, they were passing around a blue vial of liquid. Do you think it was a drug?"

"Could be."

"Then there is one more person I need to talk to." Deme pushed her dirty pajama sleeves up and marched to the stairwell door.

She climbed the steps two at a time, Cal keeping up with little effort.

Once on the second floor, she aimed for Rachel's room.

She got only halfway down the hall when Zoe Adams stepped out of her room in front of her. "What's going on?"

Deme came to a complete stop, her jaw tightening. "Why don't you tell me."

"Tell you what? That you're breaking the rules of the dormitory by bringing a man in after midnight?" Zoe cocked her eyebrows up into the sweep of her blond bangs. "I could have you fired for that."

Deme didn't back down. Instead she took another

step forward, putting herself toe to toe with the sorority leader. "What did you give the girls that made them forget what happened in the garden, Zoe?"

"I'm sure I don't know what you're talking about."

"I can have you kicked out of the dormitory and the school for drugging students, so don't mess with me."

"I'd like to see you try." One lip curled upward in a smirk. "My father is a major contributor to this school. You can't kick me out of anything."

"No matter how much money your daddy contributes, drugging others without their consent is illegal." Cal stepped up beside Deme, his hand resting at her waist.

Despite her self-righteous anger, Deme had to admit she was intimidated by Zoe's sordid, cocky self-assurance, and Cal's show of support made her feel better.

"Like I said...I don't know what you're talking about."

"Where's the blue vial you were using in the garden ceremony just a few minutes ago?"

Zoe frowned. "I wasn't in the garden a few minutes ago."

"What about the dirt on your feet and scratches on your legs? How do you explain that?"

She glanced down at her legs. "Well, you're right. There are scratches and dirt on my legs." She tipped her head to the side. "Now, how did they get there?" Zoe glanced up, her eyes narrowing. "You wouldn't have had anything to do with that, would you?"

Deme stared at the girl. She wanted to believe that Zoe was lying, but her confusion at the dirt and scratches was too convincing. "Good grief, Zoe. Go clean yourself up. Oh, and Zoe, something isn't right around here, and I intend to get to the bottom of it."

Zoe's gaze narrowed into a squint. "I can't tell you how this happened tonight, but I can tell you the Gamma Omegas stick together. Not one of them wants out of the sorority. They like what it's done for them and they won't go back." She turned on her bare heel and stomped back to her room, closing the door with a thump.

"What do you think she meant by they won't go back?" Cal asked.

"I don't know. But I'm getting really tired of Zoe's attitude." Deme sucked in a deep breath and let it out. "I want to check one more room then I need to distribute ointment and bandages." Exhaustion was dragging her down fast. No sleep and being attacked by a possessed garden had taken its toll.

"Where to?" Cal looked at the remaining doors.

"Rachel Taylor's room." Deme moved down the hallway and tapped on the door. "Just so you know, my sister used to occupy this room." Deme didn't wait for a response from Cal. She raised her hand and knocked on the door. The door swung open to darkness.

Cal reached inside and flipped the switch. Light filled all four corners...of an empty room.

Chapter 9

Cal didn't sleep the rest of the night. Though Deme insisted that she would be okay without him there, he hadn't gone far. He'd camped out beneath a tree where he could see the Gamma Omega dormitory.

Twice, the campus cop had circled. Twice, Cal had ducked into the shadows to avoid questions. As the campus maintenance man, it wouldn't do for him to be caught more or less stalking a dorm full of girls. Especially given the fact they'd had several attempted rapes. Despite the danger of getting caught and blamed for what he was trying to stop, Cal stayed put, managing to nod off near dawn.

Not until the sun shone down on his face did he awaken. Students passed by on the nearby sidewalks, carrying books to the commons for breakfast and a cram session before class.

Cal stood and stretched, checking his cell phone for

any text messages or missed calls. None. He dialed Deme's number and hit Send, only to punch the end call button before the first ring. She needed her rest, and he felt certain nothing else had happened since the garden incident.

With the grunge of a restless night making him feel sticky, he straddled his bike and headed for his apartment and a warm shower. He had to report for his first day of work as maintenance man in less than an hour, and he was certain that he would have a lot to do besides investigating the case.

After a shower, he headed back to campus, swinging through the local gourmet coffee shop for a strong dose of caffeine. Gritty eyes and an empty stomach didn't seem to be the best way to start the day. He had toilets to fix, drains to unstop and lightbulbs to change out, based on the repairs list his supervisor had given him the day before. He also wanted to ask a few questions while he had the opportunity.

Cal stepped into the maintenance shop fifteen minutes before his shift was due to begin.

Fred Knowlton sat at his desk, staring at the computer. "Damned thing is slower than molasses," he muttered.

"Morning, Mr. Knowlton."

"Fred. Call me Fred or I'll fire you on the spot," he groused, without looking up. "Know anything about computers?"

"A little." Cal stepped behind Fred and looked over his shoulder.

"Can't get this application to come up."

"Mind if I drive?"

"Not at all." Fred stood and let Cal take his seat. "I have a kind of love-hate relationship with these things.

I love to hate 'em. I had the work schedule up and was adding your name to the list of employees when it locked up on me."

Cal checked the task manager and canceled the program that was locked up and restarted it. "That should do it." He stood and let Fred resume his seat.

Fred spent a few seconds keying in information using the one-fingered typing method and pressed Enter. "There." He grinned up at Cal. "You saved me a lot of heartburn. What can I do for you this morning?"

"I was just curious about the guy I'm replacing. What happened to him? I heard rumors he disappeared."

Fred frowned. "Damnedest thing. I gave Kyle his list of repairs and sent him off about three weeks ago. Guess he didn't like the kinds of repairs and decided it was time to quit. He didn't come back that afternoon to clock out, didn't call and tell me he was quitting, and I haven't seen him since."

"Did you report it to the police?"

Fred shrugged. "I told the campus cop and HR. Figured if they were worried, they'd follow up. In the meantime, I've had some of the other guys working to pick up his slack. Glad you've come on board." His eyes narrowed. "You will let me know if you decide to quit, won't you?"

Cal grinned. "Don't worry. I will."

"Here's an updated list of repairs for the day." Fred handed him a printout. "If there's anything on the list you need help with, give me a call."

"What was on the list you gave Kyle when he disappeared?" Cal looked down at his list and back up. "Not anything on this list I hope."

"No. I seem to recall the only major repair was to a steam pipe in the basement of the student commons.

At least he fixed it before he disappeared." Fred stood, clipped a tool belt around his waist and stepped away from the desk. "Still have a lot to do today. Been short-handed so long, I've been helping out, as well." He slapped a campus maintenance hat on his head and handed another to Cal. "Here." He pulled a set of keys from his pocket and handed them to him, as well. "The master key should get you in most places on campus. Oh, and you should be able to find a coverall in the locker room that will fit you. See you at quittin' time."

Cal followed Fred to the locker room and the older man left him there with a map of the campus and a stack of coveralls in various sizes.

Dressed in a coverall and the maintenance cap, Cal hoped to blend into the woodwork. He quickly tackled the replacement bulbs in a couple of the lecture halls, keeping his ears open for anything out of the ordinary. Working through the list took up most of his morning, more than he would have preferred. But his next stop was a leaky faucet in the student commons kitchen. He wanted to check out the basement while there and see if he could find a clue to the missing maintenance man, Kyle.

It didn't take him long to replace the washer in the faucet, successfully stopping the drip. Then he located the stairs leading down into the basement. The doors were locked, but the master key Fred had given him worked to open them.

The first thing he noticed was the rumble of machines, completely obliterating any other noise he could hope to hear. If he worked down here long, he'd require earplugs or suffer hearing loss.

The basement was a maze of pipes, air-conditioning ductwork and stuff Cal didn't recognize. The lighting was less than adequate, forcing him to pull out the flashlight he'd grabbed out of the toolbox he'd been assigned. He searched the length of the basement, checking in, around, behind and over everything. He located several steam pipes Kyle could have worked on, none of which were leaking steam.

When he thought he had exhausted every inch of the space, Cal turned toward the stairs, in the process of hitting the off switch on his flashlight. When the beam swung across the concrete floor, it flashed on something beneath the metal stairwell. His hand froze on the switch. He'd missed it before because it wasn't all that obvious. Beneath the metal stairwell, he noticed metal rivets standing out on the floor. An iron ring the size of a softball stood vertical, as if it had been used not long ago and the rust caking the hinge kept it from dropping back down.

This was the basement. What could be below it?

Cal reached for the iron ring and tugged.

The door didn't budge. He searched for a lock, hoping he had a key to match. No lock. Which meant the door should open. He pulled again, putting his back into it.

This time the door creaked upward, but the weight of the door pulled it back down, dragging Cal with it.

Determined to get the door up this time, he used both hands, bent his knees and pulled with all his might. It took a lot of effort to get it open, but once he did, it was as if whatever suction had hold of it from below let go.

The door swung upward and clanked against the concrete wall beneath the steps. With the door's opening the stench of rot, sewer and damp wafted up into his face, making him gag. He pulled the collar of his coverall over his nose and shone the beam of his flashlight into the hole.

Metal ladder rungs led down into a dark abyss, the sublevel of the building. He knew that Chicago had an entire labyrinth of tunnels beneath the city. Could this be part of it?

His heartbeat kicked up the pace as he placed his foot on the first rung while holding on to the staircase above. He wondered if he'd find Kyle down here, and if so, would he be dead and decomposing?

Cal braced himself for the worst as he stepped another rung lower. In the back of his mind he thought maybe it wasn't such a good idea to go below without backup. He'd about decided to come back up when the cell phone vibrated in his jeans pocket.

His jeans were buried beneath his coverall. In order to access it, he had to climb back out of the hole and unzip his coverall.

The caller ID indicated Deme. He punched the talk button and pressed the receiver to his ear. "Deme? Are you all right?"

"Cal? Where are you?"

"In the basement of the student commons. What's up?"

"Gina's been working in the library all morning and found something interesting. I'm headed that way. Can you join us there on the second floor in the east-side stacks?"

"I'll be there." He flipped the phone shut and stood for a moment shining his light down into the darkness and obscurity of the subterranean level below. It would have to wait. He'd check with Marty and see if he knew anything about the tunnels before he ventured farther.

As he lowered the heavy iron door to the ground,

he could swear he heard something like a groan from down below. An unwanted chill spread through his skin right down to the bone. All the talk about magic had his imagination working overtime.

He jerked the door open again. "Hello!"

No response. Not even an echo, as if the ground below swallowed his call.

Maybe he'd imagined it.

He lowered the door again. The hinge gave with an eerie creaking sound almost like the cry of a child. That must have been it. Nothing a little oil wouldn't cure. He left the trap door and walked up the staircase into the student commons, feeling as if a weight had lifted from him.

But the creepy feeling he'd gotten followed him all the way across campus to the library.

Deme knew the exact moment when Cal entered the building. The vibration of his movements were his alone, and she recognized it from the many weeks they'd dated. Each time he'd entered her apartment complex, she'd known, her body anticipating their greeting and the tumbled mess they'd make of the sheets on her bed. Every minute of every day had been spent thinking of him and what he'd do to her when they finally got together. She'd been so completely obsessed with him, it had ultimately scared her into running.

Even now, every one of her nerve endings alerted her to his presence. She'd arrived a minute before him and hadn't met up with her sisters yet. But her feet wouldn't take her farther, forcing her to wait near the central staircase. Her pulse quickened, her breathing becoming more ragged in anticipation of seeing him again.

No amount of self-chastisement slowed her beating

heart. She really had to get a grip on her reaction to the man's presence. When they found Aurai, Deme would be on her way back to St. Croix and the thriving private investigation business she'd established there. Cal had said in no uncertain terms he didn't believe in magic. Therefore he'd never understand her.

Not that she'd been dabbling much in magic. She preferred to live a normal life much as Aurai had aspired to, touching on magic only to help solve investigations no weightier than finding a missing pooch or a cheating husband.

The distance from Cal hadn't lessened her longing for him and the physical ache of not having him to lie next to her in bed. Even now, she wanted him.

This is ridiculous. She couldn't go on mooning over a man she'd left behind a year ago.

Deme turned away, determined to move on and join her sisters in the stacks.

A sound behind her made her look over her shoulder.

Cal stood at the top of the stairs. Dressed in a Colyer-Fenton College maintenance uniform, he looked no less handsome. The tool belt hanging from his hips actually increased his appeal.

Her heart flip-flopped in her chest, her cheeks burning, the heat flooding her body, dipping low into her belly. The apex of her thighs flamed, and ached with longing.

Cal reached out and cupped her face. "Are you okay? You look a little feverish."

Deme almost laughed out loud, her face smoldering with heat. "It's a bit warm in here." She told herself to turn, to walk away from where this man stood touching her cheek. But she couldn't. She wanted to lean into his palm and press a kiss there. Again, she couldn't.

"Come—" Deme squeaked, cleared her throat and started again. "Come on. Selene and Gina should already be here."

As his fingers left her cheek, the cool library air barely helped to bring her temperature back under control. Her feet finally cooperated and she moved one step at a time toward the east-side stacks.

"Aren't you afraid of blowing your cover?" Cal asked. Deme shook her head. "Gina chose this location because no one uses this corner of the library. We should have no problem as long as we keep it quiet."

Gina and Selene leaned over a microfiche reader, pointing at the screen. Brigid stood beside them, her arms crossed, her brows pushed low.

"They still use those things?" Deme leaned over Gina's other shoulder.

"The librarian said they're in the process of converting everything to digital format. They just hadn't gotten this far back." Gina spoke without glancing up. "Look at this." She maneuvered the film backward to the beginning of a copy of an article from an old *Chicago Tribune* newspaper.

The headline read Five Sisters Die in Colyer-Fenton Fire.

"What the hell?" A cold hand squeezed Deme's heart, making her chest hurt almost as if the old article was a portent of her and her sisters' deaths. Which was crazy. "What's the date on that paper?"

Brigid stared at Deme. "It'll be exactly thirty years ago tomorrow."

All four sisters were silent.

"It doesn't mean anything to us," Gina finally said. "What's interesting is the location. Apparently the fire occurred in Lion Hall and it was burned completely to the ground." She looked around at the people assembled. "Anyone have a copy of the campus map?"

Cal pulled a wrinkled paper out of his pocket and handed it to Gina.

She spent half a minute scanning the page and the legend detailing the names of the buildings. "Just like I thought. There isn't a Lion Hall."

Brigid shrugged. "Which means they didn't rebuild the hall after it burned. So?"

Deme leaned over Gina's shoulder, reading down through the entire article, skimming over the details of the emergency response. The more she read the colder the room became until a shiver shook her from head to toe. "Says here in the article that it was the central building in a spokelike design. The five adjacent buildings suffered minimal damage."

"You think the forbidden garden is where Lion Hall used to be?" Gina asked.

Selene stood straight, her eyes closed, her body swaying. "Yes. That's exactly it. And the five sisters have to be the voices calling to me in my night and day dreams." She pressed her fingers to her temples. "Thank the goddess. I thought I was going crazy. I hear them now."

Deme shot a glance at her sister. "Really? Can you hear what they're saying?"

Selene's brow scrunched. "No. But the closer I get to the garden, the more I hear them and the more chaotic their voices are."

"Has to be where Lion Hall stood. That's why you can hear the sisters. They burned with the hall thirty years ago."

Brigid touched Gina's shoulder. "See what else you can find during that time frame. Any strange happenings, unexplained events, attacks, problems with students?"

Gina nudged the microfiche tray, skimming across several days' worth of newspapers, searching for anything related to Colyer-Fenton College.

A headline on the front page of the *Tribune* captured Deme's attention. "Go back."

Gina eased backward slowly, coming to a halt on an article.

Local College Coed Attacked on Campus

Deme read over Gina's shoulder. "'A young woman was attacked on the Colyer-Fenton College campus late last night. Miss Baker is being treated for injuries at an area hospital. The police questioned the victim, who was so traumatized she spoke of a huge beast, ravishing her.'" Deme looked up at Cal. "Sound familiar?"

Gina continued reading aloud, "Doctors and psychiatrists are working to help her in the aftermath of the ordeal. The president of the campus has hired additional security personnel to keep students safe, but some parents have pulled their students out of school until the perpetrator is caught."

"See if you can find the full name of the girl."

Gina swept across film, but no other news mentioned the campus or the student.

Deme straightened and paced the length of a shelf of books. "We need to get into student records."

"I'll see what I can do." Cal pulled a lightbulb from his coverall pocket, a smile tugging at his lips. "Surely there has to be a lightbulb burned out in there."

Deme almost laughed, glad he was there and helping them find her sister. "My gut tells me that the building that burned and the sisters who died in it are related to what's happening now. It's too much of a coincidence, especially considering there are five sisters involved now."

"I'll keep looking through the newspaper articles and historical records of the college," Gina offered.

"Good." Deme looked to Brigid.

Brigid rolled her eyes. "I'll check out City Hall and see what records they have on file for the buildings on campus back then. Although I'd rather be kicking ass than digging through moldy old papers."

Deme touched her sister's arm. "Thanks, Brigid."

Brigid's expression hardened. "Anything for Aurai."

"I have a class to teach right now in the theater. I can ask around and see if anyone knows where Rachel disappeared to," Selene said.

A student carrying a huge stack of research books passed by where they stood, casting a questioning look in their direction.

When he'd passed, Deme sighed. "We should meet off campus later this evening. I don't want too many people seeing us together. If someone on campus is causing all these problems, we don't need them to find out they are being investigated."

"Right." Brigid tapped a finger to her temple. "I'm outta here."

"Me, too." Selene slung the long handle of her bag over her head and across her chest, looking every bit the artistic drama teacher. "Wish me luck. I've never taught drama."

Deme smiled at her. "You'll do great. It's all about empathy and expressing emotions. Exactly what you're good at."

"Thanks. I just wish I could get rid of this headache. It's dragging me down."

Deme stared at her sister, for the first time noticing

the dark shadows beneath her eyes. "Are you sleeping at all?"

She shook her head. "Not much. I'm having nightmares about being sucked into the earth by a wind tunnel."

Deme's breath caught. "You, too?"

Brigid, three steps away, turned back, her hand raised. "Me, three."

The three of them turned to Gina.

She nodded, her mouth set in grim lines. "Is the dream about Aurai?"

All the girls nodded as one.

Deme was the first to break the long silence. "Well, let's get to work and find our sister."

Brigid and Selene left.

Gina bent over the microfiche reader.

Cal touched Deme's shoulder and motioned her aside.

"Are you going to be all right?" Cal asked.

Deme frowned. "I can handle myself. If you can find out about the students who were here thirty years ago that could be a big help."

"I'll come up with an excuse to get inside the records."

"And Cal, find out anything you can about Zoe Adams, Mike Hubbs and Rachel Taylor. If we can get an address, we might want to check with Rachel's family and see if she made it home."

"Will do." He closed the distance between them, cupping her face. "Be careful, will ya?" His thumb brushed across her cheekbone, his gaze capturing hers.

Deme stared into his eyes, trying to read into his mind and soul. "Tell me, Cal. After last night, do you still think magic is a bunch of talk?"

"Let's say I'm teetering on the fence."

"You can't deny what you saw in the garden."

"No. And I have no explanation for it. But like you said, I'm a black-and-white kind of guy. It's going to take time for me to accept the gray." He touched her lips with his, briefly, bringing his head up so fast, Deme thought she might have imagined his kiss.

"Did you just kiss me?" she asked.

"Looks like it."

"No. This is a kiss." She wrapped her hand around the back of his head and drew him down to her, kissing him hard and long. Her tongue pushed past his teeth to claim his, twisting and tasting. Her chest pressed into his, and she wished with all her heart she were naked in bed with this strong cop who'd saved her ass the night before.

A discreet cough reminded her where she was.

Deme pulled back, brushing her hand across her lips. "Sorry, I didn't mean to put on a show."

Cal grinned, then sobered. "Don't be sorry. Just be safe." He kissed her again, his lips pressing hard against hers. Then he left.

Deme watched him until he rounded the corner and disappeared. She sighed and turned toward Gina.

Her sister sat facing her, arms crossed over her chest and a smirk on her face. "Wanna tell me what's going on with you two?"

Deme straightened her shoulders. "No."

"Oh, come on. What are sisters for if they can't share the sordid details of their love lives?"

"Shh." Deme glanced around at the empty section of the library. "We've been here long enough. If we stay any longer someone's bound to see us together."

Having been the oldest sister forever, she had never

shared her life with her younger sisters, feeling the need to hold herself to a higher standard while her siblings struggled through hookups and breakups during their teens. Not that Deme hadn't struggled. Being a witch with "talents" had its own kind of strain on every relationship she'd ever been in. When she'd finally found Cal, she'd been gun-shy and afraid to let herself care too much.

Her voice little more than a whisper, Gina continued, "Really, Deme. We're all adults now. You don't have to be the model sister anymore."

Gina's comment hit too close to home, knocking a chink in the wall Deme had built to hold herself up. "It's just…"

"He's a mortal and you're a witch?" Gina's brows cocked upward.

Deme sucked in a deep breath, finding it difficult to let go and share after carrying the burden alone all those years. "Yes."

"So?" Gina shook her head. "And here we all thought you were the smart one." Her sister tsked. "So disappointing."

"See?" Deme flung her hands in the air. "That's why I never shared. I couldn't let you see how messed up I was. You all counted on me to be the perfect sister, to lead by example."

"And you're not so perfect." Gina stood and wrapped her arms around Deme. "Which makes you all the more lovable and perfect in my eyes." She held Deme at arm's length. "Do you realize how hard it is to live up to your example?" Gina grimaced. "It's exhausting."

Deme stared at her sister. "Really?"

"You're a tough act to follow, and some of us would rather give up than try."

Deme's eyes widened. "Brigid?"

Gina nodded. "I've hit a few roadblocks myself in the path to being Deme."

"I'm sorry." Deme hugged her sister close. "I didn't know I was being a pain."

"Well, you are." Gina brushed a tear from her cheek and pulled away. "Speaking of pain, I need to check the archives in the basement. The librarian said there are boxes of old documents and manuscripts down there that haven't been converted to microfiche."

"I'll go with you. The Gamma Omegas are probably all in class about now."

"Good. I didn't want to go there by myself. It's dark and creepy."

"My kind of fun." Deme nodded at the microfiche reader. "Let's print off copies of what we've found so far. As we collect more data, maybe it'll all fit together like a puzzle."

"And we'll find Aurai."

Deme's body chilled, her heart squeezing hard in her chest. "Do you think she resents me?"

"Aurai?" Gina snorted. "Never. She worships the ground you walk on. Why do you think she wanted to live a *normal* life?"

"Because of me?" Deme shook her head. "She does not want my life. I've screwed it up so much, she'd be crazy to be like me."

"Looks like you have an opportunity to make it right," Gina said, avoiding Deme's glare. "I sure would make it right if your maintenance dude was the Right in the Mr. Right."

"Sharing is over." Deme gave Gina a pointed look. "Aren't you supposed to be cleaning aquariums?"

"Did the big one on the main level. I'll work the one

on this floor and the third floor tomorrow. Poor fish were swimming in algae."

"Well, make yourself at least look like an aquarium cleaner while I print those articles." Deme parked in the chair behind the microfiche reader and located the articles they'd scanned earlier, printing out copies. When she was done, she paid the librarian and left ahead of Gina, headed for the basement.

As she descended the steps to the main floor, her head reeled with the realization that she'd been holding herself up to a standard too high for any normal person to live up to. She was allowed to have faults, foibles and to screw up every once in a while.

And her biggest mistake was leaving Cal. Was it too late to tell him she'd been wrong?

Chapter 10

Cal entered the administration building. The first office he came to was filled with middle-aged women answering telephones and giving out information concerning admissions and costs for the college. When one of the women hung up, Cal asked where he could find the student records archive room. "Someone mentioned a light out in there." He held up a bulb for good measure.

The other ladies in the room all turned their attention toward him, their gazes sweeping over him.

"I'll show you." The first woman he'd asked jumped from her chair and hurried toward him.

Cal resisted groaning. "No need. I don't want to disturb your work." He'd have a tough time going through student records with someone looking over his shoulder.

"No problem. I needed a break." She waved over her shoulder at the other women and trotted down the hall ahead of Cal, the color in her cheeks high. "My name is Monica."

"Nice to meet you, Monica."

"You're new around here, aren't you?" She smiled back at him.

"First day."

"Well, I hope you'll stay. We can't seem to keep the cute ones around here."

"What do you mean?"

She paused at a closed door marked Records and faced him, her blush deepening. "Like you don't know you're cute." Monica giggled. "Look at me flirting with a younger man."

"No, what did you mean by not keeping the cute ones?"

"I assume you took Kyle's place in maintenance."

"You knew him?"

"Yeah, he changed the outlet in the wall by my desk." She sighed. "Nice guy and closer to my age. Not that I wouldn't go for a younger man if the opportunity presented itself." Monica winked. "This is the place. I'd better get back to my desk. Let me know if you need anything else."

"Thank you, Monica. I'll keep what you said in mind." Cal smiled at her, just a little, not wanting to encourage her flirtation, but liking the frankness of the woman.

He made a show of fiddling with his keys until Monica disappeared around a corner. Once the hallway was clear, he pushed the master key into the lock and entered the room.

Rows of files stood in long rows. The edges of paper stuck out in many places, aging, turning yellow.

Starting at the first one he came to, he noted they

were in alphabetic order, many of the files dating back over twenty years. No new students were in this menagerie, those records and signed documents scanned and saved online. He spied a computer terminal in the corner, making a mental note to attempt to research Rachel, Mike and Zoe through the database.

After scouring the first three rows, he finally made it to the records dating to the year Lion Hall burned.

With only one name to go on, he quickly searched the records for a Miss Baker, locating several. On a small notepad, he jotted down the first names of the girls in the files and the last known addresses. All together there were five girls with the last name of Baker—Diane, Brenda, Katherine, Lisa and Paula. He spent a moment in each record, looking for anything out of the norm, then he moved on to the task of finding the five sisters.

How in the heck was he supposed to know which ones belonged to the girls who'd died in the fire? He didn't even have a name to start with.

In most circumstances, he'd consider the effort futile. What could students from thirty years ago tell him about what was going on today?

Given what had happened in the garden, he didn't want to leave any stone unturned, even the really weird and bizarre. Last night's fight with killer roots had left him questioning all his beliefs.

He started with the *A*s and worked his way through to the *C*s when he came across two files where the pages were packaged in large envelopes and written across the top was the word *Deceased*.

The last name on top of the first one read *Chattox*.

Cal's skin went cold as he read the first name following the comma.

Deborah.

He breathed again and moved to the next file. Again the last name was Chattox. The first name Ellen.

Only two files.

He opened Deborah's and scanned the admissions data. Under family, he noted other siblings were Ellen, Francis, Georgia and Hannah, ages ranging from twenty to twenty-six years old.

These had to be the sisters who died in the fire.

That they had the same last name as Deme gave Cal the willies. What were the chances? And as Deme had reminded him, there was no such thing as coincidence.

Had fate sent Aurai Chattox to this school? And if so, what did fate have planned for the rest of the sisters who'd followed? Would they end up like the other Chattox sisters?

A dark lump of dread settled in Cal's gut and his hand shook as he shoved the documents back in the envelope.

He tucked the two files into his coverall and zipped it. After rifling through the rest of that year and the years on each side, he didn't find any more Chattoxes. He moved on to the computer in the corner, sat down and brought up the menu.

The computer required a log-on and password. Without the ability to hack into the system, Cal had done all he could do here. He left the room, locking the door behind him.

Once out of the administration building he headed for the quiet of the library, hoping to catch Deme and Gina to share what he'd found.

As Deme descended the staircase into the basement, the walls, air and atmosphere changed, growing darker and more oppressive.

"You'd think they'd improve the lighting in here." Gina stepped past a table laden with several boxes of old books. "Basements always seem so dark." A shiver shook her frame.

"You feel it, too?"

She nodded. "It's more than just the dark, isn't it?"

Deme found a light switch against the wall and flipped it, eliminating even the little bit of light they had to begin with. "Oops, sorry." She switched it back on and moved toward the dusty stacks arranged in rows. "Let's get this done and get back topside. I don't like it down here."

"I'm with you." Gina rubbed her arms, hugging herself as though the cold was seeping through to her bones. "What exactly are we looking for?"

"Anything that can shed a little light on what's going on around here." Deme's mouth twisted into a rueful grin. "No pun intended."

"Right. That should be easy." Gina wandered past the first stack. "You can have this row. I'll start at the other end. We can work our way to the middle."

Deme skimmed over the titles of ancient books whose bindings were well-worn, some crumbling due to the damp. "Why would they store books down here? With all the pipes and dampness, you'd think they'd relegate the old stuff to the attic instead."

"Who knows." The sound of books being placed back on shelves came from the back row where Gina worked. "All I know is it's been more than three days since Aurai disappeared and we still don't have any leads on what happened."

Nothing on the first row jumped out at her as important. As Deme passed to the second row, Gina moved another row closer, as well. A look passed between them, their light banter forgotten as the dank air pressed in around them.

"Not liking this, sis," Gina called out.

"Me, either."

"Hey, I think I've found something here," Gina's voice was more muffled, barely making it through the stacks of books and documents. "There's an entire room filled with binders and schematics of the Colyer-Fenton campus—"

A loud thunk cut her off before she could finish.

"Did you drop a book?" Deme walked to the end of her row and looked to the rear of the room, where Gina had gone.

Gina appeared around the corner of a row. "No, I thought you did."

Deme moved toward Gina, placing her feet gently to avoid additional noise. "It came from your direction."

"No, it came from yours." Gina moved toward Deme, peering down each row as she passed. "We are alone, right?"

"I thought so." Deme glanced down a row. Nothing moved, nothing looked out of place.

As they converged, Deme looked down the only row they hadn't checked. A book lay on the floor, its pages open and yellowed with age.

Deme shot a glance at Gina. "Coincidence?"

Gina shook her head. "I wasn't anywhere near it to knock it off and neither were you."

They both looked over their shoulders before advancing down the row toward the book.

A draft of frigid air wafted over them, lifting the pages of the book, one after the other. The draft stopped as suddenly as it began, the pages settling.

"As if we didn't get that this was weird," Gina muttered.

Deme stared down at the book. "Someone's trying to tell us something."

"Wish Selene was here. Maybe she'd know who." Her sister glanced up at Deme. "Do you want to, or should I?"

With a deep breath, Deme squatted and lifted the book, careful to keep it open at exactly the page it had landed on. "I need more light."

"Over here." Gina led the way to the end of the stack to a table that stood against the wall. A bare lightbulb hung down from a cord, shedding a convenient glow over the tabletop.

Deme flipped the book over to read the binding. *Tales of Myths and Monsters.* A draft didn't precede the chill snaking down Deme's spine this time. "I don't know about you, but I'm not liking this any better."

"Something tells me little sis is in bigger trouble than we thought."

Deme didn't need the reminder to spur her into action. She flipped the book back over and glanced at the ink drawing of a creature, reading the title of the page out loud. "'The Chimera, Myth or Reality?'"

"Do we have a choice?" Gina quipped.

At a sharp glance from Deme, Gina raised both hands in surrender. "Okay, okay, I'll keep my comments to myself. Read on."

"'The Chimera is fabled to be a fire-breathing creature with the body of a lion. It has two heads—one of the lion, one of a goat—and it has a serpent for a tail.'"

"I haven't seen anything like that, have you?"

Deme closed her eyes, recalling the image in the window of her dorm room after her sister's face disappeared. She'd thought the vines on the window were teeth. Could they have been a lion's gaping jaw?

She squeezed the bridge of her nose, closing her eyes briefly before going back to the text, eyes wide open.

"'The Chimera has many weapons at its disposal that it can use in multiple dimensions. Some say it has telekinetic abilities as well as the ability to force thoughts into the heads of the weak or impassioned.'"

"Holy crap," Gina whispered. "The attempted rapes."

And her violent sex with Cal. Deme's hands shook.

"Is this what we're up against?" Gina asked.

Deme forced herself to continue. "'The Chimera draws on the magical powers surrounding it, twisting it to suit its own evil purposes.'"

"That's why when I tried to call on the goddess to help the girls in the garden, my magic turned against us." Deme breathed in and out, trying to calm her racing heart. "Wow, we might be in over our heads here." She looked across at Gina. "If Aurai tried to use her powers, the Chimera could have turned them against her, as well."

Gina clasped Deme's hand. "Aurai is all right. You heard Selene, and you feel it. She's still alive. We will find her and free her from whatever has her."

"Damn right we will." Deme glanced down at the book. Though it mentioned what the creature was capable of, it gave no advice on how to deal with such a being.

"We need to show this to the others," Deme said.

"What I want to know is where it's coming from." Gina's eyes opened wider. "And I might have that answer." She headed to the back of the basement. "I'd found a room filled with schematics of the buildings on campus, dating back to when it was originally built," she called over her shoulder. "I'll bring them out here where we can see them under the better light."

"I'll keep looking through the rest of the stacks for anything else that might be important, then I'll join you. Maybe there's a historical account of the college somewhere in here." Deme scanned the rows of books, brushing aside dust to read the titles, the book of myths and monsters tucked under her arm.

When she'd reached the end of the stack, a sharp scream pierced the rows of books, followed by a loud slam.

Deme's heart stopped in her chest then shot into overdrive. She ran to the end of the stack and raced toward the back of the basement where Gina had gone.

As she neared the last row of books, water pooled around her feet. "Gina!"

"Help!" Her cry came from the other side of a closed door. "I'm in here."

Deme tried the handle. It wouldn't budge. "The door is locked. Unlock it."

"I can't. It's dark in here. The light blew out."

"Hang tight. I'll see what I can find to break down the door."

"Hurry. Look out, Deme, a man tried to attack me. I called on the goddess of water…" Gina sobbed. "You were right. The Chimera is turning it against me. The room is filling with water."

Deme glanced behind her. When she saw no sign of a man waiting to jump her, she looked at the base of the door. Liquid leaked from beneath it. "How big is the room?"

"Not very. It's already up to my knees."

Deme's gaze shot right then left. Nothing struck her as useful in prying a door open.

She spun, heading back to the table. If she could break a leg off it, she might be able to pry the door open before the water got too deep.

As Deme ran past the stacks, something long, dark and thick slithered out on the floor in front of her feet.

Too late to stop herself, her foot caught on it and she flew forward, landing on her belly, knocking the wind from her lungs. She lay in the seeping water until she could catch her breath. Then she lunged to her feet.

An arm reached out to grab her from behind, hooking around her neck. Dank, moldy rot filled her nostrils as a filthy coverall sleeve pressed into her throat, cinching off her air. Her fingers pried at the arm to no avail, the pressure increasing until the air around her grew fuzzy, her vision blurring.

She had to get loose. Having lost one sister, she'd be damned if she'd lose another. Deme grabbed on to the arm, lifted her feet and pushed hard against the closest shelf of books.

Cal entered the library and took the steps to the second floor two at a time. He swallowed his disappointment when he couldn't find Gina and Deme. Retracing his steps to the first floor, he stopped in front of the information desk.

The librarian manning the computer didn't look up.

"Did you see a redhead and a sandy-blonde woman go by here?"

"A lot of people go by here." The librarian glanced up, her gaze raking over Cal and his coverall, a blush replacing the placid, bored look of a moment before. "Oh, do you mean the two who went to the basement to research the college?"

"How long ago?"

She glanced at her monitor. "Fifteen minutes."

Before the last syllable left her lips, Cal had reached the door to the stairs leading down to the basement. God, he hated basements. Like hospitals, basements had unique smells…not all good.

The concrete-and-metal stairs clanked with every footstep as he ran down. A sense of foreboding filled his chest the lower he went. The same damp, decaying scent that he'd experienced from the trapdoor in the basement of the student commons filled his nostrils, gagging him.

When he reached the bottom, he landed in a puddle of water.

What the hell? His gaze swept across a floor, the lights above reflecting across the inch of water spreading to all corners. Where was Deme?

A loud crashing sound, followed by another, followed by another roared through the cavernous area. He ran toward the sound, splashing through the water, and rounded a corner to see stacks of books toppling one after the other in a domino effect. Each shelf and tons of books slammed into the next, headed directly for where he stood.

Cal dodged to the side, hugging the wall beside him as the shelf in front of him hit the one beside him, slamming it to the floor. Books spewed out to the side and bounced upward with the force of impact, the ground quaking beneath his feet.

"Deme!"

She didn't answer. The swirl of dust was so thick it fogged the limited lighting, making the view impenetrable. "Deme!"

Sounds of a scuffle alerted him that he wasn't alone.

He picked his way across the fallen books and shelves, his feet slipping and sliding on the shifting books.

As dust and shelves settled around him, he finally saw Deme.

Someone had her by the throat.

Deme hung on to the arm with her fingers, her feet flailing, trying to gain purchase.

Adrenaline pumped through Cal's veins, pushing him forward, faster and faster as he leaped and slid toward her, slamming into her attacker.

Not until he was right on him did Cal realize the man holding her wasn't right. His face was black with decaying skin and the rot of polluted earth. Blank, soulless eyes stared at nothing. As if powered by some unseen force, he continued to choke Deme.

Cal hit him in the side, taking the man and Deme down in a flying tackle.

The arm holding on to Deme loosened and she managed to scramble free.

As she crawled across a pile of books, the creep snagged her ankle with a clawlike grip.

Cal rolled to his feet and stomped the man's wrist, again and again until the hand released Deme. "Run!" he yelled.

She crab-crawled over fractured bookshelves and the mess of tumbled books to a clear area where shelves still stood, the books still neatly aligned. Deme reached for a wooden splinter the size of a sword sticking up from a jumble of broken shelves and damaged books. She headed for the back of the room.

The vacant-eyed man pushed to his feet and lumbered toward her.

"Look out!" Cal yelled, his feet moving, but the

books slipping from beneath him hampered his progress. He wouldn't get to her before her attacker did.

"I don't have time for this." Deme raced around one of the shelves still standing and rammed into it with her shoulder. "Get back, Cal!"

The shelf teetered toward the creepy dude and back at Deme. She hit the shelf again. This time it leaned far enough to fall, crashing down on the guy in the dirt-caked coverall.

Cal jumped back, avoiding the worst of the wreck.

Deme didn't wait for the dust to clear. She dove behind the next stack, disappearing out of Cal's sight.

His heart hammering in his chest, and with Deme out of sight, Cal could imagine all kinds of horrible things happening to her. He leaped over the downed shelf and the piles of ruined books, splashing through two inches of water.

When he rounded the corner of the last stand of shelves, he found Deme.

She had the large splintered board in hand, shoving it against a door frame. "Help me!"

"Where's Gina?"

"In here. We have to get her out."

Cal ran the last few steps, his hands closing around her shoulders. "Move."

"But it's locked. We can't get in and she's going to drown." Deme hit the door with the board, tears running down her cheeks.

Cal took a deep breath and threw all of his weight into the door. The door frame split, but the lock held. Water leaked from beneath the door at an alarming rate. "What the hell's happening in there?"

"She tried to use her ability to influence water to slow down the man who attacked me. Only she got locked in and water is filling the room now. We have to get her out before—"

Cal stepped as far back as he could get and slammed into the door. Pain shot through his shoulder, but the door gave enough for the lock to break loose, water rushing through the gap at chin level.

"Help me!" Gina called through the crack as the pressure of the water forced the door shut again.

"Get back," Cal yelled.

Deme joined him this time, and together they hurled themselves at the door.

Once they had the door open a foot wide, Deme shoved a book in the opening sideways as high up as she could reach, creating a six-inch gap.

Water rushed through.

Gina squeezed into the space, creating a damming effect, the water pushing against her back, running over her head. "I can't do it," she gasped.

Cal grabbed her hand and leaned as hard as he could on the door panel. He pulled her through, water gushing out, carrying Gina past Cal and Deme. The pressure on the book made it pop out of position, forcing the door closed again.

Gina washed to a stop, sprawled across the soggy books, coughing and sputtering, soaked to the skin and pale. She sat up, pushing hanks of blond hair out of her eyes. "What the hell happened?"

"That's what I'd like to know." Deme rushed to her sister's side and helped her to her feet. "Are you okay?"

"I'll live, but I don't understand what happened with my precious water. It's as if it turned on me."

Deme hugged her sister. "Things just aren't right around here."

Gina laughed and coughed. "You're telling me."

"The man who attacked you didn't look right, either. I want to get a look at him." Cal walked over to the shelf unit beneath which their attacker lay. He shoved and tugged, lifting the heavy case off the man.

Together he and Deme dug through the books until they reached him.

Deme reeled back first, and Cal followed, the stench from the man more than either could stand.

"He smells dead." Gina held her hand over her nose and mouth.

Cal reached out and felt for a pulse, finding none and the skin cold and sticky. "If he wasn't dead before, he is now."

With her hand over her nose and mouth, Deme shook her head. "He looks and smells like he's been dead for days."

"That's impossible." Cal flipped the man over. Beneath the dirt and stains, he recognized the coverall of the Colyer-Fenton maintenance staff. "He attacked Deme."

"And a room filling with water isn't any less impossible?" Gina asked.

"One thing is for sure." Cal stood and wiped the grime against his trouser leg, his mouth set in a grim line. "I think we've accounted for one of the missing persons."

Beneath a smudge of grease, the name tag read Kyle Scruggs.

Chapter 11

"You found who?" Brigid straddled the chair in the diner, her black, leather-clad leg bouncing with the tapping of her booted foot.

"Kyle Scruggs," Deme repeated. "The maintenance man who'd gone missing three weeks ago."

"Well before Aurai disappeared." Selene shook her head. "What's happening now didn't start with our dear sister's disappearance."

"It started with the beginning of the semester when Aurai arrived on campus." Deme stood and paced next to the table. "From the looks of it, the girls of the Gamma Omega sorority are playing with fire."

"Do you think they've really conjured some kind of evil?"

Deme tipped her head toward Gina, whose hair was almost dry from her battle for life in the basement of the library. "Before the basement flooded, we found a book on monsters."

"Monsters?" Brigid's brows twisted. "Seriously?"

Deme nodded, her gaze steady on Brigid. "Seriously."

"The book actually found us," Gina added.

"How so?" Selene asked, her face open, curious.

"It fell out of a shelf on an aisle neither of us were anywhere near."

Brigid stood. "Could the Scruggs guy have pushed it out?"

"I don't think so." Deme paced again, coming to a stop in front of the table. "I think the sisters who died when Lion Hall burned down died fighting whatever it is we're up against now. And I think they were trying to tell us just what it is by showing us the book."

"And what is it?" Brigid asked.

Deme's gaze caught and held Gina's. "A Chimera."

Selene stared straight ahead, her eyes bright, far away. "Body of a lion, tail of a serpent and two heads, one of the lion and the other of a goat." She closed her eyes. "It has great power. It was what pulled at me back in Deme's dorm room."

"Are you sure?" Deme asked.

She nodded. "Yes. The voices…my dreams…were the sisters warning us away."

Cal, who up to this point had sat in a chair and held his silence, suddenly sat up straight and reached inside his coverall. "I forgot all about this." He pulled out two folders and handed them to Deme. "I think I can help you with names of at least two of the sisters who died in the fire. Seems there have been Chattox sisters on this campus in the past."

"Chattoxes?" Deme accepted the files and laid them out on the table. "Where did you get these?"

"In the student records room."

She ran her hand over the files, a strong current flowing through her fingertips. "Feel this." She guided Selene's hand to the folders.

Her other sisters reached out and the package glowed, levitating off the tabletop.

Deme slapped it down, glancing around nervously. "That wasn't supposed to happen."

"But it did." Selene looked up at Deme. "Which proves it's them."

"What are the chances of running into a group of sisters with the last name Chattox?" Deme demanded.

"One in a bizzilion." Gina's voice was unsteady, her hand shaking as she pulled it away from the files.

Deme sat down hard. "I'm not liking this at all. It's way out of our league."

"Speak for yourself." Brigid crossed her arms over her chest. "I've been following strange occurrences for the past year in my efforts with the Chicago Police Department."

"You've had something like this happen before?"

"No, but some of the people I've come across in our investigations have been pretty darned scary."

"But as powerful as a Chimera? A creature that has been legended to manipulate others for its own gain?"

Brigid shrugged. "So it can manipulate others. We're smart, and now that we know, we can be ready."

Gina stared down at her hands, her face pale. "But we can't use our own powers. They work against us."

"Then we use our heads." Brigid's mouth thinned into a tight line.

"Whoa, wait a minute." Cal held up his hand. "And

you think *you're* out of your league. I have no clue what you're talking about."

"I told you, cop, we're witches," Brigid said. "We have a certain amount of powers when we choose to use them." She smacked the back of her hand against his chest. "Keep up with us."

Deme smiled across at Cal. "It's true. When something isn't sabotaging our power, we can do some pretty amazing things." Her smile faded. "Up until now, we chose not to, preferring to keep a low profile so as not to draw attention."

"Why?"

"I personally have no desire to be dissected by some wacko scientist," Brigid said.

"It tends to make people look at you differently." Deme's gaze refused to meet Cal's. "Some of us just want to live normal lives."

"But you can't." Cal shook his head. "I have to admit, I didn't believe in all that crap about magic, but I can't begin to explain what's been happening on this campus. Unless someone is a truly gifted illusionist, which I doubt."

"So you believe us when we say we think there is a monster on this campus?" Gina asked him.

"I don't know what to believe anymore." Cal pushed a hand through his hair, standing the dark strands on end.

Deme noted how her sisters' gazes followed his movements. And why shouldn't they? He was a single, very attractive man. But that didn't help how her heart squeezed in her chest and her fists tightened.

Cal's hand dropped to the pocket on his coverall. "I have five names that could be the student who was attacked thirty years ago."

Brigid held out her hand. "I'll look into those since it doesn't have to be done on campus."

"Good. I want to check in with the lieutenant back at the office." Cal stood and stretched. "I'm almost afraid to get too far from campus now, given all that's happened. None of you are safe."

"And neither are Aurai or the students." Deme gathered her rental-car keys and handbag. "I should be getting back."

"Stay vigilant." Cal looked directly into her eyes. "Especially going near the garden."

His look and words warmed Deme all over. She wanted to walk into his arms and let him hold her until all the ugliness went away.

"You don't have to tell me twice," Selene said. "I have to go. Play practice is at five." Selene left the café.

"Me, too. Think I'll follow Cal back to the station and see what I can find online." Brigid slipped her helmet over her head and snapped the strap in place, her black hair flowing down her back.

"I'm going to search through the copies of articles we made and do more research on the Chimera." Gina gathered her purse, slinging it over her shoulder. "There has to be a way to stop it before it does irreparable harm."

"Seems it already has." Deme tapped the article at the top of Gina's pile of pages, the one about the burning of Lion Hall and the demise of five sisters just like them.

A shiver shook Deme from head to toe.

"I'll be at the hotel I'm sharing with Selene," Gina said. "You might check on her while she's at practice. That theater is on the garden axis."

Deme nodded as Gina slid by and exited with Brigid,

tossing a wink over her shoulder as she let the door close behind her.

That left Deme and Cal alone. Well, as alone as they could be in a diner with a waitress, a cook and a cashier waiting for the evening rush of patrons.

Deme smiled. Her sisters were setting her up. She moved toward the door, pushing through to stand outside in the cool evening air.

Cal closed the door behind him and captured her hand, pulling Deme up against him. "I meant it. Be careful." He touched her cheek. "What happened earlier…"

"Won't happen again. We all know now not to use our powers." Deme closed her eyes and leaned into his palm. "Thanks, Cal."

"For what?"

She opened her eyes and stared into his. "For being there when I needed you." They stood so close, Deme could almost feel his heat. If she leaned nearer, she'd feel the beat of his heart against hers.

Cal closed the distance, leaning down until his lips hovered over hers. "Wouldn't have it any other way." He kissed her, drawing her into his arms and holding her tight. When their lips parted, he didn't release her, pressing his cheek against the side of her temple. "I don't think I've ever been more afraid in my life than when I saw Scruggs choking you to death." He chuckled. "Unless you count the time in the garden when the roots were pulling you into the earth." He sighed, his chest rubbing against hers deliciously.

Deme flattened her palms against him, loving the feel of his muscles beneath her fingertips—all that power tensed for action. "That's two times you've saved me in the past twenty-four hours. This could become a habit."

"Don't let it." He squeezed her again and set her at arm's length. "Go. I have work to do. If I stand here much longer, I'll forget what it was." His hands slid down her arms to clasp hers. "I'll come by and check on you later tonight."

Deme wanted to tell him not to, that she could handle being in the dormitory on her own, but her lips wouldn't let the words through. She wanted him to come. Wanted the reassurance of his presence in that creepy room she was obligated to occupy until they found Aurai and resolved the problems on campus. "Later."

She pulled her hands from his grip and turned to her car.

Behind her, the rumble of a motorcycle engine drew her attention.

Cal, straddling his Harley, roared out of the parking lot and into the traffic headed toward the station.

Deme wanted to be on the back of the bike with him, urging him to get far away from Colyer-Fenton and the craziness they'd found there.

Sisters, come to me! Aurai's call echoed in her head, reminding her of what had to be done. Standing around mooning over an ex-boyfriend wasn't getting her any closer to finding her sister.

Before the courthouse closed, Cal stopped in the records department and asked for help locating schematics of underground tunnels in the area of Colyer-Fenton College.

The lady behind the counter frowned and glanced at the clock. "We close in fifteen minutes."

Loading all his charm into one big, sweet smile, Cal leaned over the counter. "Please?"

The woman, probably in her late fifties, plump, graying and overworked, blushed. "Well...okay." She wheeled her mouse across the mouse pad, clicked her fingers on the keyboard and hit Enter with a flourish. "That should do it." She looked over the top of her reader glasses. "Mind you, it's old and probably not accurate anymore, what with the newer tunnels and subways built, but it's the only schematics I have on file." She stood, walked toward a printer and returned with a single sheet of paper. She handed it across the counter. "You might also try the Metropolitan Water Reclamation District of Greater Chicago for the Deep Tunnel schematics, as well. I haven't compared them to these so I don't know how they relate." She glanced at the clock again and gathered her purse from under her desk. "I have to catch my train, or I'd stay and chat."

Cal smiled. "Thank you." He left, tucking the schematic into his jacket before climbing on his motorcycle and heading for the station.

Traffic being hell, he didn't arrive until well after five, narrowly missing being hit at least three times by motorists too busy talking on their cell phones to pay attention to those around them.

Lieutenant Warner sat behind his desk, an empty coffee mug beside him, staring at the computer screen.

Cal knocked on the door frame and leaned into the office. "You look busy."

"Please, deliver me from reports." Marty pushed back from the keyboard and rolled his shoulders. "I miss the days of being a beat cop."

"Know what you mean."

"Whatcha got?"

"Been a busy day on campus." He filled in the boss on the activities of the night before and the incident in the basement of the library to include the names of the victims of similar events thirty years ago.

Cal looked at his boss, expecting him to question the roots grabbing people and the water issue in the basement, but he didn't even blink.

When Cal finished his report, Marty nodded, his brows drawing together. "You mean to tell me these two sequences of events might be related?"

With a nod, Cal pulled the schematic of the rail tunnels from his jacket and laid it across the desk. "Another thing. While I was in the basement of the student commons, I found a trapdoor leading to a level even lower than the basement."

"Lower than a basement? How can that be?" The lieutenant slipped a pair of reader glasses onto his nose and leaned over the schematic.

Cal pointed to the map, his finger on the street running through the Colyer-Fenton College campus. "As you know, beneath the older streets of Chicago is a labyrinth of railroad tunnels built for the movement of freight during the early nineteen hundreds."

"Yeah. I remember stories the old cops used to tell about troubles with vagrants finding their way down in there. They did a big push to seal off the entrances to keep them out."

"Well, I think they missed one." His finger traced the line beneath the campus that ran through the five-building circle surrounding the closed-off garden at the center of campus. "I'll check the basements of the other four buildings in this area to see if they have similar access to the train tunnels."

"Good idea." Lieutenant Warner looked up. "Are we

to the point where we should evacuate students from campus?"

Cal drew in a deep breath and let it out before answering. "No. I'm not sure who all is involved in this. If there really is a creature traversing the tunnels, that's one thing we'll have to deal with. If someone human is making it appear to be a creature, we need to catch him in the act. Right now, I haven't even got a suspect. I need more time to investigate."

"That missing girl doesn't have time."

"Tell me about it." Cal's chest tightened. Deme took personal responsibility for every one of her sisters. To lose one would be devastating.

"Are you ready for reinforcements?" the lieutenant asked.

"Not just yet."

"Even to check out the basements?" Marty shook his head. "After the near-drowning incident, you don't think you need help? Sounds to me like you do."

Cal's fists clenched. He'd almost been too late, and he didn't even want to think about that. Deme and Gina would have been lost. "We managed."

"Barely, by the sounds of it." Lieutenant Warner nodded. "Fine. I'll wait another day before sending more help. In the meantime, what can I do for you?"

"Help Brigid find more information on the names I gave her. She's not as familiar with some of the systems available here."

"I'll get one of the detectives to assist." He looked over the top of his glasses. "Anything else?"

"Yeah." Cal crossed his arms over his chest. "You didn't even bat an eyelash when I mentioned the abnormal attacks. Why?"

Lieutenant Warner's lips turned up briefly. "I've

been working this city a lot longer than you have, Cal. Some crazy stuff has passed over my desk and before my eyes. I don't take anything for granted, and neither should you."

"You believe all this magic stuff?"

"All I got to say is keep an open mind and watch your back."

Cal went straight for the war room, where he found Brigid hard at work on the computer. "Any luck?"

"You're not going to believe what I've found." She turned the laptop toward him and maneuvered the cursor to a tab on the browser, then clicked. The website was the courthouse records page. On it were the names of Diane Baker and Richard Masterson.

"That would make her married name, assuming she took her husband's surname, Diane Masterson."

"Bingo."

"I need to let Deme know."

"Right. Nothing is coincidence. And look at this." She clicked on another tab and a genealogy site appeared with a family tree dating all the way back to the early sixteen hundreds of Pendle Hill, Lancashire, England. At the top of the tree were five women, all by the surname of Chattox. To the far right was one Anne Chattox. "It gets weirder." Brigid clicked on Anne Chattox's name, bringing up a new screen with a full-length story of the Pendle Witch Trials of 1612. With it was a drawing depicting a figure of an old woman dangling by the hangman's noose.

Brigid's body shook. "I get a chill every time I look at that picture." She rubbed her arms.

"Can't say that I blame you. Bring up the previous screen."

She clicked the back icon and the tree reappeared.

"If you follow it through the centuries…" She scrolled down through the names of each generation until she came to bottom. "Voila! There we are. The five Chattox sisters of the present. Gives me the creeps." She rolled the screen up a little. "And there are our counterparts from thirty years ago. Apparently not every sister has five girls, but at least one in every generation does and they keep their maiden name to pass on to their daughters."

"Did your mother know about this?"

Brigid snorted. "I always thought she was a throwback to the women's liberation movement, that that was why she kept her maiden name and had it inscribed as our maiden name on the birth certificate. Wish she was still alive. I have a lot of questions for her."

"Are any of your aunts still alive?"

"As a matter of fact, yes. Aunt Rose lives in Portland. I think we're about due a familial visit."

"A phone call will do for now. We need you too much here."

"Gotcha. I'll check with Deme and see if she'd like to do the honors."

"Do you always check with your oldest sister before making decisions?"

Brigid cocked a brow at him. "Seriously?" She shook her head. "No. But when it comes to our search for Aurai, I defer to her. I want my sister back as much as the rest of us."

"Good work. I'll check out Dr. Masterson's office and see what I can find."

"How you gonna get in without her knowing?"

Cal held up the set of master keys his supervisor had given him that morning and smiled. "It pays to be working on the inside."

"No fair. Next time I get the undercover job."

"Next time?"

"Yeah. You don't think this is the only case you'll be working for the Special Investigations Team, do you?"

Cal hadn't thought of that. "You've been working with them for a year?"

"That's right. Mostly on arson investigation cases."

"Your forte is fire, right?"

"You got it. I have an uncanny sense of smell where fire is concerned. I can tell exactly where a fire started and even visualize an arsonist as he's lighting it."

Cal nodded. "Impressive. What else can you do?"

"I've been known to throw a few fireballs when needed." Her eyes opened wide and she smiled. "Oh, and I have some pretty cool friends. Check this out." She snapped her fingers and two bright spots of flame appeared out of thin air, hovering over her hand like spirits. Then they took off and flew around the room, buzzing past Cal, singing the hair around his ear.

"Hey!"

"I call them dragonflies."

Cal ducked and batted at the little creatures as they dived toward his head. "Yeah? Why?"

"They have nasty little tempers and they breathe fire."

As Cal swatted at the pests, one of them turned on him and shot a stream of flame at him. Cal grabbed a pad of paper and held it up in front of his face. "Call them off."

Brigid snapped her fingers again and the two dragonflies disappeared in a puff of smoke. She waved her hand to clear the air. "Sometimes they set off the fire alarms." She smiled across at him. "Still a disbeliever in magic?"

"You put on a very convincing show."

"It would have gotten me hanged in the witch tri-als, hands-down." She stood, crossing her arms over her chest. "So what's up between you and my big sis?"

Unprepared for her sudden change in conversation, Cal didn't have a canned answer. "I don't know."

She pinned him with a dark-eyed stare. "Are you the one she ran away from a year ago?"

He shrugged, reluctant to discuss Deme with her sister. "If you mean were we seeing each other a year ago and she left for another job, then yes."

"She not only left Chicago, she left the country." Brigid took a step closer, her hands dropping to her hips. "What did you do to her to make her run?"

Cal shook his head and smiled. "I asked her to marry me."

Chapter 12

Deme paced her room, afraid to get comfortable, ultra-sensitive to anything that might even remotely be construed as using her powers. When she'd arrived in her room, she expected things to be out of place, the vine at the window to be tapping, something weird.

Instead, the room appeared like any other college dorm room. Normal and generic. Except for the missing comforter on her bed.

She strode to the window and glanced down at the darkened garden. The vine had retreated from her window, hopefully for good. Exhausted by the lack of sleep the night before and the trying events of the day, Deme still couldn't imagine closing her eyes to sleep.

The elusive moon hid behind a thin layer of cumulus, turning the edges of the clouds a silvery blue. The ground below was nothing more than a black abyss, trees and shrubs hidden from view.

A light blinked on in a building across the garden. A lone figure stood silhouetted in a window.

Crossing the room to the folder she'd been given upon acceptance of the resident assistant position, Deme pulled out the campus map. With the map in hand, she returned to the window, orienting the map to the lay of the structures surrounding the garden.

The administration building stood across the garden and to the right of the Gamma Omega dorm. When Lion Hall had been standing, none of the surrounding buildings faced each other. Not so now. Although she couldn't make out the features of the other person, instinct told Deme who it was. The president of the college, Dr. Diane Masterson. What was she doing in her office this late?

With half a mind to go over and confront the woman, Deme hesitated. What could she ask without alerting the woman to her investigation of the staff and students? No. She couldn't barge in and demand to know why the woman stayed so late into the night. Likely she was as concerned as the police about the recent attacks and disappearance of one of the students.

For a long moment, Deme stared across at the other woman, wanting to extend a little magical nudge to read the woman's mind.

Deme tugged at the collar of her shirt, the air in the room feeling stuffy, muggy and dense. She looked away and beneath her breath muttered, "No magic. No magic. No magic." She hoped that by reminding herself constantly she'd remember not to cast even a simple spell. Not that she performed magic on a daily basis, but sometimes she sent a quiet prayer to the goddess for help or protection, or she used a little of her influence to tap into thoughts. After what happened in the garden and the library basement, she was afraid to speak to the goddess at all.

When Deme looked across the garden again, the woman had disappeared. At that exact moment, the light blinked out.

With nothing to stare out at but darkness, Deme resumed her pacing.

The more she paced, the more her legs dragged until finally she pulled a clean tank top and a pair of shorts from her suitcase and prepared for bed and another sleepless night.

Before she lay on the sheet-covered mattress, she checked the room thermostat. Why was it so hot and humid in the room? Eighty degrees? Good Lord. She maneuvered the dial to a cool sixty-eight. No wonder it was so hot.

Cal had promised to come by before he called it a night. Where was he? The digital alarm clock on her nightstand glowed a bright green eleven forty-five.

The air in the room didn't seem a bit cooler with the change in the thermostat. Deme checked it again. It was back at eighty. She tapped the box, cursing her inability to fix anything mechanical. Maybe when Cal got there he'd take a look at it. In the meantime, she reset the dial to sixty-eight, for what it was worth, grabbed a washcloth from her suitcase and dampened it with cool water. She pressed it to her warm skin, dragging it across her face and down her neck to her breasts.

So damned hot.

As she lay on the thin mattress, Deme pushed aside the sheets, fanning the cool, damp cloth over her and then draping it over her face.

With the cloth blocking the overhead light, Deme

closed her eyes and breathed deeply, letting her body relax. Sleep would come if she'd just let it.

The air in the room thickened, and the effort to draw a breath grew more labored. Deme couldn't seem to bring a full deep breath into her lungs, so she took shorter, faster breaths until she panted like a dog in the full summer sun. The faster she breathed the more light-headed she felt.

So tired from her day, she didn't care, couldn't move more than to raise her hand to her chest. She lay still, the only thing stirring her fingers, trailing across her breasts. The air around her seemed to swirl and lift her hand, guiding it lower.

Half-asleep, not fully awake, she let her hand travel down her belly, to the juncture of her thighs. That throbbing area low in her body, aching for a touch, a stroke, a gentle hand to soothe away the tension. Or better yet, to create more.

Deme's fingers slipped beneath the elastic band of her shorts, lacing through the mound of curly hair. When she found that spot, she caressed it with the tip of her finger, stroking, coaxing, teasing.

Her back arched from the bed, her hips lifting to greet the steady ministrations of that magical finger. Her body tensed, climbing up the ragged peak to the climax. Intense vibrations rocketed through her body, sending her spiraling to the top of who knew where, lifting her higher with each minuscule brush of her finger.

A groan filled the air. She was surprised it was her own. In her body, but not, Deme couldn't control her responses, couldn't back down from the most intense orgasm she'd ever experienced. So intense she sensed it was wrong, but she couldn't stop herself from riding the wave on and on like a surfer on a never-ending crest.

The exquisite ache built into a painful desire, growing and changing with each passing moment. Deme's groans transformed into low guttural growls, her fingers curling into claws, scratching at her belly, tearing at her shirt.

Naked, she had to be naked. She ripped the cloth from her heated face, clawed at her shirt, ripping it away in shreds. Her shorts fell to the floor in nothing but tatters. Her eyes remained closed, the darkness a balm to the strengthening desire racking her body.

This is wrong.

The small voice whispering in the very back of her mind fought to push aside the animal expanding within, only to be beaten back, slammed against the wall of doubt.

Help. The essence of Deme struggled to surface from the quicksand of darkness drawing her down.

Piercing the darkness, a voice called out in a clear, sweet tone, *Deme, fight it!*

Aurai? Deme tried to open her eyes to see her beloved sister, but no matter how hard she tried, she couldn't.

Don't let it win!

I can't fight it. It's so strong.

You have to fight or it will consume you.

Deme shoved and pushed against the inky darkness, her body weakening, her will dissolving. *It's too strong. Need help.*

He'll come.

Cal raced along the Eisenhower Expressway and took the exit leading to Colyer-Fenton College, a sense of urgency he couldn't justify pushing him faster and faster.

Since he'd left Brigid at the station, he'd had an increasing sense of doom the closer he got to the campus. If he believed in intuition, he'd say someone was in trouble there.

Deme.

When he arrived at the Gamma Omega dormitory, he drove up on the lawn and parked his motorcycle in front of the door, hopping off before the engine stopped roaring.

He hit the door at a full run, slamming into the locked glass so hard he banged his nose.

Damn. He squeezed the bridge of his nose to stop the stinging, his eyes tearing. He'd forgotten the doors were locked at eleven o'clock. Only those with a pass key could enter.

He whipped out his master key and inserted it into the lock, twisting hard.

Down the hallway to the staircase and up two at a time, he ran. When he arrived on the second floor, girls lined the hallway in varying states of dress, from baby-doll nightgowns to sweats and T-shirts. One girl stood wrapped in nothing but a towel. All of them had one thing in common. They stared ahead, their eyes blank, their footsteps stilted like so many zombies in a horror film.

When Cal tried to dodge past one, she stepped to the side, directly in his path.

"Excuse me." He grabbed her by the shoulders and set her to the side, eager to clear the path to Deme's room.

Sounds of muffled screams and animal roaring

drifted from the end of the hall where Deme stayed. Cal had to get to her. Something wasn't right.

"It's with her." The girl Cal remembered as the president of the sorority, Zoe, stood in front of him, dressed in a sheer nightgown that left nothing to the imagination, her blond hair hanging down over her shoulders,. "Wouldn't you rather have me?"

"No." He reached out to grab her arms, but she moved fast, closing in on him, wrapping her arms around his neck, her legs lifting to clamp around his waist.

He staggered with the surprise attack and the impact. As he struggled to pry her off his body, the other girls closed in around him.

The closer they came, the louder the roars from the room down the hallway.

He had to get past these girls and get to Deme.

Cal pried the legs from around his waist. As he worked at the arms clinging to his neck, Zoe wrapped her legs around him again. For a thin young woman, she had surprising grip and strength in her thighs. She squeezed her legs together, making the contact more painful.

This time Cal pulled her arms free and jerked one up behind her, then with his free hand, he got one leg free and slung her around, knocking several of the girls aside in the process.

With little gentleness, he pushed and shoved the young ladies out of the way and raced for the end of the hall.

"Deme. Let me in," he called through the door.

Guttural growls were the only response.

He pulled his master key from his pocket and inserted it in the lock. When he pushed the door to open, it pushed back.

Cal leaned his shoulder into it and the door flung open.

Darkness greeted him, the overhead light covered in a thick layer of what looked like moss. The walls had the same coating. The air was as thick, humid and dank as though he was deep in the rain forest, not a Midwest college dormitory.

The light from the hallway shone across the green algae-covered floor to the single bed in the corner.

Levitating above the thin mattress was a naked woman, long red hair splayed out as though charged with static electricity.

"Deme!"

Her body jerked, her back arching. She turned to face him, but her eyes were closed.

"Deme!" Cal rushed forward, stopping a foot away, unsure what to do, how to bring her back from wherever she was. "It's me, Cal," he said, his voice cracking. "Deme, what is it doing to you?"

One slender hand reached toward him.

He took it. "Deme, please."

Her eyes opened, the pupils golden, like those of a lion.

Cal staggered backward. This wasn't Deme, but it was.

"You can't have her," he said, his tone intense, almost as much of a growl as he'd heard from Deme.

Deme's body twisted and dropped to the mattress, then like a cat, she flung herself at him, her arms and legs wrapping around his body, clinging to him in a choking hold.

Cal struggled to breathe, no clue how to handle the

possessed Deme without hurting her, but if he didn't get her to loosen up, he'd be the next victim taken by the Chimera.

"Deme." He clasped her cheeks between his hands. "Look at me." He gazed into her eyes, determined to make her see him. "You have to fight whatever has you."

The tension in her body eased a fraction. "That's what…Aurai…said." Deme's gaze softened, the irises more green than gold. For a moment, Cal thought she was back. Then a growl rose up from her throat and she dug her nails into his skin, her legs wrapping even tighter around his middle. "Take me." One hand raked over his shoulders and down below her bottom, where she worked the rivet on his jeans.

Cal covered her feverish fingers just as she loosened the button. "No, not like this." He raised her hand to his face and pressed a kiss to her palm.

She stared at the place where his lips had touched, as if mesmerized by the gesture, the gold irises fading into emerald-green. Until she blinked, her eyes narrowing, her lips curling back into a feral snarl.

Her tongue snaked out to lick a coarse path along his neck to his earlobe, where she bit down hard.

"Ouch!" Cal jerked away from her teeth. "I won't let you have her, damn it. She's mine." He dragged her face close to his, almost nose to nose. "I love you, Deme, damn it, and you love me, too." His voice was low, determined, insistent, begging Deme to come back from the hell the Chimera had her in.

Her legs loosened and her feet dropped to the floor. A broken sigh escaped from her throat and she was leaning into him. "Help me," she whispered. Her arms circled his waist where her legs had been and she pressed her face into his shirt.

"I'll help you, Deme. Just don't give up on me." He stroked her hair.

"It's stronger than me."

"No one is stronger than you."

Her body jerked, her head flung back, her eyes widening, the lion eyes back. Rumbling growls rose in her chest, her fingers curling into his skin.

"Fight it, Deme."

Her teeth clenched, her lips pulling back. "I am," she said through clamped jaws.

Thumbs slipped into the waistband at the back of his jeans, shoving them downward. He swatted at her hand, knowing it wasn't Deme doing this, but at the same time he couldn't ignore desire straining against his zipper. "Not like this. I won't make love to you when you're like this."

"You will," she said, her voice low and raspy, nothing like normal. Before he could stop her, her hands snaked to the front of his jeans, whipped the zipper down and shoved the denim downward.

His engorged cock sprang forward into her hands.

Despite all his attempts not to react, he sucked in a gasp and held it, teetering on the verge of knowing he should do the right thing, and wanting to slam into her, burying himself to the hilt.

Her hand wrapped around him, a slow smile rising on her lips, her golden eyes narrowing. She pressed her face into his neck, her breasts crushed against his chest, sliding across the fabric of his shirt.

Naked wouldn't be close enough. Cal groaned, resisting the overpowering wave of desire washing over him. He couldn't make her stop when she shoved his jeans down around his ankles, couldn't find the strength to halt the progress of her hand, sliding up his leg between his thighs.

She had him by the balls before he could voice even a mew of protest.

Breathing like a man topping a steep climb, he grabbed her hand, drawing it up to his chest.

The growl in her throat was only the beginning of her protest. She whipped her hand free and ripped his shirt in half from hem to chin. Clawlike fingers traced a line down his torso to the jutting member pressing into her belly.

"Not like this," he repeated like a mantra to her and himself. With every ounce of control he could muster, he smoothed a hand over her hair and along her neck. "When I make love to you, I want to make love to the Deme I know and care for." He pressed a kiss to her temple. "You, Deme. Not some creature from the Black Lagoon." He trailed his mouth along her jawline until he brushed across her lips. "Kiss me, Deme. Only Deme."

For a long moment, the woman in front of him remained poised, gaze on his lips, her irises crossing from gold to green and back to gold. Finally the green solidified, the pupils returning to normal.

Deme reached up to cup his chin. "Cal? When did you get here?"

He laughed low in his belly, his breath catching in his throat. "A few minutes ago."

She blinked, her gaze capturing his. "How did you get in?"

Cal cupped her chin with both hands and brushed his thumbs across her lips. "Master key." He bent to take her lips. "I'm glad you're awake."

"Was I sleepwalking?" She turned her cheek into

his palm and pressed her lips against his skin. "I don't seem to remember."

"You were having a bad dream."

Her eyes turned toward the ceiling and the green moss coating it. "Am I still dreaming?" She moved, her breasts rubbing against his naked chest. "I must be. We're both naked." She smiled, a hand trailing over his shoulder and down his arm. "I like the way your skin feels against mine."

Cal wanted to laugh, cry and yell all at once. Deme was back, but she didn't remember any of what had happened only a moment ago.

Deme's hand continued downward to his hips, circling behind to press him closer. "Were you about to make love to me?"

"To you, yes." He did laugh and kissed her. "Only you, babe." He kicked off his boots, shed his jeans and came to her, hard and fast. The tension of fighting his desire fueled his passion. He lifted her. Unwilling to wrap her legs around his waist, he settled her on the solitary mattress, her legs falling over the edge.

She parted her knees, opening to him.

Invitation accepted, he drove inside her, burying himself deep. Her tight channel engulfed him, coating him with the juices of her own desire, only a moment ago fueled by a demon.

As he thrust in and out, the tension building, rising, bursting over the edge of sanity, he remembered what he'd told her to get her back. He loved her.

He still loved this woman. No matter what happened after they found Aurai and returned Colyer-Fenton to a safe place of learning again, he would always love her. Even if she didn't return his feelings.

Having bared his soul to her once, Cal had no intentions of doing it again. Deme had some kind of misguided perception about who she was and what he'd be willing to accept. Until she got over it, he'd do his best to keep his dreams of a white picket fence and children running around the house as just that. Dreams.

The more he stroked her inside, the more ragged his breathing ran. If he wasn't mistaken, the room temperature had risen at least ten degrees since he entered her. Perspiration slickened his body and hers until the smack of skin on skin sounded more like slaps.

Deme planted her feet in the mattress and rose to meet every thrust with one of her own, her hands clenching around his waist, guiding him in and out, faster and faster. Her eyes closed, her breasts bounced as she dug her nails into his buttocks and slammed him into her.

With his body strung so tight, Cal catapulted over the edge, so intent on milking every last sensation from his body and hers. As he drifted back to earth and to Deme, he sucked in a deep breath. "I've missed you."

Deme didn't respond at first, her eyes still closed. Then they opened and a smile slid across her lips, her bright gold, feverish eyes staring up at him. "I missed you, too."

Chapter 13

Deme woke to sun streaming in through the window, the sheet draped over the lower half of her body and her head aching. With the brightness of the light shining into her eyes, she couldn't see the rest of the room.

Movement at the far corner captured her attention, but the angle of the sun blurred her vision. "Cal?"

"Afraid not." The figure moved out of the corner and closer until Deme could see who it was.

"Dr. Masterson?" Heat rose in Deme's cheeks as she pulled the sheet up to her neck, hiding her naked breasts she was sure the president of the college had already gotten an eyeful of. "What are you doing here?"

"I regret to inform you that your services are no longer required as the resident assistant of the Gamma Omega dormitory."

"What?" Deme sat up straight, dragging the sheet with her. "Why?"

"Several of the girls have informed me that you've broken the most important rule of the dormitory. A rule you, as the resident assistant, are supposed to be enforcing."

Guilt raised the temperature even higher on Deme's body thermostat and she gulped. "Which rule?" she asked, knowing full well that fornicating with a man in your dorm room was top on the list of no-no's of the Gamma Omegas, although she was positive a majority of the girls had violated that rule more than once.

"If you'd bothered to read the manual, you'd know." The college president lifted the folder with the manual inside and tapped it against her palm. "No men in the dormitory after the door is locked at eleven o'clock." Her brows rose on her forehead as her gaze skimmed over Deme and her rumpled sheets. "I'm sure you've broken other rules as well, based on your state of undress."

"My apologies, Dr. Masterson." Deme forced what she hoped was an apologetic smile. All the while her head ached as if she'd been on an all-night bender. "Would it help to tell you that I won't let it happen again?"

"No." Dr. Masterson crossed her arms over her chest. "It wouldn't surprise me to get calls from some of the parents with their concerns over their daughters' well-being."

"You're telling me," Deme muttered.

"What was that?" The older woman's eyes narrowed.

"Understood. I'll need time to arrange for alternate accommodations. I'll let you know the moment I find some."

Even before Deme finished her sentence, the older

woman was shaking her head. "I want you out by this evening."

Deme gasped. "I can't. We won't be finished." Hope plummeted to her belly.

Ms. Masterson's jaw tightened, her arms still firmly crossed over her chest. "Finished?"

Back-paddling like a kayaker facing a waterfall, Deme grasped for the first thing she could think of. "I'm working on a project with some of the students. I need to finish it before I can go apartment hunting."

"That would be your problem."

"Please, Dr. Masterson. The other girls are depending on me to make sure we get it right." She sat up straighter, hating to beg to a woman she'd had doubts about last evening. "Let me stay another day. That's all I ask."

The president of the college drew in a long, deep breath and let it out slowly before saying, "One day." She followed quickly with, "Too many strange things are happening around here. I don't want your involvement to make things worse." She pointed at Deme. "If you do, you'll discover that I can be your worst nightmare. Do you understand?"

A cold chill raced down Deme's spine and didn't dissipate even after the other woman left the room, closing the door firmly behind her.

Just what did she mean by she could be her worst nightmare? Did Dr. Masterson have any idea what Deme's nightmares had been about lately?

Deme tossed the sheets aside and got out of bed, her legs sore, the place between her thighs tender. She must have been really tired when Cal had visited her last night. Her memory was pretty sketchy on a few things. Based on her nakedness and soreness, she could assume they'd done more than just sleep. Why she couldn't say no to the man was beyond her level of comprehension.

Her brows drew together as she stared around her room. Nothing looked out of the ordinary. The plain white walls needed some form of decoration to make them less sterile, but other than that, the room was no more threatening than any other dorm room on campus.

Deme scratched her head. Had she dreamed of being in a jungle last night? Something about moss-covered walls, heat and humidity tugged at her subconscious, but not enough to wrap her mind around. Next time she saw Cal, she'd ask him if she'd talked in her sleep.

Deme slipped into a bathrobe and tossed a clean towel over her shoulder before emerging from her room. A shower sounded damned good about now. Then she'd get on with the investigation. She had only one more day to eke out any information she could from the Gamma Omegas before her cover was blown. Just as well. Enough time had passed since her sister's disappearance.

Halfway to the bathroom, the muffled sound of sobbing reached Deme through Rachel Taylor's closed door. Really wanting the shower, she almost ignored it and moved on, but the sobbing grew louder.

Deme raised her hand and knocked on the door. "Rachel?"

"Go away."

"It's me, Deme, the R.A." Okay, so she technically wasn't the R.A. anymore, but Rachel probably hadn't spoken with Dr. Masterson yet. "Let me in."

The sobbing subsided. After a full minute and a half, just when Deme thought the girl was going to ignore her, the door opened a crack and Rachel looked out, her hair hanging like so much black straw around a face deeply marked with acne scars.

Deme gasped. "Rachel?" She could have kicked herself as soon as she made the sound.

Rachel's eyes welled with yet more tears and she slammed the door.

Thankfully, Deme got her foot in the crack before she could shut it all the way. But the impact on her toes made her cry out in pain. "Holy cow! Open the damned door before you cripple me."

Rachel clapped a hand to her mouth and flung the door wide. "I'm so sorry. I didn't mean to hurt you."

Playing on the girl's guilt, Deme winced. "I'll be okay, I hope." She moved into the room and closed the door behind her. "Now tell me what all the crying is about."

Rachel turned away. "I can't do it anymore. I can't be someone I'm not."

"What do you mean?"

"The sorority. I've asked to be moved to another dorm. I can't take it anymore."

Deme gripped the girl's arms and forced her to look her in the eye. "Take what?"

"The lies, the secrecy, the rituals. I don't care if I'm ugly on the outside."

Deme studied the girl, who a day ago had been another Zoe clone, perfect complexion, perfect hair and face. Today, she met the exact description Aurai had given Deme about her roommate—hopelessly homely, but sweet. "You aren't ugly, Rachel."

"I wasn't when you met me, but I am now." She stared into Deme's face with red-rimmed eyes. "Look at me!"

Deme choked back a lump in her throat. This girl

wanted so badly to fit in she'd practically sold her soul to the devil to be beautiful. "You're more beautiful to me now than any of the Zoe clones in this dorm." She hugged Rachel to her and stroked the back of her head as the younger woman's shoulders shook with the force of a new wave of weeping.

"I wanted to be pretty, just once." Rachel's tears soaked through Deme's robe.

"We all want to be accepted."

"But not the way they're doing it." Rachel pushed away, scrubbing her sleeve beneath her nose. "It's wrong."

"Tell me, Rachel." Now was her chance to get to the bottom of the Gamma Omega shenanigans. "What rituals are they performing?"

Rachel strode across the room, wringing her hands. "Apparently Zoe found a book in the library. A book of spells. She decided to use it as part of the sorority initiation, only it didn't work out exactly as planned."

"How so?"

Rachel looked across at the empty bed that used to be Aurai's.

A lump the size of Texas rose in Deme's throat, and she fought back the ready tears thoughts of her youngest sister inspired.

"That night was horrible." Rachel buried her face in her hands, her body shaking. "They swore me to silence, but I can't be quiet anymore." She looked up through her tears straight into Deme's eyes. "My roommate disappeared that night." She shook her head side to side, her eyes glassy as if seeing the drama replayed over and over. "She was lifted into the air, her robe wrapping around her like she was in a funnel cloud."

Deme took a step toward Rachel. This was the most

she'd heard about her sister's disappearance from any-one. "Then what?"

"The candles had blown out and there weren't any lights coming from any of the nearby buildings. A cloud must have passed over the moon because it got really dark. I could hear her scream as though she was being drawn into a vacuum, dragging her away in a final blast of wind." Rachel blinked, her brows drawing down low over her eyes. "You see why I couldn't tell anyone? Who would believe me?" She clutched at Deme's arm. "You believe me, don't you?"

Deme pulled Rachel into her arms and hugged her again. "Yes, sweetie, I do."

After a long minute, Rachel pulled away enough to brush the tears from her cheeks. "Now Mike is in the hospital because of me."

"Why do you think it's your fault?"

She snorted. "My vanity. I wanted so much to be like the other girls. The spell Zoe used made it happen."

"What exactly was this spell?"

"It makes ugly girls like me…" She ducked her head, her cheeks reddening. "It makes them pretty."

"You are pretty without spells and rituals."

"That's what Mike said, but when I drank from the vial, I became beautiful and Mike couldn't control him-self around me. It made him an animal." She wrapped her arms around her middle. "It made him attack me… and made me attack him."

"What's in the vial?" Deme took Rachel's hands. "Are you sure Zoe didn't drug you?"

The younger girl's mouth drew into a tight line. "No. It was the spell."

"But she could have put some kind of date rape drug in the bottle."

Rachel shook her head. "The spell and the potion in the vial are what made me beautiful and then aggressive. I've never hurt another human being in my life. Neither has Mike. When he found out what he'd done, he couldn't live with himself." Rachel's voice caught on another sob. She swallowed hard and continued. "He tried to commit suicide. Thank God he failed. I told him it wasn't his fault, but he wouldn't listen. That's when I decided enough was enough. I stopped drinking the potion. I haven't been out of my room since. They'll know as soon as they see me."

She held up a blue vial and pressed it into Deme's hand. "Here, take it. I won't be needing it. I'm done with Gamma Omega. I was just fooling myself to think I'd ever fit in."

Deme took the vial and Rachel's hand. "You're doing the right thing. You don't belong with Zoe's group."

Rachel nodded, her shoulders sagging.

"Not because you're not beautiful, but because you're beautiful where it counts." Deme touched her hand to her chest. "Don't let anyone tell you that you're ugly. Do you hear me?"

Rachel nodded. "Yeah. That's what Mike said. If only I'd listened, he'd be okay, not in a coma." The younger girl slipped her arms into a hooded sweat jacket, pulling the hood up over her head. "I'm going to the hospital now to visit him. Maybe he'll be out of the coma today. Wish him luck, will you?"

"You bet." Deme stepped out of the room with Rachel and ran right into Zoe.

This girl had caused enough trouble with Rachel and Aurai to remain on Deme's blacklist for life. Even if something else was manipulating her actions, Deme couldn't seem to forgive her at this moment. "What do you want?" Deme asked, none too gently.

"Nothing. Should I want something?" Her gaze went over Deme's shoulder to connect with Rachel's, her eyes narrowing at the girl's appearance. "Just checking on my Gamma Omegas. This sorority sticks together, don't they?"

An implied "or else" hung in the air between Zoe and Rachel, making Deme's blood boil.

"Look, Zoe." Deme stepped in between the two coeds and stood nose to nose with the striking sorority president. "If anything happens to my new friend, Rachel, you'll answer to me. Got that?"

Her beautifully arched brows rose into her low-slung bangs. "I don't have a clue as to what you're talking about."

"Then I suggest you get a clue and leave us alone." Deme pushed past her and marched to the exit, shoving Rachel in front of her.

Deme had had her fill of Zoe Adams.

Cal had a job to do, or he would have stayed until Deme woke up. As it was, he'd eased her eyelids open to get a glimpse at her emerald-green eyes before he'd climbed out of the bed and dressed for work in campus maintenance. No more cat eyes. Whew!

Most of the night he'd lain awake, watching out for a return of the Chimera. He must have dozed off because when he woke, the room had returned to normal, no sign of algae, moss or the jungle humidity that had greeted him earlier.

Convinced the threat had abated for now, Cal rose from the bed, put on his jeans and slipped out of the dorm shirtless. The one he'd worn in had been ripped to shreds by the Chimera-possessed Deme. One thing was certain, she could not sleep in that room another night. He'd talk to her about it later.

First major stop on his list of assigned maintenance duties had to be the office of one Dr. Diane Masterson. What he hoped to find, he had no idea. Maybe he'd run into her and discuss her past and the attack that happened on this very same campus thirty years ago.

He couldn't imagine any woman in her right mind returning to a place where she'd been brutally raped. And to overlook the area where it had occurred day after day...

Cal couldn't begin to fathom the woman's reasoning. He hurried through the morning tightening faucets, unclogging toilets, replacing hinges and door handles, unjamming locks and performing the myriad other duties required by his supervisor. By noon, he was just heading for the administration building when his cell phone rang.

"Black speaking."

"Cal?" The voice sounded like Deme.

Cal's heartbeat quickened. "Deme?"

"No, it's Selene. Something weird's going on here at the theater. Think you can come give us a hand?"

"I'll be right there." His heart pounding, he dashed past the student commons, weaving his way through the maze of students lounging on the grass or sitting at the outdoor tables.

It never ceased to amaze him how the sun could go on shining when crazy, soul-defining and dangerous events happened. People could be dying and the sun would continue to rise and set.

He arrived outside the theater in time to see a stream

of students gathering in front of the door, waving at their friends to come.

Cal ran past them and pushed through to the door. Gina stood in front of the glass double doors, refusing to let the students pass. When she saw Cal, she motioned him forward. "Thank goodness you're here." She opened the door and let him slide through. "I was here cleaning the theater aquarium when it started. Selene and Deme are on the stage."

The auditorium was half-full of gawking students, some pointing toward the stage, others pressing hands to their mouths, their eyes wide.

Selene stood on the stage looking up into the rafters. Deme stood beside her.

Cal's groin tightened just at the sight of Deme. He squelched his reaction and climbed the steps up the side of the stage.

"Have you tried to talk her down?" Deme had her back to Cal and didn't see him approach.

"I've tried everything short of calling the fire department. I thought since you are her R.A., you might have more luck." Selene glanced around. When she spotted Cal she blew out a long breath. "Blessed Be, you're here. Maybe you can help."

"What's going on?" he asked, his gaze sweeping over Deme's face, noting the dark smudges beneath her eyes.

"Not what—who." Deme pointed up at the catwalk twenty-five feet above the stage. "Shelby Cramer is up on the catwalk and won't come down."

"And she's acting really funny," Selene added.

"Funny how?" Cal stared up into the shadows of the catwalk.

"She's growling and hissing at anyone who tries to climb the ladders."

At first he couldn't see the girl. Then a movement caught his attention and he spotted her. Crouched on the metal mesh, the pretty blonde stared down at the people gathered below.

A student hurried forward, handing Selene a flashlight.

"Oh, thank the goddess." Selene shined the light up at Shelby, the beam reflecting an intense red off the girl's eyes.

Shelby shrank back and hissed.

"That's not normal," Selene stated.

"Goes along with the way she's acting." Deme stared into her sister's eyes. "When did she start acting this way?"

"I don't know. She was quiet when she showed up for rehearsal, but she wasn't acting strange until halfway through the first act." Selene's gaze shifted to the young woman in the rafters. "Do you think the Chimera has her?"

Deme nodded. "That's where I'd put my money." She turned to Cal. "I'd have gone after her, but I'm not much bigger than she is. Can you help me take her?"

Cal's jaw clenched. "I'll get her." Before he could take two steps toward the ladder in the far corner of the backstage area, Deme's hand shot out and grabbed his arm.

"I'm going with you."

"No."

"She's acting like an animal. If you chase her one way, she'll run the other. We need to come at her from opposite directions. Corner her."

"I don't want you up there." He didn't want to tell Deme what he was really afraid of. If Shelby was possessed by the Chimera, what was to keep the beast from possessing Deme as it had last night?

"I'm going." Deme took off toward the ladder leading up into the rafters.

Cal grabbed her shoulders and forced her to stop. "I don't want you up there."

"Why?" she demanded, her green eyes blazing, the air practically crackling between them. "Don't you trust me?"

"You, yes. The Chimera, no." His grip relaxed. "Do you remember any of what happened last night?" He asked the question softly enough only Deme and Selene could hear.

Deme frowned, rubbing her temple. "Not much. You came over late and we must have done something because I woke up naked."

Selene's lips twitched and she opened her mouth to comment. At a glare from Cal, she closed it.

Cal's face softened and his fingers rubbed her shoulders. "Let's just say you weren't quite yourself last night."

"Really?" She looked up at him, her frown deepening. At last she shook her head and planted her hands on her hips. "Well, I am myself this morning, and you can't do this without help."

Cal stared at her long and hard. Metal rattled overhead as Shelby ran along the catwalk, ducking low to stare at them beneath the thin handrails. "Okay, but you take direction from me."

"Fine."

Cal ran to the far backstage corner while Deme headed for the other. They arrived at the same time. Cal pulled himself up the ladder, keeping his eye on Shelby and Deme alternately.

He reached the top first and he waited for Deme. When she stood on the catwalk, he motioned her forward.

Shelby crouched in the middle of the walkway, her head swinging back and forth as she watched the movements of Deme and Cal. A low rumble rose from her chest, ending in a teeth-baring hiss.

Cal edged closer from his end. "Shelby," he called out, appealing to the girl buried beneath the Chimera's trance. After what had happened to Deme last night, he knew how easily the Chimera could manipulate others. He also knew that the person was still there and could be reached if you were persuasive enough. "Shelby. Come with me and you'll be all right."

Deme moved faster, closing the gap between herself and Shelby more quickly than Cal.

He picked up the pace, afraid that Shelby would attack Deme before he could reach her.

Shelby crouched lower, her catlike gaze shifting from Deme back to Cal. Her hands curled into claws, her body tensed. She was going to pounce.

"Watch out!" Cal yelled.

The girl let out an ear-piercing animal scream and leaped at Deme.

Deme, standing her ground, refusing to let the girl by, was hit full force in the midsection. She staggered, fell backward and landed on her back, Shelby on top of her. The structure shuddered, metal creaking, followed by a loud pop.

The old strut beside Deme that attached the catwalk to the ceiling beams broke.

The footbridge tilted sharply toward the front of the stage.

A collective scream rose from the students in the

audience as Deme and Shelby slid toward the edge and the twenty-five-foot fall to the hardwood flooring of the stage.

Deme hooked an elbow around the strut on the opposite side and wrapped her legs around Shelby's middle as she slipped over the side.

His heart hammering against his ribs, Cal's first instinct was to dive for Deme and grab her before she fell. But he was too far away. Instead, he held tightly to the handrails until the shaking stopped. Then he was running down the listing walkway toward the two women. If they fell the way they were, both could die or be terribly injured.

After a full year without her, Cal couldn't lose Deme again.

The muscles in Deme's shoulder burned, the weight of her own body enough to make her cry. The additional weight Shelby represented was making it nearly impossible for her to hold on.

Footsteps pounding toward her on the grate alerted Deme to Cal's approach. Hope surged inside. But shifting metal beneath her killed that hope. "No!" she gasped. "Stay back! If you come any closer, the other strut will break."

As if to emphasize her point, the structure creaked loudly and the catwalk shuddered again.

Shelby clawed at Deme, trying to climb up her onto the catwalk. Her eyes were wide and feral.

"Shelby Cramer, I know you can hear me. Listen up, girl!" Deme yelled, her back and legs straining. She had to get through to the young woman. If she didn't, the Chimera would take them both to the ground in a very uncomfortable landing. One they might not survive.

The woman stopped clawing and stared up at Deme, her eyes narrowing, her lips pulling back over her teeth.

"You don't own her." Deme's arm was going numb. She reached up with her other hand and clutched at the strut to relieve the pressure on her elbow. She wouldn't last much longer. "Shelby, take your body back. It's yours!"

"I can get closer," Cal called out.

"No!" Deme said between clenched teeth. "It's too dangerous." With every muscle in her body screaming for release, Deme forced her voice to calm. "If you let her die, you die with her. What's it going to be?"

Shelby stared up at Deme, her chest rumbling with a low, wicked growl. Her eyes flashed red and then back to gray. The girl's head lolled backward.

Then as though coming up for her first breath of air, Shelby gasped, her eyes wide, her body rigid. "What the hell?" She looked down and twisted violently, almost jerking Deme loose from her hold on the strut. "What's going on? Help!" She wrapped her arms around Deme, clinging tightly, pressing her face into Deme's belly.

"Shelby...keep calm." Deme's arms and legs shook. "Can you reach up and grab on to the catwalk?"

"No! Oh, God. Help. Oh, God." She hung on to Deme with a death grip, refusing to let go.

"I can't hold on much longer, Shelby. You have to help yourself."

"Deme, we have to risk it." Cal inched forward. "I'm coming to you."

"It'll break." By this time, Deme's refusal was weakening. If she didn't get some relief soon, it wouldn't matter, they'd fall anyway.

Shelby turned her face toward Cal.

Cal lay flat on the catwalk and crawled toward them,

distributing his weight across a broader surface to ease the strain on the lone strut standing between the two women and a tragic fall. The metal creaked but held.

When he got within two feet of Shelby, he reached out a hand. "Take my hand, Shelby."

"I can't." Her voice shook and she buried her face in Deme's belly again.

"Yes. You. Can." He scooted forward a little more.

Deme's arm was slipping, and her legs couldn't hold up under the strain. Shelby was sliding farther down her body.

"Give me your hand now," Cal shouted.

Shelby cried out and slapped her hand into his.

Deme's legs lost their grip on the girl and she slid free. "No!"

Shelby screamed. The metal of the catwalk groaned and jerked as the girl's weight shifted from Deme to Cal.

Deme, her arms shaking, struggled to pull herself up to the section of catwalk still firmly attached to the roof. She lay facedown, breathing hard. As the blood rushed back into her arms, the pain of a thousand pins and needles stabbed into her.

Dangling from Cal's grip, Shelby hung twenty feet above the hard wooden floor of the stage. "Help! Oh, God, please," she sobbed.

"I've got you," Cal said, his voice low, steady, calm. He reached with his other hand and pulled her up a little more.

"Why is this happening to me?" Shelby whimpered.

"Everything is going to be okay," Cal said.

Across the broken catwalk from Cal, Deme let Cal's words wash over her, warming her where she'd felt so cold. If he hadn't been there today...

When Cal finally had Shelby close enough, he grabbed the back of her jeans and hauled her the rest of the way onto the walkway, scooting her back to the undamaged portion.

As Deme lay gasping for breath, arms aching and her face pressed against the catwalk's grate, Cal's words washed over her. *Everything is going to be okay.*

She pushed to a sitting position, then stood, her resolve hardening. Tired of reacting to every curveball the Chimera threw at her. Deme realized the only way everything was going to get better was to make it happen.

Chapter 14

Cal worked with Fred to stabilize the catwalk, repairing the damage and reinforcing the struts so that they wouldn't fail again. Not until nearly quitting time did he get a chance to check out Dr. Masterson's office. He told Fred he had one more thing to check on his way back to the locker room and not to wait on him.

"What you did for that girl…" Fred patted him on the back. "You do good work, Cal. Get some rest."

Cal used his key to enter the administrative building through a side utility door accessed only by maintenance personnel. Most of the staff had already left for the day, leaving the desks empty and many of the lights off. He quickly located the college president's office and knocked on the door. When no one answered, he let himself in.

The walls were lined with framed diplomas from the University of Illinois. He scanned all of them, taking pictures with his cell phone. Not even the undergraduate degree read Colyer-Fenton College, as if the attack had driven her from the college to complete her education elsewhere.

"With this arsenal of education, why did you come here?" Cal wondered out loud to the empty room.

"I had to come back," a voice said behind him. "To face my fears."

Cal froze, his hand in the air in the middle of snapping another picture of her doctorate diploma. Lowering his arm slowly, he turned to face the woman. "Of what?"

"I spent years hiding in my room, only venturing out to go to and from class. I was so afraid of every shadow. Not until I decided to come back here did I find purpose."

"What were you afraid of?"

She rolled her eyes. "Don't play stupid with me. I saw what you did for that girl in the theater. You're not some Cal Smith, the maintenance man. You're here because of the happenings on campus."

Cal didn't respond. By not replying, he agreed. "So what are you going to do?"

"I don't think you're responsible, if that's what you mean. And if you can help find what's causing all this chaos, all the better." She walked across the room to sit behind her desk. "I'm of the opinion that whatever it is, it has been here before."

"Thirty years ago?"

She steepled her fingers, looked directly at him and nodded. "Just do me a favor."

"And what's that?"

"Keep me in the loop, will you?"

"I can't make that promise."

"I can have you thrown off campus."

He tipped his head. "Yes, you can."

Her lips twisted into a wry smile. "But I won't. I owe you for Shelby."

"Thanks. Do you mind my asking what happened thirty years ago?"

She laughed, the sound harsh in the fading light from the window. "The news article didn't give you enough?"

"Only that a young woman was raped."

Dr. Masterson stood and faced the window, the one looking out onto the garden. "That's all there was to the story." Her tone didn't invite further questions nor any hope of additional answers.

"Then I'll be going. If you can think of anything else that might help solve this case, I'll be around."

Silhouetted against the window, Dr. Masterson looked dark and alone. "Next time, wait to be invited into my office. I'm kind of particular about people invading my privacy." She looked back over her shoulder, her eyes narrowed. "And do be careful whom you associate with. There are those on campus who aren't what they appear to be."

His lips curled up on the corners. "Like me?"

"You'd be surprised. And so might they."

Somehow, he didn't doubt that. Cal left, closing the door behind him. His last view of Dr. Masterson was of her looking out her window, down into the garden.

Deme spent the day talking to sorority sisters and searching every inch of the Gamma Omega dormitory for any evidence leading her to find Aurai. Having come up empty, she'd turned her search to the student commons and finally returned to the library, where she'd called a meeting of Brigid, Gina and Selene in the relative privacy of the second floor east stacks.

"Relatives!" Gina gasped.

"Coincidence be damned," Selene said in an unusual display of frustration. "You know what this means, don't you?"

Deme nodded. "We're on this campus for a reason. Apparently the same reason the five sisters had been here."

Brigid held up a finger. "With one difference…" She planted her hands on her hips. "I don't plan to die taking down the big, bad Chimera."

"Right," Deme agreed. "And I'll be damned to eternal hell if one of my sisters pays the ultimate price. We're a family and we will all emerge intact, if I have anything to do with it."

"Here! Here!" Gina clapped.

"Sounds all well and good, but you listen to me." Deme's eyes narrowed as she looked into the steady gazes of her sisters. "Don't try to fight it alone. The Chimera is strong. You saw what it could do to a regular girl when it took over Shelby. It seems to turn our powers against us, so beware."

Gina put her hand into the center of the circle of sisters. "Be safe, sisters."

Deme's palm covered hers, and Brigid and Selene piled a hand on top. "Blessed Be."

A whirl of wind lifted their hair, and the women smiled at each other.

Deme's eyes misted. "Same goes for Aurai," she said softly.

"We will find her." Selene's arm circled Deme's shoulder. "We have to believe that."

"I do." The responsibility of being the oldest sibling

weighed more heavily than ever before. "Look, you guys get off campus and get some rest. We have more work to do tomorrow."

After her sisters left, Deme couldn't give up. She spent the rest of the evening searching through more news clippings for anything else she could find on the five sisters. There had to be something useful to lead her to Aurai.

Fatigue pulled at her eyelids long before she closed the books and packed it in. She hated to admit that fear of last night's black hole of memories made her reluctant to return to her room, thus she had pushed on longer than she should have.

When she finally left the library, Deme trudged toward the dorm, not at all looking forward to staying another night alone in the room against the garden. Having seen what the Chimera could do to a young college coed, she shuddered to think what it could do with her as semiconscious as she was.

A man pushed away from a light pole and ambled her way.

Deme's pulse sped. She could tell that walk anywhere. Cal Black moved like a panther, his steps smooth, measured, lean and sexy.

After the day she'd had, she couldn't think of anyone she'd rather see. She needed a few answers to questions she had concerning what had happened in her room the night before. Questions aside, she was glad to see him. No amount of self-denial would change that, and frankly she was tired of fighting her attraction. Hell, she was flat-out tired, period.

"Tough day at the office?" he asked.

She fell in step beside him, heading for the parking lot. "Yeah. I'm glad you came by."

He chuckled. "That's a change for the better."

His laughter filled the emptiness threatening to drag her spirits ever downward. "Mind if I ask you a few questions about last night?"

"Can it wait for a few minutes?"

"Sure."

He hooked her arm with his big, rough hand and took off across the campus lawns toward the parking lot.

The tallest of her sisters, even Deme's long legs had a tough time keeping up with Cal. She arrived at his motorcycle slightly out of breath. "Needing a little exercise, big guy?"

"Huh?" He looked up as if he hadn't realized Deme was beside him all the way.

"You're hitting the old ego hard these days." Deme laughed. "If you want to be by yourself, why didn't you say so? I'd understand."

"No, I don't." He shook his head, his frown showing his confusion. "I want to be with you."

Cal's words had an instant warming effect, leaving Deme feeling more alive than she had since she'd almost plummeted to the stage that morning. She didn't respond to his comment. Didn't feel as if she had to.

He shoved a hand through his hair and breathed deeply. Then he handed her a spare helmet. "Get on."

She looked down at the helmet and shrugged. "Okay. Where are we headed?"

"Somewhere…anywhere…away from here. I need to get my head on straight." He climbed onto the bike and kicked the engine to life, the roar echoing across the quiet campus.

Deme climbed on behind him and wrapped her arms around his waist.

The motorcycle shot out onto the road and soon entered traffic on the Eisenhower Expressway, headed east toward Lake Michigan.

As Cal dodged vehicles, Deme leaned into him, letting herself go for the few short minutes she could, the wind blowing the cobwebs from her mind and clearing her head. Away from campus her mind wasn't clouded with the oppressive presence of the Chimera. She needed this break in order to think straight and plan her next move.

Cal dropped off the expressway, heading south. He came to a stop on Lake Shore Drive near the John G. Shedd Aquarium.

After the short, swift ride, Deme was more alert and awake than she'd been in days.

Cal parked the bike, removed his helmet and took hers from her, securing it to the motorcycle. Then he grabbed her hand and led her along a broad, concrete walkway. The flotilla of sailboats lining the bay on Lake Michigan, the night skyline of Chicago and the Navy Pier spread out before them.

"Where are we going?"

"Shh…" He left the sidewalk and crossed over grass, pulling her along behind him. "It's almost time."

"Time?"

Over the steady hum of traffic, a loud *pop* sounded across the water toward the Navy Pier and a trail of color shot into the air high above the lake, where it exploded in a burst of brilliant pink light.

"Oh, yeah. I'd forgotten all about the fireworks." She stood beside Cal, staring up at the display as, one after another, rockets shot into the air. "Our mother used to bring us here in the summertime. We'd spend the afternoon on the beach and stay until the fireworks ended. Aurai would fall asleep before they started."

Cal slipped an arm around Deme and pulled her against him. Nothing sexual, but it had a tremendous pull on her in the area of her heart.

She'd expected him to make love to her on the beach, or try to kiss her in the moonlight, but to just stand there and hold her while they watched the fireworks…

Tears welled in her eyes. How had she gone so wrong where this man was concerned? He'd once asked her to marry him. She'd answered by running away.

How could she make it right again? All because she was strange, different…a witch. "I don't lead a normal life."

"Neither do I."

"I can make things happen with earth, plants and vegetation that would scare most people."

Cal shrugged. "I chase bad guys and get shot at."

"Everything about me and my sisters is bizarre and unusual."

"Is that a bad thing? Some people would kill to have what you and your sisters have."

"Something has." She stood in silence a moment, reflecting on the people who'd been hurt or killed by the Chimera's manipulations. "All we wanted was to lead normal lives, have careers, maybe fall in love…" Her voice faded off. She hadn't meant to mention that *L*-word, but there it was.

Cal let the word pass, instead asking, "What do you remember about last night?"

"Not much. I was hoping you could fill in the blanks." Deme stared up at him, his face illuminated by the night sky, brightened occasionally by the flash of the pyrotechnic display.

He stared up at the fireworks exploding high above Lake Michigan. "You weren't quite yourself."

"The Chimera had me, didn't it?" A shiver raked over her body, shaking her all the way down to her toes. "Was I as bad as Shelby?"

He chuckled. "You had your moments."

"Did I hurt you?"

Cal hesitated, his gaze remaining on the lights of Navy Pier. "No."

Deme didn't believe him. "Show me your shoulders."

"You didn't bite me this time. Except on the ear." He reached up to touch his earlobe. "But it's fine."

"Then how else did I hurt you?" Deme couldn't help but feel he wasn't telling the whole truth. Her lapse in memory frustrated her.

"You didn't." His arm tightened around her. "Look, I just came to see the fireworks."

Deme faced the display, a thousand questions racing through her mind. Had she said something hurtful to him while possessed by the Chimera? He'd once asked her to marry him. After she'd disappeared for a year, he probably harbored some pretty ill feelings toward her. Had she jabbed at that pain? Did he even care anymore?

Her heart squeezed inside her chest. Though she'd run away from him, hoping he'd forget her and move on to a normal life with a normal woman, she couldn't help wishing he still loved her.

She glanced up at him, wanting more than anything to ask if he still loved her, but she couldn't. Her gaze returned to the pier and she forced herself to say, "The fireworks display is pretty, isn't it?"

"Yeah. My father only brought us once while my mother was alive. She loved it. When she died, he couldn't bring himself to return."

"I'm sorry."

"Why? It was a long time ago."

"You must have been close to your father."

His hand dropped to his side. "It was a long time ago."

The fireworks died away and a stream of vehicles made a slow, lighted procession out of the Navy Pier parking area. Families on their way home after a fun-filled day. Life couldn't be more beautiful and simple for some.

Only Deme's could never be that uncomplicated. Hadn't her mother said from the moment she could understand that because she was blessed, she had a responsibility to use her gifts to help others? She'd told herself that was what she was doing with her private investigative service in St. Croix. But she'd really only been lying to herself.

Trying to live a normal life ignoring her talent except to further her own financial pursuits had given her what? A great, big empty feeling.

What Cal had hoped to accomplish by bringing Deme out to watch the fireworks was a mystery to himself. He'd spent the past couple of days working nonstop to discover anything there was to know about a missing girl. The discoveries had been more than weird, shaking his knowledge of the world he lived in. It was a lot to comprehend and believe, all being shoved at him one frightening incident after another.

Standing on the shores of Lake Michigan, on the edge of the city he'd called home for his entire life, he had to admit, he knew less now than he thought he'd known last week.

He needed this. A chance to stand back and evaluate.

"I spoke with Dr. Masterson." Cal broke the silence. Deme shot a glance his way. "And?"

"She more or less admitted she was the woman raped thirty years ago."

"Why did she come back?"

"She couldn't move on until she laid her ghosts to rest."

Deme snorted. "Like that's going to happen now?" She breathed in and let it out. "Sorry. I don't mean to be sarcastic, but I have a feeling it's going to get a whole lot worse before it gets better."

He nodded, his hand tightening around her waist. "I'm afraid you're right."

"Did you learn anything else?" Deme asked.

Cal had yet to tell Deme of what he'd found in the basement of the student commons, but he couldn't keep it from her long. Sooner or later, Lieutenant Warner would spill the beans to Brigid, and she'd be all over him for not letting her in on the secret tunnels sooner. "I found out there is a labyrinth of tunnels beneath the city."

"The old freight tunnels they used back in the early nineteen hundreds? Yeah, so?"

"I did a little research and got with an engineer friend of mine." He faced Deme. "Did you know that one of the tunnels runs directly beneath the Colyer-Fenton campus?"

Deme's eyes widened. "Do you think that might be where the Chimera is hiding?" Her hand clutched his sleeve. "It could have Aurai there." She turned toward the parking lot. "We have to go."

Cal grabbed her arm and pulled her to a stop. "Whoa, wait a minute."

"Why? You could have found her."

"We don't know what's in the tunnels or even if the

air is breathable. You can't go chasing down there until we get the right equipment."

"But Aurai could be down there. If the air isn't breathable, she'd be…"

"Dead."

Deme gulped down the lump in her throat. "But she's not. We felt her. She's still alive."

"The place where she is might be okay, but getting to her could be deadly, not only because of the Chimera, but poisonous air."

"Cal, we have to go. If there's any chance at all that she's down there, we have to find her."

"And we will." He pulled her into his arms and held her. "Tomorrow. I have a tunnel expert meeting us at the diner in the morning. He'll bring breathing apparatus and the equipment we need to test the air."

Deme stared up into his eyes a long time before her shoulders slumped. "You're right. We need to do this correctly. I don't want anyone else hurt."

He held her arms, his hands squeezing tighter. "Deme, only me and the tunnel expert are going down."

She jerked out of his hands and backed up a step. "No way."

"I can't risk losing you or another one of your sisters."

"I'm going with you. You tell your expert to bring enough equipment for me to go, too."

"No."

"Come on, Cal. You knew how I'd respond to this. If you didn't want me to go with you, you might as well have kept it to yourself. The cat's out of the bag now." She fisted her hands on her hips, her legs planted wide, daring him to refute her claim.

And he wanted to. The thought of Deme getting hurt

in the nasty, smelly, dank tunnel below the campus made him crazy. But with her standing there in front of him, her green eyes blazing, the wind off the lake lifting her wild red hair around her, she looked like a Valkyrie ready to do battle with the devil himself.

A smile crooked the corners of his mouth, spreading into a grin. "Okay. But only you. The rest of your sisters will have to remain ignorant until we know more."

She stuck out a hand. "Deal."

Cal grabbed the proffered hand. Instead of shaking it, he pulled her into his arms. "Now, we need to get some sleep. I haven't had a good night's rest in three days."

"You can drop me off at the campus."

"Not sure that's a good idea. Not after what happened last night."

"You never did give me all the details." She fit perfectly against him, her breasts rubbing against his chest with every breath. "There are a few memories missing from that particular event. Are you ever going to tell me what happened?"

"Maybe someday." He leaned down and kissed her. "As for now, I think we should make some new ones." His lips pressed against hers, his tongue slipping into her mouth to taste hers. Yeah, this is what he'd wanted. Far away from the influence of the Chimera, he could be certain that the woman he kissed was indeed Deme, not some jacked-up creature from the underworld.

Her hands slid beneath his shirt and up across his back, her fingernails lightly scraping his skin.

Cal tensed.

When she didn't dig deep, he relaxed and tugged her shirt from the waistband of her jeans, letting his own hands roam across her warm, naked skin.

Not until a cool breeze off the water caressed the side of his face did he come up for air and remember where he was. He set her at arm's length, removing his hands from beneath her shirt. "We better go before we're arrested for indecent exposure."

Deme leaned into him, her fingers finding his nipples beneath his shirt. "But we still have our clothes on."

His hand slid up her arms, gripping her shoulders. "We won't for long at this rate." He pushed her away and took her hand, leading her up the grassy slope to the concrete walkway.

In silence, he climbed on the motorcycle. Deme slipped on behind him, the inside of her thighs sliding around his. Cal almost pulled her into his lap and made love to her there in the park. Instead, he kicked the engine into life and revved it, shooting out onto Lake Shore Drive, headed for his apartment.

When he passed the exit off Eisenhower Expressway to the Colyer-Fenton College campus, Deme shouted, "You missed my exit."

He shook his head and kept going. No way in hell he'd let her sleep in that room one more night.

When he pulled into the parking lot of his apartment and parked the bike, Deme hopped off the back, her face set in grim lines. "I need to go back to campus."

"No." He took off his helmet and headed for the stairwell.

She stood beside his bike, refusing to follow. "Then I'll just call a taxi."

He stopped and turned around. "You can't."

"Can't call a taxi?"

"No, you can't sleep in that room tonight."

"Why?"

"I don't want what happened to Shelby today to happen to you…again."

Deme's eyes rounded. "It had me last night?" She walked toward him, slowly, as though in a trance, her gaze seeking his in the dimly lit parking lot. "How bad was it?"

He took her into his arms. "It made Shelby look like a kitten stuck up in a tree."

Deme leaned her forehead into his chest. "Damn."

"Yeah."

"But I can't impose on you."

"Who said you were imposing?" He swung her up into his arms. "I would have taken you to your sisters if that had been the case." He gazed down at her. "I still can, if that's what you want." His breath held in his throat as he awaited her answer.

Chapter 15

Deme wrapped her arms around Cal's neck. "No. This is what I want." She leaned forward and pressed her lips to his. Every nerve in her body burst into flame, blood rushing low in her belly to that aching, throbbing place at the juncture of her thighs.

She wanted Cal. Tall, sexy…naked…Cal.

He carried her up the stairs, as if she weighed nothing. When he reached the upper landing, he wasn't even breathing hard.

"You know, I could have walked." She kissed his lips and laughed. "But it was more fun watching you play the he-man."

"And here I thought I was impressing you with my chivalry." He dropped her feet to the ground and jammed the key into the lock.

As soon as the door opened, Deme pushed through,

ripping her shirt up over her head and tossing it to the corner. "What's taking you so long, Detective?"

Deme couldn't explain the feeling of coming home. Was it the amount of time that had passed, the distance she'd traveled, the events of the past couple of days or the emotions evoked by returning to Cal's apartment after a year? She couldn't put a finger on the one thing that made her want to grab for what little happiness she could find and hold on. Tomorrow was another day of trouble, but tonight was hers and Cal's.

She shimmied out of her jeans and kicked them off, standing there in her bra and panties, her chest rising and falling with the rapid breaths of a sprinter.

Cal closed the door behind him and leaned against it, his arms crossed, his brows raised. "Is this the reason you think I brought you here?"

A moment of doubt struck Deme as her skin cooled, her stomach fluttering with a sudden attack of the nerves. Her arms wrapped around her middle. "Didn't you?"

He shook his head.

Deme's eyes narrowed and her arms dropped to her sides. Was he testing her, or did he really not want to make love to her? "Not interested?" She walked toward him, her hand slipping up her back to unclasp her bra.

He tipped his head to the side. "Thinking."

Deme held the cups of her bra in place, letting the straps slide down her shoulders.

Cal didn't move, but the flare of his nostrils gave him away.

Oh, he wanted her all right.

Deme let the bra fall to the end of the fingers on one hand and she lifted it in the air before tossing it across a lamp shade. "Still thinking about it?"

He pushed away from the door but didn't close the distance. "Yup."

After a day full of stress, this little game of cat and mouse should have pushed Deme over the edge. Instead, it was reviving her, making her want more.

Standing in nothing but her black bikini panties that left very little to the imagination, she straightened her shoulders, pushing out her chest, proud of what genetics had blessed her with.

Still he stood there waiting for her to make the next move.

Deme remained rooted to the floor three feet away from Cal, her body on fire, ready and waiting for him to take her. Apparently he wasn't ready and it was up to her to make him want her as badly as she wanted him.

Deme let her fingers trail slowly across her belly, sliding into the indention of her belly button, tracing a path upward. When her hands reached her breasts, she cupped them, squeezing gently, lifting them and massaging their firm roundness.

The nipples peaked, hardening into tight little nubs. With the tips of her fingers, she tugged at them, pinching and teasing.

Her breathing became more erratic, what she was doing to entice Cal making her hotter and more needy with each stroke.

With one hand on her breast, continuing the sensual massage, she slid her other hand downward to the apex of her thighs, beneath the elastic of her panties.

She threaded her fingers into the mound of hair, parting her folds to caress the sensitive little nubbin hidden between.

Deme's breath caught in her throat. Her hips thrust forward as her finger stroked the sweet spot.

Her head fell back, her hair brushing over her back and lower to the top of her buttocks, the swish of the fine silken tendrils as erotic as a man trailing feathers over her nakedness.

Lost in her own sensual arousal, Deme didn't realize Cal had moved until he grasped her face between his palms. "Look at me."

She blinked her eyes open, unaware she'd even closed them. When she looked into his deep brown eyes, she could see a fire burning bright.

He stared for a long moment before he let out a steady breath. "Good, it is you." His hands skimmed down her neck and over her shoulders to cup her breasts in his palms. His lips pressed into the pulse thrumming along the side of her throat, his tongue flicking and tasting a path down to her collarbone.

Deme's head fell back, exposing the mounds of her breasts to his lips. "What is that supposed to mean?"

"Just what I said." He pushed her breast up with his hand and took the nipple into his mouth, teasing it with the tip of his tongue. One hand glided down her waist, edging beneath her panty line to join her hand there in a sensual stroking motion.

Deme gasped, pressing her breast more fully into his mouth. "Were you expecting someone else?"

His lips left her breast to kiss her full on the mouth. "I was hoping we were alone so I could do this." He backed her up until her bottom hit the edge of his dining table. With a rough thumb, he hooked the elastic of her waistband and dragged her panties halfway down her thighs. Then he lifted her until her bottom slid across the table, her knees draping over the side. With her perched above him, he dropped to his knees and finished the job of taking off her panties, one agonizing inch at a time, pressing his lips to every inch of exposed skin all the way down to her ankles.

When he finally pulled the panties free, Cal parted her legs, pulling them over his shoulders, bringing her aching entrance within inches of his lips.

Deme cupped the back of his head, urging him closer. All the worries of the day were washed to the back of her mind. The only focus she had was on what Cal's mouth could do to her.

Cal pressed his lips to the inside of her thigh, mere inches from heaven, sliding his tongue closer.

Her body throbbed, nerves jumping as his fingers parted her folds, thumbing the center with gentle precision. When his tongue replaced his thumb, Cal teased and flicked, dropping lower to thrust into her, laving her channel with warm, wet strokes.

Deme's hips pushed forward, meeting his thrusts and wanting more. When he transferred his attention back to her own point of desire, the little nubbin of tantalized nerves, Deme's hands braced behind her, her bottom rising off the table.

A brilliant explosion of sensations, every bit as spectacular as the Navy Pier fireworks display, burst through her, rocking her world into a bliss so intense, she didn't know she'd screamed out until the sound of her voice echoed in her ears. She rode the wave of pleasure, hips rocking, breathing erratic, her heart beating a thousand times a minute.

As the intensity diminished enough so she could breathe, a new burgeoning need swept over her. She grabbed Cal's ears and pulled him up.

"Hey. Do you mind?" He climbed to his feet, eager to get ahead of her pull on his ears, and stood between her thighs.

With her breath still coming in erratic heaves, Deme yanked at the rivet on Cal's jeans. "You have…" She breathed out and sucked in another breath. "Too many clothes on," she said, her words coming out in a rush. With a quick flick, she had the button undone and the zipper down.

Cal's erection sprang forward into her palm and she guided it swiftly into place.

With one hard thrust, he filled her.

Deme let out the breath she'd been holding and sucked in another, her legs wrapping around his middle, drawing him closer.

Cal started slow, sliding in and out.

Deme had no patience for it. She wanted him hard and fast. The more punishing, the more alive she felt. With both hands on his buttocks, she set a pummeling pace.

As she climbed that tension-filled peak yet again, she let go of her hold and lay down across the table, her fingers digging into her folds, coaxing more from her climax as she catapulted over the top.

With one final thrust, Cal clutched Deme's hips, holding her hard against him for one last second, sliding free before he spilled inside her.

Replete, fulfilled and completely satisfied, Deme lay across the table, her legs falling over the edge, her body limp. After several cleansing breaths to refill her starving lungs, she sighed. "I can't move another muscle."

"Yes, you can." Cal pulled his jeans up around his hips without buttoning or snapping. Then he scooped his hands beneath her legs and back and lifted her. "You can hold on so I don't trip carrying you to our bed."

Surprisingly, her arms did work as she draped them

around Cal's shoulders. "Hey, why is it I'm naked and you're not?"

"My error. I haven't mastered pulling my jeans off while still wearing boots. When you come up with the magic that will do it for me, let me know."

"I'll work on that." Deme liked the feel of his cotton shirt rubbing against the skin of her hip and the way his fingers curled around her thigh and beneath her breast. That he could make a joke about spells was icing on the cake.

In his bedroom he laid her across the comforter and straightened, staring down at her. "You're so beautiful, I'm beginning to think you've cast a spell on me."

She leaned up on her elbow, letting her legs fall open. "So, Mortal, when did you decide you believed in witchcraft?"

"Since I met you." He started to work on the buttons of his shirt.

Cal sat beside Deme at the diner the next morning. With her thigh pressed against his, heat singed a path to Cal's groin, making him wish they were back in his apartment twisting in the sheets. Or better yet, making it on the table.

Cal was eying the table in front of him with more than casual interest when Lieutenant Warner and Dustin Zoeller, the Chicago tunnel expert, slid onto the bench across from him.

Heat rose up in his cheeks as he worked to squash images of a naked Deme lying on the smooth tabletop in front of him.

"Good morning." He cleared his throat and extended a hand across the table to Dustin. "Glad you could make it."

The lieutenant nodded toward Deme. "You must be one of Brigid's sisters."

"Deme Chattox." Deme held out her hand to the lieutenant and to Dustin. "I'll be going on this little spelunking expedition with you this morning."

Cal cringed. Nothing like Deme taking the lead on the happenings of the day.

Dustin's brows rose along with the lieutenant's. "What's this?"

Cal jumped in. "I didn't have time to tell you that there's been an addition to our little group." He hadn't had time because he'd been buried inside their little addition, making love to her into the wee hours of the morning. A bit of information he had no intention of sharing with his boss.

Dustin shook his head. "No can do. I can't authorize a civilian to enter the tunnels. It leaves the city open for lawsuits."

Deme smiled. "Sorry. I didn't mean to put you on the defensive, but my sister is the victim here. I know things you can't possibly understand. You need me."

"We could get Brigid to go. She's at least on the payroll," Lieutenant Warner offered.

"No. I'm the oldest. My sisters are my responsibility." Deme's eyes narrowed. "I take it you haven't told Brigid about the tunnels yet, am I right?"

"No." The lieutenant frowned. "But—"

"Good. Let's keep it that way until we know what we're dealing with."

Cal chuckled. "You see what *I'm* dealing with?"

"Remind me to recruit her, will you? And while you're at it, I want to meet the rest of the Chattox women." Marty grinned. "I have a feeling they are Chicago's best-kept secret."

The tension in Cal's shoulders lessened. He thought he'd have to fight his boss to get Deme on this mission. She'd been right that she understood more about the world of magic than any of the men did. She could feel things they didn't, maybe even sense trouble before it happened. They needed her or someone like her when they descended into the bowels of the city.

"Sir, I don't think it's a good idea," Dustin protested again. "She's not an expert in the tunnels. How can she know more?"

"She has other special talents."

"What? Like a psychic?" Dustin snorted and blushed. "No offense."

"None taken. But I'm going." Deme smiled sweetly. Cal recognized the spark in her emerald eyes as one of challenge. She wasn't going to be easily dissuaded. He almost felt sorry for Dustin. The man obviously didn't know who he was up against in Deme Chattox.

The tunnel expert appealed to the lieutenant with raised brows.

Lieutenant Warner's jaw firmed and he glared at the younger man. "She goes. If anyone takes the heat, it'll be my ass."

The expert's lips pressed into a thin line. He wasn't happy, but the lieutenant was in charge. The man finally shrugged. "It's your life, lady."

Deme laid a hand on the expert's arm. "It's my sister's life we're talking about."

A surge of pure jealousy so strong it surprised him ran through Cal's veins like a shot of adrenaline. Not until Deme removed her hand from Dustin's arm did Cal's pulse slow back to normal. He couldn't even attribute his jealousy to a mind-manipulating Chimera this time. They weren't anywhere near the campus.

Cal drew in a deep breath and concentrated on what Dustin had to say.

"I have breathing equipment, ropes and a device that can test air quality as we proceed down into the tunnels. I prefer to have a full team of rescue personnel on hand to pull us out if things go south." The man held his hand up when Cal started to protest. "I understand we're on a college campus. We need to protect the entrance location to keep others from finding it and misusing it."

"I've got it covered." Lieutenant Warner grinned. "I've arranged for the fire department to conduct a recruiting demonstration on campus today. The chief will be on call in case of emergency. He's loaning two of his finest to our efforts in the basement of the student commons. They'll be there under the pretext of performing an annual fire inspection."

Cal nodded then asked, "What about weapons?"

Dustin shook his head. "We don't know if any of the gases down below are flammable. If you discharge a weapon in a flammable environment, you could blow half of Chicago to hell in a heartbeat."

"Whoa." Cal held up a hand. "No weapons? Do you have any idea what we're up against?"

Dustin looked from Cal to Lieutenant Warner and back. "I thought we were looking for a kidnapping victim. I assumed we'd be looking for her and her kidnapper. Is there more than one?"

Cal glanced across at Lieutenant Warner.

The lieutenant shook his head, just enough for Cal to get the message not to share any more than necessary. Why would the lieutenant keep information about a monster running loose beneath the city to himself?

Cal almost laughed out loud. As if he'd have believed it a few days ago? Not likely. He'd originally thought it was a big hoax and that anyone who'd believe such bull needed his head examined. Yeah, maybe the lieutenant was right.

"Look, if you'll get us down there and show us how to use the equipment, we'll take care of finding our girl."

Deme tapped her foot as the group converged in the student commons basement thirty minutes later. The sooner they got moving, the better. After four days being held captive by the Chimera, Aurai would be getting weak. Given the beast's methods of attack, Deme guessed it didn't have access to its own physical form, moving through the actions of others, or as in Aurai's case, by manipulating their talents to capture them.

Dustin Zoeller gave them a brief training session on the dangers of being in the tunnels, the gases that could be poisonous and how to use the air-testing device.

He then showed them how to wear the oxygen tanks and masks and checked all the equipment for proper functionality.

"I feel like I'm going scuba diving." Deme fitted the breathing mask over her face and adjusted the elastic straps.

"The subterranean environment can be just as deadly." The tunnel expert pulled the straps holding the mask to Deme's face tighter.

The heavy metal door beneath the stairwell stood open, the dark cavity already sending chills across her skin. How she wished her sisters were there for moral support.

She had chosen not to inform them, sure they'd insist on accompanying her into the tunnels. Deme couldn't let them. Not until she knew more.

Cal hooked his D-ring to the rope the firemen would use to haul them out if need be and climbed onto the top rung of the metal ladder. He paused, giving Deme a thumbs-up. "Ready?"

"As ready as I'll ever be." Her heart hammering in her chest, she edged toward the tunnel, every instinct in her screaming for her to keep out.

"Deme!" The clatter of footsteps on the metal staircase rang out as several people clambered down from the main level of the student commons. "Deme, wait!"

Deme turned to face an angry phalanx of sisters as Selene, Brigid and Gina reached the basement floor, breathing hard, eyes blazing.

Brigid led the charge. "What the hell are you doing?"

Deme pushed the mask to the top of her head. "I'm going after Aurai."

"Without us?" Gina stepped up beside Brigid.

"I didn't want to worry you."

"Bull." Selene, the usually calm, collected sister, glared at her. "You didn't want us here."

They'd caught her and nailed her. She yanked the mask off her head. "That's right. I didn't want you here."

"I thought we were in this together." Gina tipped her head to the side, her blue-gray eyes reflecting her disappointment.

"Only when it's convenient for her." Brigid planted her hands on her black-leather-clad hips. "You aren't our mother."

Deme flinched. "I never said I was."

"Yeah, but whether we wanted you to or not, you've been calling the shots since Mother died."

"I had to." Who else would have kept them together?

"No, you didn't. And for the record, this past year

while you were in St. Croix, we were on our own." Gina crossed her arms over her chest, a frown drawing her brows together. "We managed fine."

The implied "without you" hung in the air.

"We proved to ourselves that we could live without Big Sis guiding our every movement." Selene stood with her hands on her hips just like Brigid. "We don't need you."

The blow hit her square in the gut, and she stepped back as if it had been a physical punch. Her eyes stung, but Deme refused to let the tears fall.

Selene reached out for Deme's hand. "We don't need you as our *mother.*"

Gina joined Selene, placing her hand over their joined hands. "No, we don't." She glanced back at Brigid.

The black-haired sister hesitated and then closed the distance, adding her hand to the rest. "We don't need you as our mother. We need you as our sister."

Deme stood, surrounded by her sisters, the love she felt for them swelling in her chest. "Sisters who need to find a missing member of the family."

"Right." Brigid was the first to break the circle. "So what's happening here?"

Deme gave them an abbreviated version of the plan. "I was going to tell you about it once we got an idea of what's down there."

"Well, the cat's out of the bag." Brigid's chin lifted in challenge. "We're coming with you."

Deme shook her head. "There's not enough breathing equipment."

"Then I should go since I have a better psychic connection," Selene insisted.

Brigid planted herself in front of Deme, hands on

hips. "No, I should go because I'm working with the city on this case."

Gina pushed Brigid aside. "I should go because... well...just because."

Lieutenant Warner pulled Deme out of the middle of the women. "Deme's going. She's been briefed on the equipment and we're running out of time. The fire department won't be on campus all day. You three can help the rest of us monitor their progress."

Brigid glared at the lieutenant. "I'll pick a bone with you later."

"No, you won't." Lieutenant Warner nodded to Cal. "Go."

Deme's pulse quickened as his head disappeared below the top of the ladder. She pulled the mask in place, tightened the elastic straps and checked the oxygen meter.

The lieutenant clapped her hard hat fitted with a headlight on top of her head. "Be careful down there."

She pulled on thick work gloves, gave the lieutenant a thumbs-up and got in line behind Dustin Zoeller as he waited for the firemen to snap the rope through his D-ring. Then he stepped over the edge and descended the rungs of the metal ladder into the tunnel below.

When it was her turn, Deme stood steady while the fireman tugged on her web seat and snapped the rope through the D-ring. It was scary to think that thin rope was their lifeline to escape if the shit hit the fan down below.

With a deep breath, Deme grabbed the ladder rungs and lowered herself into the darkness. The only light chasing back the shadows was the thin beam from her helmet. She leaned over, pointing her head at the ladder below her, catching a glimpse of the top of Dustin's head and the tiny glow from his headlight. She couldn't see past him to Cal, making her want to hurry her progress to the bottom.

With the mask fitted tightly to her face, Deme couldn't smell the air, but she could feel its coolness through the long-sleeved coverall the tunnel expert had provided. The dampness of the air made her exposed skin sticky.

The descent took longer than she expected. Just how deep were the tunnels? After five minutes, claustrophobia became a real concern. The not knowing how much farther had her breathing harder. Several times she had to stop and remind herself to breathe slowly so as not to use up all her oxygen before she had a chance to look around.

When she thought the ladder would never end, she emerged from the vertical tunnel into a horizontal tunnel large enough for a man to stand up straight without hitting his head on the pipes and conduit hanging above.

Before she could make the last four rungs, Cal grabbed her from behind and set her on her feet. She turned in his arms and clung to him for a few seconds, more relieved than she cared to admit in front of the tunnel expert.

Dustin stood in the middle of a train track, holding the bright yellow toxic-gas monitor. After five minutes, he slid his mask off. "Hydrogen sulfide's a little high, as is the carbon monoxide, but not enough to be alarmed. At this point, the air's breathable. You might want to conserve your oxygen."

Cal and Deme switched their oxygen off and removed the masks.

The dank, metallic scent of wet rocks filled her nostrils.

Cal unclipped the chem light from his web harness and clicked it on, flooding the tunnel with light.

Dustin unfolded the tunnel map he'd brought along and shined his headlight down at the lines. "We're headed toward the foundation of Lion Hall—the one that burned down—right?"

Now that she was down here, Deme just wanted to get this whole adventure over with. The same oppressive feeling she had in her dorm room of being watched by a malevolent being hung in the air, making it difficult to breathe. She was tempted to put her mask back on, but knew it wasn't the lack of oxygen that was doing it to her.

If her sister was down here, she had to find her or some evidence that this was where the creature had her trapped. She couldn't draw on her ability to "feel" for her sister on the off chance the Chimera would tap into her powers and trap her, as well.

Frustration made her impatient. "Which way?"

The tunnel expert nodded to his left. "That way. Should be a junction in fifty feet that will take us there." He hesitated. "Are you sure we don't need additional backup?"

"If you want to go back up, do. Just leave the air monitor with us."

"No, no. I'll go." Dustin tucked the map in his pocket and unbuckled his chem light from his web belt, holding it out in front of him like a weapon. "Lead on."

Cal took point, moving ahead carefully, stepping over old pipes, discarded equipment and crumbled bricks.

Picking her way across the uneven ground was slow but gave Deme a chance to study her surroundings, to feel without pushing too much into the consciousness of the Chimera. Hypersensitive to being manipulated now, Deme kept firm control of her mind and senses, determined to keep the beast at bay.

She kept a close eye on the tunnel expert, as well. Cal knew what was ahead. Dustin hadn't a clue. She and Cal had discussed it with the lieutenant and decided to stop short of their destination to keep the other man safe.

The closer they moved toward the center of campus, the heavier her steps, as though something pushed her down, making it harder and harder to move.

"You all right?" Dustin asked from behind.

"Yeah," Deme said, feeling anything but right.

"Should be an open area one hundred yards ahead right below the old foundation of Lion Hall."

Deme pushed forward, determined to get close enough to see what they were up against, without placing Cal or Dustin in the line of fire. Problem was, she didn't have any idea how close was too close.

A waft of air lifted the loose tendrils of her hair that had escaped the rubber band securing a ponytail at the back of her head. Dust particles stirred and floated in front of the chem lights. The closer they came to the foundation of Lion Hall, the stronger the wind current until the three were bent double, straining to take another step. They stayed close to enable them to see each other as the dust particles thickened.

"This isn't right!" Dustin yelled. "There shouldn't be this much air moving through the tunnel."

His words whipped away, but Deme heard them and agreed. She knew what was causing it, and it made her blood boil.

The Chimera was manipulating her sister's power.

At this point, they'd reached the end of the rope. Unless they unclipped, they couldn't go any farther.

Cal dropped back and grabbed Deme's shoulders. "This is as far as you two go."

"No way." She shook off his hands and tried to step around him, the wind slamming her backward into Dustin.

"This is getting too dangerous," Cal shouted above the gale ripping through the tunnel.

"It's my sister! She's in there!" Deme unclipped the D-ring from the rope, ducked around him and dashed forward, head tucked low, shoulder to the force pushing against her.

Chapter 16

Cal pointed to Dustin. "Stay here."

When he ripped the rope out of his D-ring and turned, he could barely see Deme disappearing into the swirling dust. He bent under the force of the wind pushing past him and hurried after her.

As he caught up, the blasting air pushed harder against him and the tunnel seemed to close in, his light nothing but a thin beam in the darkness.

Deme came to an abrupt stop at the end of the leg of tunnel. Roots climbed the arching walls, twisting and interlacing with each other to form a tight web, blocking their path.

Still pushing hard to catch up to Deme, Cal wasn't prepared for the sudden cessation of wind. He plowed into her, slamming her body into the web of roots blocking the passageway into the cavernous chamber below the expired Lion Hall.

He grabbed Deme and tugged at her, attempting to pull her away from the vines that had quickly wrapped around her wrists and ankles. Even as he yanked and jerked at the snagging vegetation, the roots inserted themselves between him and Deme, pushing him away as they pulled Deme forward.

Cal reached for the knife attached to his belt and hacked at the roots winding around Deme's wrists and ankles. As he sliced each one away, more appeared and replaced the damaged ones.

When a vine wrapped around his wrist, Cal caught the knife in his free hand and sliced it clean away from him. Before the plants could draw Deme through the web, Cal cut and hacked, finally yanking Deme free. Like a fireman running from a burning building, he hitched her up over his shoulder and hauled her several yards away, where he set her on her feet. When she lunged toward the web again, Cal wrapped his arms around her waist. "Deme, I won't let the Chimera have you."

Deme strained against Cal's arms, leaning toward the seething, slithering mass of living plant life. The roots and vines waved in the air, crawled ten feet into the tunnel and stopped, as though an invisible barrier barred their ability to spread.

"Please," she cried. "Let me go."

"It seems the Chimera is unable to manipulate your powers outside the perimeter ring of buildings surrounding the rose garden."

Deme swayed toward the cavern, her eyes glazed, her face pale. "Can you feel it?"

"Feel what?"

"The energy sucking me in. It's draining me, pulling me toward it."

"I've got you, babe, and I'm not letting go." He hugged her against his body, his wrists locked around her waist.

"You have to let me go. Aurai is in there. I know it. The Chimera used her power of wind to push us away."

"If it wants you to come now, why did it try to push you away? And why the web of roots blocking our approach to the Lion Hall foundation?"

"It wants me, not you." Deme's eyes closed. "Aurai is calling me. She's there." Her eyes opened and she clawed at Cal's arms. "Let me go. She's in there. Aurai is in there, and she's alive."

Cal clenched his teeth and held on tightly even as Deme's fingernails dug into his skin. "I can't let you go, Deme. You'll end up trapped just like Aurai."

"I have to get to her."

"We will. But we need to work it out with your sisters. The Chimera has too strong a pull on you. It defeated your younger sister. You're strong, but it has manipulated you, as well."

Deme ceased her struggles and looked up into Cal's eyes, tears shimmering in the meager light from the top of his helmet. "I can't abandon her."

"You're not. *We* are going to regroup and come back with a plan to free her. Right now I have to get you out of here."

"No!" she shouted, renewing her efforts to claw her way free of his arms. "I can't leave my sister."

"Deme!" Female voices sounded behind him. Cal and Deme ceased their struggles and turned as one to face the three sisters they'd left topside in the basement.

"I thought we told you to stay put." Deme planted her fists on her hips.

"We couldn't." Gina snorted. "We passed the tunnel expert a few minutes ago. He was shaking and scared."

Deme glared at her sisters. "What if the air down here wasn't breathable?"

"Obviously it is." Brigid started forward, her gaze moving past Deme to the wall of interlaced roots and vines blocking their entry into the area beneath where Lion Hall had once stood. "The Chimera wants us, doesn't it? I can feel its lure."

"Don't get too close," Deme warned. "It tried to drag me through but pushed Cal away." Deme tugged at Cal's hand holding her back from charging into the Chimera's lair.

He refused to release her hand in case the Chimera managed to make another grab for her.

Brigid pushed past Deme and Cal and stood as close as she could get to the blocked entrance without being snagged by the waiting vines. "Why you and not him?"

Gina joined them. "We have the power."

Selene stood behind Cal, her eyes wide, her face pale. "It wants our power."

"The Chimera already has Aurai's power. We can't risk it taking the rest of us."

"It would be catastrophic." Selene's voice shook.

Deme turned toward her brown-haired sister. "Do you know what would happen?"

Selene stared straight ahead, looking at neither her sisters nor Cal, her focus on something none of them could see. "If the Chimera has all our powers, it will be undefeatable."

"Then we won't let it have the rest." Brigid flicked her wrist, cupping her hand. "And we're taking Aurai back." A ball of flame erupted in her palm.

The flame startled Cal and he stepped backward, loosening his grip on Deme.

"No, Brigid. Don't use your powers." Deme made a dive for the entrance to the underground chamber beneath the rose garden.

As if sensing her approach, the vines and roots parted, lashing out to snag her wrists. "Damn!" Deme fought with all her might to free her arms and legs, twisting and kicking to push back the onslaught of vegetation dragging her into the Chimera's lair.

Cal reached for his knife as he ran for Deme.

Before he got more than three feet, Brigid put out a hand, stopping him. "Let me."

"No!" Deme yelled. "Remember what happened to Gina."

His hand on the hilt of his sheathed knife, all Cal could do was watch.

With the ball of fire swirling in her palm, Brigid reared back like an all-star pitcher and launched the fireball into the web in front of Deme.

The roots shrank back, absorbing the fireball, and then with a whoosh of air, they shot it back at the people standing in the tunnel.

Gina ducked, and Selene cried out and fell against the side wall.

Cal dove for the uneven floor, his knee crashing against a fallen brick, sending a sharp pain lancing up his leg.

The fireball ricocheted off the ceiling and bounced back and forth from side to side on the walls, growing in size and intensity, filling the gap behind them, creating an impenetrable wall of fire. Heat built in the confines of the tunnel.

Cal glanced up at the piping carrying natural gas

throughout the city. If the pipes grew too hot, they'd explode, possibly leaving a gaping hole in the Chicago cityscape. "We have to get out of here before the gas lines blow."

Deme screamed as vines slithered around her neck and sucked her toward the interior of the chamber. Her cry ended as the air was cut off to her windpipes, the creeper cinching tighter around her throat.

Cal pushed to his feet, yanking his knife from the scabbard. He attacked the vines, slicing them in two and pulling them away from Deme's throat.

Brigid's hand curled again.

"Don't!" Selene and Gina yelled.

Another vine snaked out and snagged Brigid's wrist before she could wind up another fireball.

The vines and roots dragged her toward the chamber. She fought them off, but for every one she freed herself from, two more appeared and wrapped around her limbs.

His hand wielding the knife as fast as he could, Cal cut away at the deadly plant life threatening Deme and Brigid.

Gina and Selene crowded against his back, the heat intensifying, edging closer.

"We'll be burned alive if we stay here." Selene buried her face in her arms, the glow of the fire making her skin red.

Gina raised her hands, closed her eyes and whispered something Cal couldn't hear.

Too busy hacking away at the vegetation intertwining around the other two women, Cal couldn't tell what was happening with the sisters at his side until a sudden swoosh sounded beside him.

His arms tiring, Cal sliced into the last vine holding Deme hostage and he shoved her behind him. He turned to Brigid and cut a root holding her wrist. When he had her free, he pushed her back, as well. The vines turned on him and lashed out.

Cal backed away, his feet splashing through ankle-deep water.

"Gina, what did you do?" Deme shouted.

"I don't know. I only wanted to put out the fire so we wouldn't burn to death."

"Hang on to something," Selene warned.

Cal turned in time to see a wall of water bearing down on them. "Grab the pipes or cables. Don't let it suck you into the chamber."

All four women wrapped their arms and legs around the pipes on the sides of the walls or ceilings.

Cal had barely enough time to latch on to the pipe above him before the wave slammed into him, nearly yanking his hand free. The tunnel around them filled with water, covering the tops of their heads.

Miraculously, the light on his helmet continued to glow an eerie yellow in the swirling fluid. Cal kicked his feet, pushing himself upward to the roof of the tunnel, where he gulped in air. Then he submerged and checked for the women. Gina was closest. Selene's dark hair swirled like black ink in the murky water. Deme kicked and fought to reach the pocket of air above her head and Brigid swam toward him, working her way back through the tunnel.

Cal moved aside and gave Brigid a push to send her on her way. He grabbed Gina and shoved her after Brigid. Selene floated toward him, her face pale, her eyes wide. He squeezed her hand as he pushed her after her sisters. Deme clung to the pipe above, her head tipped back, her mouth and nose pressed against the roof. A ghostly white root slipped through the water toward her.

Cal yelled, the sound muffled by the liquid. He bunched his legs and thrust himself toward her, cleaving through the water, his lungs burning with the need to breathe. He reached Deme at the same time as the root did.

He grabbed Deme and shoved her after her sisters, the movement sending him backward toward the chamber entrance, right into the clutches of the root.

With the ease of a snake, it slipped around his ankle.

Desperate to breathe, Cal kicked and fought to reach the roof and the pocket of air. But the root yanked him down, refusing to let him surface even for a moment.

He'd lost his knife in the blast of water. Cal had nothing to defend himself from the Chimera's hold on him. If he didn't get air soon, he'd die.

Several yards down the tunnel, Deme emerged from the water and slid across the floor into her sisters' legs. "What the hell just happened?"

Brigid, Gina and Selene reached for her and hauled her to her feet. "The Chimera used Gina's water against us."

"Cal?" Deme spun to face a wall of water, held in place by the force of a being far beyond her limited powers and comprehension.

Selene shook her head. "He hasn't come out yet."

"Damn!" Deme's heart raced, her breathing coming in gasps. She couldn't lose Cal. Not now. She cared too much about him. Hell, she loved him.

Deme shook off her sisters' hands.

"Don't, Deme," Brigid yelled. "He can get out on his own."

"And I should stand here and wait?" Deme sucked in a deep breath and dove back into the water. The light from her helmet provided a narrow beam in the cloudy water.

She swam as fast as she could, using the sides of the walls and the floor to kick off, propelling her forward.

Where was he? Her chest hurt, her lungs desperate for air. Light reflected off something shiny on the tunnel floor. Deme recognized Cal's knife, scooping it up as she swam forward. If the vines had him in their clutches, he didn't have a way to fight them off.

When she finally caught a glimpse of Cal, he was thrashing around in the water, kicking against a thick root that had him by the ankle.

Careful to stay far enough away to keep from being caught up in the same trap, Deme reached for Cal, pressing the knife into his flailing hand.

As quickly as she handed it to him, he sliced through the root and kicked free, bumping into her as he pushed farther away from the web of vines and roots.

Not until he'd gotten several yards away from the wicked vegetation did he swim to the top of the tunnel. Deme joined him, gasping in huge gulps of air. "I thought you were right behind me," she said between breaths.

"I would have been." He grabbed her hand and squeezed, letting go almost immediately. "Ready? Let's get back."

Deme dragged in another deep breath and pushed off the wall, headed back to where her sisters waited.

The farther they moved from Lion Hall, the more shallow the water became until they emerged on their feet, slogging through the tunnel toward Selene, Brigid and Gina. They stood in the dark, their irises contracting as the lights from Cal's and Deme's helmets illuminated their surroundings.

The sisters fell on Deme, hugging her close. "We thought you weren't going to make it out." Gina hugged her so tightly, Deme couldn't breathe.

"But I did." Deme looked back toward the chamber. The water had drained away. The passage appeared as it had when she and Cal had first walked down it what seemed like a lifetime ago.

"We have to go back." Deme took a step back that way. "I can still feel Aurai in there."

"Me, too," Selene whispered.

Cal blocked the tunnel, his feet braced wide, his arms crossed over his chest. "You're not going back. Not now."

"But we have to," Deme insisted. Aurai's voice called to her, desperate, afraid.

"No." Cal twisted her around and slung her over his shoulder. Ducking as low as he could, he ran back down the tunnel.

The wind picked up, this time clutching at him like a giant hand trying to suck them back toward the garden and the subterranean levels below the foundation of Lion Hall.

Deme bounced along, the air whooshing out of her lungs with each jarring step Cal took. Her sisters ran behind them, keeping pace.

When Cal reached Dustin Zoeller, he shouted, "Get out of here!"

Dustin, eyes wide, his face pale, spun on his heels and ran back in the direction of the student commons basement where they'd entered this maze.

When they reached the vertical tunnel, Dustin didn't

slow, but grabbed the steel bars of the ladder and pulled himself up, his monitor bumping against the rails.

Cal dropped Deme to her feet and turned her toward the ladder rungs. "Go, Deme. Get out of here. Now."

She hesitated.

Cal lifted her hand and curled it around the ladder sides. "Please." He kissed her neck, his hands cupping her butt, then he shoved her up the ladder.

Pushing her every step of the way, Cal arrived at the top, breathing hard and exhausted.

Deme's sisters emerged behind them, all of them talking at once.

Beyond her endurance and fresh out of steam, Deme swayed, her eyes rolling backward in her head. Before she could respond to any of her sister's questions or concerns, she fell, darkness consuming her.

Cal was there, scooping her up into his arms.

"Is she going to be all right?" Lieutenant Warner asked.

"I don't know." Cal stared down at Deme, lying limp in his arms.

"I tried to keep the other women out, but they wouldn't be deterred." Marty glared at the sisters. "What happened down there?"

Cal snorted, hitching Deme higher in his arms. "The Chattox women are a force unto themselves."

"Holy crap!" Dustin Zoeller joined them, ripping his mask off the top of his head and throwing it to the ground. "I've never seen that kind of wind in the tunnels before." He shook his head. "It shouldn't be that strong. I don't get it." Then for the first time he noticed the others were soaking wet. "How did you get all wet?"

"Slipped in a puddle." Cal locked gazes with the lieutenant, unwilling to enlighten the tunnel expert. The fewer people who knew what was going on beneath the city streets, the better off the residents of Chicago. They couldn't afford a mass panic and the resulting exodus that could cause more deaths than the Chimera could achieve on the campus of Colyer-Fenton College. "We need to get Deme and her sisters away from here."

"I know where we can take her." Brigid nodded toward the steps leading out of the basement. "Let's get her to my apartment. It's only a couple miles from campus. Far enough away that nothing here can affect us." She closed her eyes and drew in a deep breath before opening them again. "I feel it even as we stand here."

Cal would rather have taken her to his apartment, but he didn't want to fight the three sisters, whose worried expressions indicated they wouldn't let him waltz away with Deme.

"We can go in my SUV." Gina hurried up the stairs, followed by Cal and Deme. The other two sisters brought up the rear.

When they arrived in the parking lot next to Gina's midsize four-door SUV, Deme's eyes blinked open. "What… Where am I?"

Cal gave her a wry grin. "We're getting you the hell off campus."

"Put me down." She struggled ineffectually against Cal's arms around her.

He shook his head. "No way."

"Why are you carrying me, anyway?" She glared at him and then noticed her sisters standing in a circle around her. "Why are you all staring at me?"

"You passed out, sis." Brigid grabbed the keys from Gina's hand and clicked the button to unlock the door. "We're getting you away from campus so we can discuss what happened and what we plan to do next."

"I felt her." Deme fought against Cal's hold, but he held tighter. "Aurai's down there. We can't leave her there."

"And we can't afford for the Chimera to take another one of us." Selene laid a hand against the side of Deme's face. "Remember, you don't always have to take care of us. We're in this together. Let's make this a group decision and effort."

"We can stand around arguing, or we can get moving." Brigid jerked open the car door. "Either way, you're coming with us. We can talk when we get to my place."

Cal squeezed Deme and set her inside the car in the front passenger seat. "I'll be right behind you."

She looked up at him and nodded, her forehead wrinkled in a stubborn frown. "I'm counting on it."

Selene climbed in the backseat and Gina in the driver's seat. Brigid mounted her Harley.

As the SUV drove away, followed by the motorcycle, Lieutenant Warner joined Cal. "I expect a full report." He held up a hand to stem the flow of words Cal had poised on the tip of his tongue. "I know...after you've had a chance to calm Deme down."

"Thank you, sir."

"I think it's time to evacuate campus. To hell with what the college president might say."

"Good idea." Cal looked back at Colyer-Fenton. With the sun hidden behind a bank of gray clouds, the campus looked hunkered down, ready to weather a tempest. As if sensing an impending storm, students hurried across the manicured lawns, clutching their books to their chests to keep papers from flying out in the rising wind.

Even as Cal observed, the wind increased, neither

from the west nor the east, but seeming to come from all around, swirling toward the center of campus and the rose garden where Lion Hall once stood.

Cal nodded again. "Yeah, get the students out."

"I'm on it." Lieutenant Warner wrapped his coat around him and charged back toward the administration building and the office of Dr. Diane Masterson.

Cal slung his leg over his motorcycle seat and reached down to insert his key in the ignition.

A slender hand reached out and grabbed his.

His heart slammed against his chest and his gaze shot up to capture the brown-eyed stare of a student he should know, but couldn't quite place.

"You're Deme Jones's boyfriend, aren't you?"

On the verge of correcting Deme's last name, Cal bit hard on his tongue and nodded, maintaining his cover story.

The girl threaded her fingers together. "Is she going to be all right?"

"Yeah."

"Tell her Rachel said hello and that I hope she feels better soon." Rachel stared down at her clasped hands. "And not to worry. I'll make it right."

Before Cal could ask her what she meant by that, she turned and ran back toward the Gamma Omega dormitory.

Cal glanced to where Gina's car had already disappeared around the street corner headed for the campus exit. He kick-started his motorcycle and drove after Gina's car. As he neared the edge of the parking lot, his gaze shifted back behind him to the girl who'd identified herself as Rachel. If he had it right, she was the young woman whose boyfriend almost raped her near the garden over Lion Hall.

Torn between following the student and following Deme, Cal turned his bike around and parked it. If the girl had any intention of going up against the Chimera, he had to stop her.

Deme had her sisters to look out for her. This college coed had no one and, from what Deme had told him in the early hours of the morning, even her sorority sisters had turned against her when she'd quit taking the potion they'd concocted to make them beautiful.

His mind with Deme and her sisters, Cal dismounted from his Harley and hurried after Rachel.

Cal had stepped into the Gamma Omega dorm and stopped the first girl who passed him. The girl had light blond hair pulled back with a headband, every hair in place. She wore a short jean skirt and a cotton-candy pink tube top that exposed more of her midriff than it covered.

Cal cringed. Another Zoe clone. "Where can I find Rachel Taylor?"

"Men aren't allowed in a girl's dorm without an escort." The blonde's perfect brows arched. "Besides, you're too old for her." She flounced away without having answered his question.

When he turned to find another girl to ask, Zoe Adams stood before him, her head tipped slightly to the side. "That seems to be the sixty-five-thousand-dollar question. When you find Miss Rachel, tell her I'm looking for her." Zoe's eyes narrowed into thin slits. "She has something that belongs to me."

"Me, too." Another girl joined Zoe, then another, and another until the hallway filled with angry Zoe clones.

Cal knew when he should cut his losses. If he really thought Rachel was in the dorm, he might push past the phalanx of beautiful women to find the ugly duckling.

But since they were looking for her, too, he decided to look elsewhere.

"Thank you, ladies." Cal tipped an imaginary hat and backed out of the building, pushing through a throng of girls who'd crowded in behind him.

Dr. Masterson hurried toward the dorm, her serviceable low heels clicking on the concrete sidewalk. "Mr. Black, perhaps you could help me clear the boys' dormitory. Lieutenant Warner insisted the students were in danger and should be evacuated at once."

"Yes, ma'am, I'll get right on it."

She paused, her brows pulling together. "You're working with him, aren't you?"

Cal was past needing a cover for his work. "Yes, ma'am."

"Well, I'm certain you'll see to the boys' safety then, won't you?"

Without waiting for his response, she hurried into the Gamma Omega dorm, shouting to the girls as she went.

Cal jogged away from the circle of buildings at the center of campus to the boys' dormitory. Inside, some of the guys had already received word of the evacuation via text message from other students across campus.

Young men streamed out of the dormitory toward the parking lot, carrying suitcases and laundry bags. He tasked one guy per floor to knock on the doors and make sure the dorm was empty before leaving. Once he'd set the evacuation of the boys' dorm in motion, he resumed his search for Rachel, the clock ticking away the minutes since the time he'd told Deme he'd be right behind her.

He returned to the Gamma Omega dormitory one more time to see if Rachel had returned to gather her belongings.

When he stepped through the doors, the dorm was a flurry of activity. All the doors were open and girls shouted across the hallway as they shoved clothing into suitcases.

With no sign of Zoe or a blockade of girls to obstruct his passage, Cal raced up the stairs to the second floor where Deme's room had been. Hadn't she said Rachel had been her sister's roommate and hadn't their room been on the same floor as Deme's?

A scream ripped through the hallway.

Cal raced toward the sound.

A door blasted open and a girl with dirty-blond hair and a pockmarked face stumbled through, her hands covering her cheeks, tears streaming from her eyes. "Where is it? I need more."

Cal grabbed her arms and made her focus on him. "Where is what? What do you need?"

"The vial, the blue vial with the potion. I need it, can't you see?" She clawed at her face, her jagged fingernails leaving deep scrapes across her already scarred skin, blood oozing from the wounds. "I can't go back. I won't go back to being pathetic."

"You're not pathetic. You're human and beautiful in your own right."

"Shut up." She shook his hands free and ran toward the stairs. "Zoe, help me. Make me beautiful again."

Cal stood in the middle of the hallway for a moment longer, then turned to face a door with the words *Rachel Must Die* written across it in black Magic Marker.

What the hell?

He grabbed the knob and tried to open the door. It was locked from the inside. With heavy, metal door frames, no amount of banging against it would open it.

Then he remembered the master key on his assigned key ring. He quickly opened the door and pushed it open.

The room was a wreck. Black fabric lay in shreds across the room, drawers had been emptied onto the floor and everything in the closet was scattered across the room.

Cal's stomach took a steep dive.

The window stood wide open, wind flapping the thin curtains hanging on each side.

He ran across the floor and stuck his head through, expecting the worst. When he looked directly below the window, he let out the breath he'd been holding in a whoosh. "Thank God."

He'd expected to see Rachel's broken body lying in the bushes. But the bushes remained as they had been before all the commotion began. And he still hadn't found her. Based on the cries of the other occupants of the dormitory, she might have found the vials of potion Deme had told him about that made the girls beautiful. If he didn't find Rachel before the sorority sisters did, the Chimera would be the least of her worries.

Cal left the room and raced to Deme's room, peering out her window into the garden below. No Rachel. The garden was empty, appearing calm, serene, no sign of the beast beneath the manicured grass.

If he didn't find the coed soon, he was sure Deme and her sisters would launch some half-cocked plan before he could get to them and inject a voice of reason. Cal left Deme's room and took the stairs to the lower floor, leaping the last four steps entirely. Rachel was nowhere to be found. Where would she have gone? He headed for the student commons. Maybe she'd gone for a bite to eat.

He frowned. Rachel didn't know about the trapdoor

in the basement, did she? His footsteps quickened until he was jogging across the campus.

An employee stood outside the glass doors of the student commons, twisting a key in the metal lock. "Sorry, got orders from the big boss, we're shutting down and evacuating campus."

"I'm maintenance staff. Are you sure everyone's out?" Cal looked over the worker's shoulder into the open bay lined with tables, the chairs scattered haphazardly as though they'd been vacated in a hurry.

"Positive."

"Did you check the basement?" Cal pulled the ring of building keys from his pocket.

"Why would I check the basement? Only staff goes down there." The employee nodded toward Cal's key ring. "You have keys, check it out yourself. I'm out of here." The young man turned toward the parking lot. "Just lock up when you leave. I don't want to get blamed if someone loots the place."

Cal didn't bother to respond, wasting precious moments finding the right key to unlock the door. Once inside, he dodged in and out of the tables and dashed through the kitchen to the rear of the building where the door led down to the basement. He ran down the stairs, arriving at the bottom, his heart racing. Where the hell was Rachel?

Chapter 17

Deme sat at the diminutive dining table in Brigid's apartment. Despite Brigid's tough-as-nails exterior, her apartment made up for it in feminine decorations, ranging from impressionistic landscapes to fluffy floral throw pillows on the white leather couch. Brigid was a contradiction, the one sister Deme could never quite connect with. The leather and motorcycle riding screamed nonconformity and a harsh demeanor.

Yet her apartment was her realm of peace and tranquility.

"You realize this is the first time I've been to your apartment?" Deme commented.

Brigid shrugged. "Kind of hard to visit when you're in St. Croix."

Deme's lips pressed together and she stared across at her second-oldest sister. "I know. I'm sorry. I deserted you. I deserted all of you."

"Why?" Brigid stepped forward, her fists balanced on her hips. "Were you ashamed of us?"

"No, never."

"Then were you ashamed of what we were? What we are?"

"In a way, yes. As much as Aurai wanted to live a normal life and attend college like any other nineteen-year-old, I wanted to live a normal life, too. But I knew I couldn't."

"So you ran away?" Brigid snorted. "Apparently being the oldest doesn't make you the wisest."

"I didn't say what I did was right. I'm just saying I had to do it at the time."

Selene stood behind Deme and laid a hand on her shoulder. "Because of Detective Black?"

Deme turned in her seat to face the sister who seemed to see right through her. Selene's image swam before her in a pool of tears welling in Deme's eyes. "I couldn't be with him, knowing he wouldn't understand who and what we are."

"And now?"

Deme huffed, a single tear slipping down her cheek. "He's handling it just fine."

"Did you ever think of giving yourself a chance? Giving him a chance?" Brigid rolled her eyes. "For the oldest and smartest, you're pretty dumb sometimes."

Deme smiled at Brigid, pushing her damp hair out of her face. "You got that right. I wasted an entire year thinking I was doing the right thing when I could have been…" She gulped back a sob.

"With him," Gina finished. "And we almost lost him today to the Chimera."

"Which brings up another issue. I don't want him involved in this anymore."

"Sorry, chica," Brigid quipped. "He's in up to his neck. You're not going to keep him out of it. Hell, wild elephants couldn't keep him away. In case you haven't noticed, he's in love with you."

Deme's face heated, an image of them lying naked in his apartment flaring in her memory. Yeah, they were highly compatible in bed, but could they build a relationship on lust alone? "I'll be glad when we get Aurai back and things get back to normal."

Gina snorted. "What is normal?"

Deme sucked in a breath and let it out. "You're right. I don't think we were destined to lead normal lives. Any of us who think we can are sadly mistaken."

Though he seemed to be handling the witch thing well, would it all catch up to Cal and overwhelm him when they finally got Aurai back, took care of the Chimera and life returned to a semblance of normalcy?

"Time's wasting." Selene slapped a heavy volume in the middle of the table, her normally sweet expression one of intensity. Her ice-blue eyes glowed with a light of challenge and determination. "We have to defeat the Chimera in order to get our little sister back."

"Right." Deme stood, pushing her chair back from the table, giving all four sisters space to gather around the *Book of Spells* their mother had given into their keeping. Deme had left it with Brigid when she'd gone to live in St. Croix. As much as she'd tried to divorce herself of her heritage, she couldn't.

Deme laid her hand on the leather binder. Brigid laid hers down on top of Deme's then Gina and Selene added theirs until all four sisters' hands rested on the book their mother had bequeathed to them. Together they closed their eyes and chanted.

"Feel the power

Free our hearts
Find our way
Be the one
With the strength of the earth
With the rising of the wind
With the calm of the water
With the intensity of fire
With the freedom of spirit
The goddess is within us
She is power
We are her
We are one
Blessed Be."

A surge of energy built beneath Deme's hand until it blasted through her, slinging their arms up and away from the book.

The tome flipped open, one page at a time, slowly at first, building in speed until the pages fluttered, creating a breeze.

Deme stood back with her sisters, watching and waiting. No one dared speak until the pages drifted to a stop, halfway through the book.

As one, each sister leaned over the book to read.

"'To free the Spellbound,'" Deme read aloud.

"'*Give shape to the victim*
with the bones of a rat
Give voice to the trapped
with the scream of bat
Give substance and life
with the seed of a thistle
Then cast out your troubles
Repeat on a whisper
The call to the caged
of all shapes and size

Repeat it five times
and watch your quarry rise
With the strength of the earth
With the rising of the wind
With the calm of the water
With the intensity of fire
With the freedom of spirit
Rise from the darkness
take shape in the light
come to our sisters
bring substance to might
When the ground thunders
it will rise through the rift
Capture it quickly
Before the grounds shift.'"

Deme glanced up at her sisters.

Brigid gave voice to the question in all their faces. "We save her without facing the Chimera?"

"No!" Selene shook her head. "We shouldn't play with magic."

"How else will we get to Aurai? We can't fight the Chimera. It's too strong." Selene pressed her fingers to her temples. "We can't." Her face scrunched in pain.

Deme lifted her sister's chin. "Why?"

"The other sisters…the ones that died…they say it's too dangerous."

"I say we go for it. Aurai's been down there long enough." Gina entered Brigid's kitchenette and opened her pantry door. "What have you got in here? Any rat bones or bat screams?"

"I'm with Gina. Aurai's been gone long enough." Brigid stared across at Deme. "I have everything you left in my care. Unlike you, I didn't plan on ignoring that part of my life."

Deme hugged her sister. "Once again, you prove to be the smarter sister. Thank you."

As she pulled away, Brigid's cheeks flushed.

Deme stood back and looked at each of her sisters. "Are we in this together?"

Gina and Brigid gave a resounding "Yes!"

Which left Selene.

"I want to believe this is the right thing to do." Tears trickled down her sister's face. "But the voices in my head are screaming for us not to. They want us to go away and never come back."

"Not an option." Deme shook her head. "We can't leave Aurai."

Selene wiped the moisture from her face and straightened. "No. We can't."

Deme went to work. "Mom didn't want us to use this stuff until we were good and ready. She didn't even want us to look through it. I have no idea if we have the ingredients we need to perform the spell."

"We have everything but the bat. And I know where we can get one of those on the way." Brigid's voice sounded confident. When the other sisters all looked at her, she shrugged. "I catalogued everything. I'm anal, so sue me."

Gina grinned and hugged Brigid. "Let's get our sister out of there."

"Damn right." Brigid switched the light on in the small pantry and reached to the top of the shelf to grab a bag labeled Rat Bones. She grabbed another labeled Thistle Seeds.

Brigid disappeared for five minutes to the top of the apartment building, returning with a bagged bat. "Don't ask how I knew it was there."

Ingredients in hand, including the live bat, the sisters returned to the Colyer-Fenton campus as the sun set.

For the first time since their mother's death, Deme felt closer to her sisters than ever. Between the five of them, they'd survive and overcome the power of the Chimera.

As Deme stepped out of Gina's SUV, the sun had set and a fat new moon slipped up the horizon, glowing a deep orange. "Ladies, do you realize the fall equinox is upon us?"

Gina reached into the SUV and pulled out the sack with the bags of ingredients and one live bat. "We will give thanks to the goddess for our bounty and for our family."

"Once we have Aurai back in our arms," Selene amended.

"Right." Brigid looked around. "Where to? The tunnels?"

Deme shook her head. "No. We return to where it all started."

"Can we go to the garden without being captured by the Chimera?"

Deme handed each sister a thumb-size leather pouch attached to a leather strap. "Put these around your necks."

Gina draped the charm over her head. "When did you have time to make a protection charm?"

"I didn't. I found these in a jar in Brigid's pantry. Mom must have made one for each of us. Seeing as our pentagrams aren't protecting us like they had in the past, I thought a little added boost might help." She slipped hers over her head and held one more in her hand. "This one was for Aurai."

"She might not be where she is now if she had been

wearing it." Selene's voice quietly echoed the thoughts Deme had had when she'd found the charms.

"We can't change the past, but we can shape our future if we choose." Deme set off for the garden, wondering where Cal had gone. He'd said he'd catch up to them and yet he hadn't even left campus. His motorcycle stood where they'd left him over an hour earlier.

With her sisters ready to take on the Chimera for possession of Aurai, she didn't dare take time out to look for him. She prayed to the goddess he was all right.

With the comforting softness of the leather pouch resting between her breasts, Deme lifted the latch of the garden gate between the Gamma Omega dorm and the student commons. The campus appeared deserted. No kids standing around chatting, exchanging notes or flirting with each other. No one hurried to a night class.

A chill shivered along the surface of her skin. She could have sworn there had been a chain and lock securing the garden the last time she was there.

Brigid nodded toward a bush where a chain, a heavy set of bolt cutters and a severed lock lay almost out of sight. "Someone beat us here."

Deme held her hands out to each side. The sisters joined hands in a circle. "We may only have one shot at this before the Chimera tries to take us down."

Gina nodded. "Hit hard and fast. Got it."

"And don't use your regular powers," Selene added.

Brigid nodded. "Yup. That's suicide."

Deme gave a short, sharp bark of laughter. "Like what we're about to do isn't?" She looked around at the familiar faces, her heart swelling inside her chest. "I love you guys."

"Ditto." Brigid's normal tough voice broke. She

squared her leather-clad shoulders and said, "Let's go get our sister."

Deme led the charge, carrying the ingredients, her gaze panning the grounds for live roots and vines ready to claim her and reel her into the Chimera's lair. Strangely, no obstacles blocked their path or tried to grab them.

"I smell a trap," Gina commented from Deme's left.

"I smell gasoline." Selene pointed ahead. "We have company."

In the center of the garden, Rachel Taylor shook a plastic gas jug over a pile of robes and little blue vials. "Die, you son of a bitch! Whatever you are. I hope you burn in hell!" Tears streamed down her face and gasoline splashed across her jeans and shirt.

Rachel flung the jug to the ground and pulled a matchbook from her pocket.

Deme's breath caught in her throat. If the Chimera didn't get her, her attempt to incinerate the trappings of the Gamma Omega's foray into witchcraft could include herself. "Rachel, don't!" Deme ran forward.

"I have to do this. I have to stop it from hurting anyone ever again." Rachel struck a match. "We need to be proud of who we are, not ashamed. This is for all the ugly girls dying to become beautiful." The match dropped to the pile of robes and flames leaped into the air, spreading everywhere the gasoline soaked.

A finger of fire raced across the garden lawn and up Rachel's leg.

The girl screamed and backed away from the bonfire growing in size and intensity.

Deme hit Rachel in a flying tackle, pushing her away from the trail of fire. In a desperate attempt to douse the flames, Deme rolled Rachel in the dirt, the flames on her pants and shirt refusing to extinguish until they had thoroughly burned through the fuel feeding them.

Gina joined her, yanking at the girl's shirt, pulling it up over her head.

Rachel screamed and fought to be free, her eyes rolling back in her head, fear and pain making her movements frantic, her young body strong in her effort to be free of the sisters.

Brigid removed her leather jacket and dropped it over Rachel's flaming pant legs, using it as a hot pad to remove the girl's jeans.

When they had her out of the burning clothes, Deme jumped to her feet and hauled Rachel up with the help of her sisters. "Get out of here! Get out while you can."

Brigid draped her jacket over Rachel's shoulders and the sisters pushed her toward the gate, shoving her through and pulling it closed behind her. Then leaning her back against the gate to keep Rachel from pushing through again, Deme shouted to her sisters, "Give me your hands." She grabbed Gina's hand and Brigid's. Gina and Brigid clasped hands, completing a circle of three, and Deme closed her eyes.

She said a silent prayer to the goddess of earth to protect the gate and keep it closed. When Deme opened her eyes, vines were pushing up through the earth, intertwining around the bars of the wrought-iron fence, wrapping around the gate to keep anyone from opening it to come in or out.

With Rachel safely outside the Chimera's range, Deme, Gina and Brigid turned back to the center of the garden.

Selene had gathered the fallen bags of ingredients and the cloth sack with the live bat, then walked toward the fire, her footsteps slow, measured, trancelike.

"What the hell is she doing?" Deme asked. "She needs to wait for the rest of us."

"Wait, Selene!" Brigid ran ahead and laid her hand on her sister's shoulder.

Selene didn't look at her, just shrugged loose and continued toward the fire.

"The Chimera must be manipulating her." Gina broke into a sprint, racing across the lawn, Deme in close pursuit.

Brigid tried to wrest the bags from her hands, but Selene wouldn't let go. Then she was running toward the fire, her pace quickening with each step.

Brigid reached her first and grabbed her around the waist to hold her back from throwing herself into the fire. She stopped her just in time. But she couldn't stop her from tossing the bags into the flames.

"No!" Brigid lunged for the bags, but she couldn't let go of Selene to save them from being burned. An agonizing, high-pitched scream filled the air as the live bat was consumed by flames.

Gina grabbed Selene and pulled her farther away from the fire. "Selene. Snap out of it. Don't succumb to the Chimera. He's using you."

Selene blinked and stared at her sister as if seeing her for the first time. "What do you mean? What's happening?"

Brigid stared into the fire where the bags had disintegrated beneath red-hot flames. "That's it? Did we just lose our last shot at getting Aurai out of this alive?"

"No." Deme grabbed her sister's hands. "The Chimera won't win. It won't keep our sister. The ingredients are there. We just need to say the spell. Do it now, before the Chimera can stop us!"

"But we don't have Aurai to complete our circle," Gina cried.

Deme turned to Selene. "Can you reach her? Can you call to Aurai and let her know we need her?"

Selene squinted, a frown drawing her brows together. "The other sisters are warning me. They say we are making a mistake."

"We have to get our sister out of there," Deme reminded her. "We have to do whatever it takes."

Selene shook her head. "They want us to leave, to get out now while we can."

The fire behind them flared higher, the heat bearing down on them.

"Bullshit," Brigid said. "We're not leaving without Aurai."

Using her best calm voice when all she wanted to do was scream, Deme entreated her sister, "Selene, ask them to help."

Selene closed her eyes, the frown on her forehead smoothing. "I feel Aurai's presence, and the sisters are here, too."

"About damned time," Brigid muttered. "Let's do it."

With one last look around the garden, Deme searched for the angry vines, sudden tidal waves or flash fires they'd been up against before. Nothing stirred and the fire behind them slowly died.

A stillness settled over the garden, so still not even a cricket dared to chirp.

Slowly at first Deme chanted the spell, her sisters joining in until their voices sounded in unison, growing in strength and determination.

With the strength of the earth
With the rising of the wind
With the calm of the water

With the intensity of fire
With the freedom of spirit
Rise from the darkness
take shape in the light
come to our sisters
bring substance to might."

The four sisters repeated the chant five times. With each repetition, the air around them thickened.

When they finished, Deme said a silent prayer to the goddess and opened her eyes, hoping beyond hope she'd find her youngest sister standing in front of her.

For a long moment, the garden remained still, an energy she couldn't see building, rising in intensity.

Wind blew in from the east and twisted in a circle around the sisters, forming a funnel and rising higher into the night toward the full moon. In the middle of the funnel a ghostly image appeared, a girl in a black robe, with long, flowing blond hair.

"Aurai!" Deme wanted to reach up to grab for her sister, but she couldn't break the ring of truth she and her sisters formed with their hands. All they could do was watch as she rose higher, her image solidifying.

Then the wind died down, lowering the sister until her feet touched the ground.

Aurai's legs crumpled beneath her and she fell in a heap of black robes and blond hair at the sisters' feet.

Deme, Brigid, Gina and Selene broke the circle and rushed forward.

When they gently rolled her over on her back, her eyes blinked open and she whispered, "I knew you would come."

"Thank the goddess, you're okay." Deme hugged her sister, tears running down her cheeks. She couldn't believe it had been as easy as that. All they'd had to do was work a spell and their sister was back among them. She hugged her sister again and sat back to give Brigid and Gina a chance to be with her.

Selene stood back from the group, hovering around Aurai, her eyes wide, her face pale. "Deme."

Deme frowned. "What is it, Selene?"

"We have a problem." She swayed, her eyes blinking closed and open again. "We've made a terrible mistake."

"What do you mean?" Deme rose to join her sister, looping an arm around her shoulders.

Selene shook, her teeth chattering in her head. "We have to stop it."

"Stop what?"

The wind that had delivered Aurai lifted the hair around Deme's face in a gentle fluff. Then it swirled again, twisting around the five sisters on the garden lawn.

"It's coming." Selene stepped back, her face tilting to the heavens. The trees in the garden swayed and lashed out in a frenzy, bending nearly double in the gale-force winds.

Clouds blocked the full moon, darkening the sky. Then they opened up and rain pounded down on the women, hard, heavy drops that slapped against Deme's face, stingingly painful. The rain came in sideways, joining the whirling funnel. The fire Rachel had started flared.

The twisting wind shifted over the flames and added their power to the building tempest. In the midst of the fire, rain and wind, an image grew and grew until it was twice the size of a tour bus.

Deme sucked in a deep breath and let it out. "By the goddess, what have we done?"

Chapter 18

The trapdoor to the tunnels stood open, the vertical tunnel a gaping, dark maw. Someone had gone down recently, might even still be down there.

Cal leaned over the black hole. "Rachel?"

No one responded and he couldn't see anything in the abyss. Without a flashlight, he'd be of no use.

Too much time had passed since he'd last seen Deme. The fool woman wouldn't wait for him to join her before she made her next move against the Chimera. Cal could only hope her sisters would hold her back, talk sense into her—make her wait until he could get to her.

Cal ran up the stairs to the kitchen and searched cabinets, drawers and a broom closet before he located a flashlight that worked. Back down in the basement, he tied the flashlight to his belt loop with a thin strap and climbed onto the ladder.

Although it had been only a couple hours since he'd

been down in the tunnels, it felt like a lifetime. And he didn't want to go down now any more than he had wanted to go then. But he had to suck it up to save Rachel from doing something completely stupid. Having seen what the Chimera was capable of, Cal knew one girl didn't stand a chance against it. Much as he'd rather be with Deme, she would want him to take care of Rachel first.

He lowered himself down the ladder, moving as quickly as possible. When he reached the horizontal shaft, he ran in the direction of the Chimera's lair. He slipped once on crumbled bricks and nearly twisted his ankle tripping over the abandoned railroad tracks. On the final turn toward the foundation to Lion Hall, he saw a light ahead—a woman's body silhouetted by its glow.

"Rachel!"

The figure paused for a moment, and the light bounced away from him. She was running toward the Chimera's lair.

Cal leaped over a rail switch and ran down the tracks, fearing he wouldn't be able to stop her in time.

Halfway to her, a roaring rumble filled the tunnel and the walls trembled. A blast of wind sucked Cal forward, lifting him off his feet. He'd been running full sprint, and with the added force shoving him along, he couldn't slow down fast enough to stop his headlong rush. The ground beneath his feet shifted so sharply, the force threw Cal forward. He tumbled, falling to his knees, rolling head over heels in a painful somersault. The flashlight flew from his hands, light bouncing then blinking out three feet from where Cal came to a jolting landing.

His head throbbed, probably from hitting the train

railing. It hurt to breathe, indicating a bruised or broken rib, and his ankle ached, but he could move. Cal patted the ground in the direction he'd seen the flashlight fall, dust filling his lungs, choking him so badly he had to pull his shirt up over his nose in order to breathe.

So far his fingers found only the ice-cold steel of the train rails and crumbled brick. No flashlight. Without a light to guide him back to the exit, Cal doubted he'd make it. He could be trapped in the dark maze for a long time. No one knew where he was, and he still hadn't reached Rachel. His chest tightened, his breathing labored as he fought a full-scale panic attack. Now wasn't the time to be thinking negative thoughts. He would find the flashlight and he would get himself and Rachel out of this mess so that he could return to Deme.

His fingers closed around a smooth, round cylinder. The flashlight. He picked it up and flicked the switch on and off. Nothing. Frustration raged through him, kicking adrenaline through his veins. "Damn it," he growled. "You're going to work." He slapped the metal tube against his palm and a beam of light flashed across the tunnel.

Dust particles filled the air, reflecting light back into his eyes but not into the distance. One slow, painful step at a time, Cal limped toward the chamber that had once been the foundation of Lion Hall. Blinded by the light reflecting off the dust, Cal could only inch along, checking his footing as he went in case he happened to trip on the woman who'd run from him.

"Rachel?"

When he thought he'd gone far enough to be at the tunnel's end, his foot connected with something soft.

A feminine groan rose up from the ground.

"Rachel?" Cal squatted, cringing as pain shot through his knees and ankles.

"Not Rachel," a lower, familiar voice said.

The woman pushed up into a sitting position and scrubbed the layer of dust from her face. "It's me, Diane Masterson."

Cal reached out to the woman. "What are you doing here?"

She laughed, the attempt bringing on a coughing fit. "I came to kill it."

"Kill what?"

"The beast. I came to kill the beast."

"What do you know about it?" Cal asked. Had Lieutenant Warner filled her in on all the details of what lay beneath campus?

"I know it can't be stopped by just anyone. I know it's evil. I know that it's what raped me thirty years ago." Her words grew louder and faster as tears welled in her eyes and made dirty tracks running down her face. "It ruined my life by impregnating me with a baby. A baby I had to abandon, to throw away because it was so hideous." She buried her face in her scuffed hands, sobs shaking her shoulders. After several seconds, she sucked in a sharp breath, raised her head, her lips pulling back in a sneer. "That beast has to die so that I can live."

Cal placed a hand on her shoulder, not sure what to do to ease the woman's pain. She had seemed so strong, so well put together. For her to fall apart... It shook him to the core. But that didn't get them out of the mess they were in.

"Can you stand?" Cal gripped her arm at the elbow.

"I think so." She reached out for her flashlight and

then leaned on his arm, letting him leverage her to her feet.

"Come on, let's get out of here before the ceilings cave."

"No!" She jerked out of his grip and stepped backward, toward the chamber where the Chimera resided. Her light panned the vast cavern.

The dust had begun to settle and as it did, their flashlight beams revealed...nothing.

Cal moved into the chamber. Only hours ago, it had been a seething mass of impenetrable vegetation. Now it was concrete pillars, pipes, old rail tracks and open space. Complete silence surrounded them, the scuffs of their feet the only sound echoing off the concrete walls.

"It's gone."

"No." Dr. Masterson stumbled forward. "It has to be here. It was here earlier. I could tell by your faces as you emerged from the tunnel. It has to be here."

"It isn't now." In Cal's gut, he knew this. Just as he knew that although it was gone from here, they weren't out of danger. That same gut feeling told him that Deme and her sisters were in more danger than ever before. If he wanted to be there to help defeat the Chimera, he had to get out of the tunnels and back up on campus. "Let's get out of here. The tunnels aren't safe."

"It isn't fair. I've spent the last thirty years living in fear, afraid of my own shadow, sleeping with lights on. Afraid of its return. It can't end like this."

Cal didn't have time to be nice. "Get a grip, Dr. Masterson. If we don't get out of here soon, it won't matter. And there are people I love up there who just might need my help." He gripped her arm and manhandled her toward the tunnel and their exit out of the maze beneath the city.

After they'd traveled several hundred feet, Dr. Masterson pulled out of Cal's grasp. "I can manage on my own." She cinched the belt on her trench coat, the jacket hanging heavy on one side.

Cal didn't have time to contemplate why. He pushed forward. If Dr. Masterson decided to stay behind, he couldn't take the time to drag her along. Deme needed him. He knew this as he knew the sun wouldn't rise in the morning for him if she wasn't in his life anymore. His long strides ate the distance and soon he was back at the ladder, staring up at the small circle of light shining down from the basement.

He turned back to see that Dr. Masterson had managed to keep up with his pace. Her light bobbed along as she hurried toward him.

Without delaying any longer, he tied his flashlight on his belt and grabbed the rungs of the ladder, beginning the long climb upward. The bang of the light hitting the metal rungs and the sound of his breathing getting heavier were the only noises he could make out. He made it to the top in less than five minutes.

"You gonna be all right?" He called down to Dr. Masterson.

"Yeah. Go on. Don't wait for me." She was only halfway up when he turned away from the trapdoor and left the basement.

Deme needs me. The mantra reverberated in his head, setting the pace, pushing him faster. When he burst through the exit doors of the student commons, he was running all out toward the garden.

When the garden came into view, Cal saw Rachel crowded against the gate, screaming through the wrought-iron bars.

He caught her by the shoulders and spun her around. "What's wrong? What's happened?"

"They're in there." Rachel pointed toward the garden.

"Who's in there?"

She shook her head, her gaze darting past him to the sky over the top of the gate. "It'll kill them."

Cal peered through the gate covered completely and held securely by twisted vines.

Wind whipped past him, the moon cloaked by sinister clouds, the light of the city reflecting off their blanketing thickness.

Thunder rumbled and lighting slashed the sky, fingering offshoots that spread out in a thousand different directions. As the thunder died down, an eerie roar started low and built until it made Cal's eardrums burn. He'd heard a similar sound like that in a zoo. The roar of a lion.

Cal ripped his knife from the casing on his belt and cut at the vines. "I...really...hate...vines!" His last word coincided with his final hack, freeing the gate enough that he could push through.

Once inside he passed a stand of bushes and trees to where the lawn opened out in a wide swath between rosebushes. What had been empty minutes before was filled with a monster that consumed the majority of the space between the buildings.

On the other side of the beast, Deme and her sisters crouched low. Only there were five women, one with pale blond hair, pushing up from the ground, her hands and face dirty, her skin white.

The beast reared back on its hind legs, its two massive heads rising as high as the clouds, one a goat with wicked horns, the other a ferocious lion with long, razor-sharp teeth. Its tail whipped around and struck at Cal, the shape of a serpent with the fangs of a pit viper.

Cal leaped backward, the snake's teeth ripping through the thick layers of coverall, missing his skin by a fraction of an inch.

Gina raised her arms to the beast and a wave of water swelled in front of her. Like a tsunami, it bore down on the raging titan. Before it could smash into the creature, the wave twisted and elongated into the shape of a giant paw, and it altered course, swatting Gina, knocking her five feet into the air. She screamed as she sailed across the garden, her cry cut off when she crashed to the earth.

Deme and Brigid advanced on the beast with nothing but their hands and their questionable powers of the pentagram to defend themselves. Deme took no more than five steps before her feet were mired in briars, enveloping her legs like concertina wire, bringing her to a complete standstill.

Brigid moved forward, eyes narrow, palms cupped, fireballs swirling and ready to launch.

She reared back and flung the first one straight at the closest head. The goat opened its mouth and swallowed the fireball.

Without pausing, Brigid launched the second at the lion's head.

It, too, swallowed the fireball. Then at the same time, the two heads shot the fireballs at Brigid.

"Look out, Brigid!" Cal yelled, but the speed was too great. Brigid didn't have time to duck or dodge the attack.

The fiery orbs hit her dead-on, knocking her on her butt and catching her shirt on fire. Brigid crab-walked backward, slapping at the spreading flame. Finally, she rolled over, smothering it out in the grass.

With Gina, Deme and Brigid incapacitated, that left Selene and a weak Aurai standing against the beast that moved toward them.

"Run, Selene," Aurai cried. "Our powers are of no use against it."

Selene stood still, her gaze pinned to the advancing monster, her arms rising out from her sides.

The Chimera roared and reared again, its paws rising above Selene. If it dropped to all fours, it would land directly on top of her.

Cal ran forward, knife drawn, yelling like a banshee.

The snake struck out.

Fast and true, Cal swung his knife, severing the serpent's head.

The lion roared and dropped down, barely missing Selene.

Before the giant could turn, Cal grabbed its mane and hauled himself up onto the demon's back.

The Chimera flung its head back and forth, roaring, angry.

Cal plunged his knife into the beast's neck again and again. The injury didn't seem to have any effect on the beast but to make it more annoyed. Its body twisted and bucked.

Cal felt himself losing grip. He flung his knife down to Deme. "Get out, Deme," he yelled, then he was flying through the air. He hit tree branches, crashing from one to another as gravity brought him down to earth, flat on his back, the wind knocked from his lungs.

For several seconds, he couldn't move, couldn't lift a finger. He just lay there stunned and immobile.

Like a one-woman vigilante, Diane Masterson charged

into the fray, her hair standing on end, tunnel dust covering every inch of her body from hair to feet. She waved a forty-five magnum and screamed like a demented Valkyrie, "Die, you son of a bitch!"

Cal sucked in a breath and yelled. "Get down!"

Aurai tackled Selene, throwing her to the ground.

Deme, having cleared the briars, dove for cover, and Brigid rolled over where she lay as a loud bang ripped the air.

Masterson was flung back, landing hard on her butt.

The Chimera flinched, the bullet having pierced its front shoulder. It reared again, spinning on its hind legs, and landed in front of the college president.

Holding the pistol in both hands this time, Dr. Masterson fired again.

The bullet slammed into the beast's chest, bringing it to a complete halt.

"That's for what you did to me. The creature you impregnated me with. For ruining my damned life!" Tears streamed down Dr. Masterson's face as she raised her weapon again. She pulled the trigger but the gun jammed.

The Chimera growled, a low gurgling sound that made the trees shake.

Diane Masterson tried to pull the bolt back to dislodge the bullet, but it wouldn't budge.

The beast stumbled forward, its lips stretching over fangs the size of butcher knives.

The college president flung the pistol to the side and crab-walked backward, scrambling to get to her feet.

Cal sucked in a deep breath, pulling air into his lungs, finally able to move again. He leaped from the ground and ran for the Chimera.

Deme beat him there. Dodging the beast's massive

paws, she dove beneath it and rolled to her feet directly below its throat. With both hands, she rammed the knife into its jugular, ripping a long gash downward. Blood gushed like a geyser.

The Chimera roared, the sound less menacing, gurgling with the fluid filling its lungs.

With its last breath, the Chimera lurched forward.

Cal dove beneath it, knocked Deme out from under and rolled to the side as the giant crashed to the earth.

Dr. Masterson screamed.

The beast landed on Cal's leg, trapping him beneath a mound of fur and bones.

Deme lay in the grass a few feet away from him. So very still.

Unable to reach her, Cal cried out to her, "Deme!"

For the longest moment of his life, Cal struggled to free his leg, his gaze on Deme.

Then her hand twitched and she moaned.

Cal's eyes misted. Thank God, she was alive. He shoved and pushed, but the weight of the creature pinned him to the ground.

"Let me help." The pale-haired Aurai stood beside him, her hands rising palms upward, her eyelids drifting closed. A gentle breeze lifted the fine strands of her hair, spreading it out to the sides like a cape of gold.

The lifeless body of the Chimera rose from the ground, just enough that Cal could slide his leg free.

His first stop was to check on Deme.

She pushed up to a sitting position. "I'm all right. What about my sisters?"

"I'm good," Brigid called from the other side of the creature's corpse.

"Me, too," Gina said, coming up behind Cal.

"And me." Selene appeared around the side of the Chimera.

"What about Dr. Masterson?" Deme asked.

"Not so good for her." Brigid rounded the front of the beast, carrying a forty-five Magnum pistol. "One of the beast's fangs pierced her heart. Likely she died instantly."

Selene shook her head. "Poor woman. What a terrible truth to live with."

"What did she mean about being impregnated?" Brigid asked.

"I don't know." Deme heaved a weighty sigh. "Now we can't even ask. At least we're all here and alive." She climbed to her feet and gathered her baby sister in a hug. "And you're back."

Aurai laughed. "I was beginning to wonder how long it would take you to find me."

Brigid, Gina and Selene crowded in for a group hug.

Cal took the pistol from Brigid and cleared the misfired round, waiting for the women to finish their reunion hug.

"We wouldn't have found you without Cal's help." Deme opened the circle of sisters and grabbed Cal's arm.

Suddenly he was drawn in and included in the family hug.

Awkward at first, he couldn't help the way his chest swelled. He hadn't felt this loved…well, since his parents passed on. He could easily get used to being a part of this family of sisters.

But for how long would Deme include him? Now that Aurai was safe amongst them, would Deme return to St. Croix?

Cal pulled free of the sisters.

Deme's brow wrinkled and she stared across the top of Aurai's head into his eyes.

"We need to talk," Cal said.

Deme nodded. "Yes, we do. Let's do it now."

With all five sisters staring at him, Cal fidgeted. "Can we go somewhere more private?"

"I share everything with my sisters. Anything we have to say can be said in front of them."

Cal gazed into five pairs of eyes so different from each other, but bearing the same stubborn streak he so admired in Deme. "Okay, then, for starters, you can't go back to St. Croix."

Deme nodded. "Agreed."

"You're staying here close to family. Your sisters need you. You need them and you need me."

"Right." Deme smiled, detangling herself from her sisters' arms and walking toward Cal.

"I don't care how much you like living on a sun-baked island in the Caribbean, you have to come back to Chicago, where I can see you every day."

She walked right into his arms and wrapped her hands around his neck, dragging his mouth close to hers. "I'm with you so far."

"And you can't leave again." He pressed a brief kiss to her lips. "Did I mention that part?" His lips found hers again, taking her mouth more completely.

"I love you, Detective Cal Black. I'm not leaving you ever again. So get used to it."

"I was just thinking how easy it would be to get used to you being around all the time. And I wouldn't mind it if your sisters came to visit us."

"Oh, really?" Brigid stood with her legs parted. "Does that mean you're not going to freak out every time one of us uses our powers?"

Cal's gazed didn't leave Deme's. "I think your powers are what make you special."

Deme smiled up into his eyes. "And here I thought you'd run screaming."

"I don't scream." He kissed the tip of her nose. "I yell on occasion, but I don't scream."

"I'll have a few loose ends to tie up in St. Croix."

"I feel a honeymoon coming on." He kissed her full on the lips, hard and fast, then dropped to one knee.

Selene sighed. "How romantic."

Aurai hugged her brown-haired sister. "I hope we find a man like Cal."

"Not me." Brigid huffed. "Men are overrated."

"Only because you haven't found one who makes your knees weak." Gina backhanded her leather-clad sister in the belly. "Shut up and let him finish."

Deme shot a quelling glare at her sisters and they fell silent.

Cal laughed and took her hand in his. "Deme Chattox, can you find it in your heart to love me as much as I love you? To live with me through thick and thin, through Chimeras and whatever else this crazy world has to throw at us? I live a dangerous life. It can be hard on a woman."

"I'm not just any woman, Cal Black. As you said, I'm special." Deme dropped to her knees and took both of Cal's hands in hers. "But let's be perfectly clear. What exactly are you asking?"

"I'm asking you to marry me and be my partner for life."

Deme sucked in a deep breath and let it out slowly.

Her pause had to be the longest seconds of Cal's life.

Then her eyes shone with moisture that spilled down her face.

For a moment, Cal's stomach clenched.

"By the goddess, if you won't say it, we will." Brigid joined hands with the other four sisters.

"Yes!" The four sisters said in unison.

"Do you mind?" Deme glared at them, then her frown cleared and a smile shone across her face. "In case you didn't get the message, the answer is yes." She closed the distance between them, cupping his face with her hands, and kissed him long and deep.

Cal threaded his fingers through her tangled auburn hair and sealed the deal, his tongue thrusting past her teeth to stroke hers.

"Ahem." Brigid rolled her eyes. "If you two could finish, we might get this place cleaned up and the kids back in time to finish out the semester."

Cal gathered her in his arms and rose to his feet, hugging her tight.

"I'll need to get a job or open another investigation agency," Deme said. "I won't be a kept woman."

Brigid walked by her, tossing over her shoulder, "Or, you can come to work for the Chicago Police Department with me and Cal."

Deme stared up into Cal's eyes. "And investigate things like what happened here?"

"It seems Brigid and I have been recruited for special projects. Lieutenant Warner thinks we have the necessary skills to tackle the weird and unusual."

"Probably because we are weird and unusual." Brigid laughed. "What do you say, sis? Want to work for the city?"

Deme's gaze never left Cal's. "You okay with that?"

"More than okay. It means I get to see a lot more of you."

Deme's smile turned sexy. "Oh, you'll get that as soon as we get back to your apartment."

"Mind keeping it G-rated?" Gina jerked her head toward Aurai. "Child here."

"I'm not a child." Aurai stomped her foot. "I'll be twenty in a couple weeks."

"Sure you can put up with my family?" Deme asked. "I don't plan on running out on them again."

"I'm positive." Cal tipped her head back and kissed her again. "Especially if it means I get to be with you."

When Deme broke the kiss, she looked around at her sisters. Aurai stood nearby, a rumbling sound emanating from her belly. "We need to get Aurai some food."

Aurai laughed, her hand covering her stomach. "I could use a bite."

Selene stood beside the Chimera, her face tipped back, her eyes closed.

"Feel anything?" Deme and Cal walked across the grass to join her.

"They're leaving," Selene said.

"Who?" Gina joined her.

"Our sisters." Selene smiled. "They said thanks for doing what they'd tried to and failed." Selene opened her eyes and stared around at her living sisters. "They need one last favor."

"What's that?"

"To help them dispose of the body."

"Civic-minded of them." Brigid walked across to Selene.

Selene held out her hands.

The sisters came together in a circle beside the Chimera, all closing their eyes and raising their faces to the full moon breaking through the clouds. Their voices rose together into the night.

"With the strength of the earth
With the rising of the wind
With the calm of the water
With the intensity of fire
With the freedom of spirit
The goddess is within us
She is power
We are her
We are one
Blessed Be."

Cal didn't pretend to understand, still mystified by the magic these sisters wielded. He stood by and witnessed the unexplainable union of their spirits.

As they repeated the chant over and over, the Chimera rose from the ground, its massive body appearing weightless in the light from the moon.

The sisters' voices grew softer and softer until they stopped as one.

On the final "Blessed Be," the Chimera's body trembled then shimmered and exploded in a cloud of vapor.

"They're gone." Selene's eyes filled with tears. "I feel empty."

"You have us." Gina slipped an arm around her waist and drew her close.

"And we have Aurai back." Brigid pulled her younger sister into the group hug.

Deme wrapped her arms around them. "We have each other."

Cal stood by, waiting patiently, feeling as if he was spying on a family gathering he wasn't a part of. He hoped to change that soon.

When Deme held out a hand, he smiled. Maybe sooner than he expected. He joined the sisters in the hug. Part of a very unique family, and damned proud of it.

Epilogue

The next day, Cal and Deme met with Lieutenant Warner and Dustin Zoeller at the trapdoor in the basement of the Colyer-Fenton College student commons.

A welder stood by to seal the metal door for good. No student or campus employee would ever descend into the maze of tunnels below the city from this entrance again.

The door stood open for the last time as the welder inspected the hinges and prepared his equipment.

"Deme tell you that she accepted the job?" Lieutenant Warner rocked back on his heels, a grin spreading across his wrinkled face.

"I told him," Deme responded.

Marty patted her on the back. "I think you'll make a great asset to the team."

Cal grinned. "Yeah, she has great assets."

Deme swatted him playfully.

Cal had spent the entire night making love to her. She definitely had assets, every one of which he intended to explore more thoroughly tonight.

"What about the Gamma Omegas?"

"They've had their sorority charter revoked and Zoe Adams was expelled from campus." Deme smiled grimly. "I confiscated the Book of Spells from Zoe's room and, since Rachel stole all of their vials of potion, almost all of the girls have reverted back to normal coeds."

"What about Rachel and her boyfriend?" Cal asked.

"Brigid visited Mike in the hospital. He's out of the coma and Rachel was with him." Deme stared at the welder's back, her mind miles ahead. "Both of them are transferring to a community college to complete their core courses and will probably go on to the University of Illinois to complete their bachelor's degrees."

The lieutenant nodded toward the vertical tunnel leading down into the bowels of the city. "Think we've seen the last of the trouble from the tunnels?"

Deme shook her head. "No."

"What makes you say that? The Chimera is dead."

"Gut feel."

Cal nodded. "I get that feeling, too. I think Chicago has its share of trouble brewing. Will sealing the tunnel stop it?" He shook his head. "Probably not. But then we wouldn't have a job, now would we?"

The lieutenant sighed. "I was looking forward to coasting into a peaceful retirement in a few years."

Cal laughed. "Not a chance. This city has a life of its own."

"You think Dr. Masterson meant anything by what she said about her baby?"

"If it's a monster, I hope she killed the thing. Otherwise, what happened to it?" Cal stared into the darkness of the tunnel.

"I had Brigid do a search on public records of births and had her check hospital records in and around Chicago. No one by the name of Diane Masterson delivered during the year following the rape. If she had a baby, she delivered it somewhere else or at home."

"Think it survived?" Deme asked.

Lieutenant Warner grimaced. "I don't even want to speculate."

The welder closed the trapdoor and set his tools out to begin the welding.

"I think that's our cue to leave." Lieutenant Warner turned. "By the way, good work on getting this case closed and cleaned up."

Despite their vow to act professional in front of the boss, Deme slipped her hand into Cal's. "We had a little help from some sisters."

"See if you can get some more help from them on your next case. I have a file waiting on Cal's desk. Don't wait too long to get started. We've had a number of attacks reported in the past forty-eight hours in downtown Chicago. One in particular stood out."

"What's special about this one?" Deme asked.

"One woman survived long enough to tell the paramedics it was a beast with a man's body and lion's head that attacked her. Maybe this lion creature is Diane Baker's missing son."

Cal looked at Deme. "Let's get to work."

* * * * *

COMING NEXT MONTH
from Harlequin Nocturne®
AVAILABLE NOVEMBER 13, 2012

#149 HOLIDAY WITH A VAMPIRE
**Susan Krinard, Theresa Meyers and
Linda Thomas-Sundstrom**

Three women find out if their vampire lovers are naughty
or nice in this collection of stories. Guaranteed to make
a cold winter's night a little steamier!

#150 SENTINELS: KODIAK CHAINED
Sentinels
Doranna Durgin

In order to save the Sentinels, powerful bear shifters
Ruger and Mariska will have to be more than strong
partners—they'll have to open their hearts.

You can find more information on upcoming Harlequin® titles,
free excerpts and more at www.HarlequinInsideRomance.com.

HNCNM1112

REQUEST YOUR FREE BOOKS!

2 FREE NOVELS FROM THE PARANORMAL ROMANCE COLLECTION PLUS 2 FREE GIFTS!

YES! Please send me 2 FREE novels from the Paranormal Romance Collection and my 2 FREE gifts (gifts are worth about $10). After receiving them, if I don't wish to receive any more books, I can return the shipping statement marked "cancel." If I don't cancel, I will receive 4 brand-new novels every month and be billed just $21.42 in the U.S. or $23.46 in Canada. That's a saving of at least 21% off the cover price of all 4 books. It's quite a bargain! Shipping and handling is just 50¢ per book in the U.S. and 75¢ per book in Canada.* I understand that accepting the 2 free books and gifts places me under no obligation to buy anything. I can always return a shipment and cancel at any time. Even if I never buy another book, the two free books and gifts are mine to keep forever.

237/337 HDN FEL2

Name _____ (PLEASE PRINT)

Address _____ Apt. #

City _____ State/Prov. _____ Zip/Postal Code

Signature (if under 18, a parent or guardian must sign)

Mail to the **Reader Service**:
IN U.S.A.: P.O. Box 1867, Buffalo, NY 14240-1867
IN CANADA: P.O. Box 609, Fort Erie, Ontario L2A 5X3

Not valid for current subscribers to the Paranormal Romance Collection or Harlequin® Nocturne™ books.

Want to try two free books from another line?
Call 1-800-873-8635 or visit www.ReaderService.com.

* Terms and prices subject to change without notice. Prices do not include applicable taxes. Sales tax applicable in N.Y. Canadian residents will be charged applicable taxes. Offer not valid in Quebec. This offer is limited to one order per household. All orders subject to credit approval. Credit or debit balances in a customer's account(s) may be offset by any other outstanding balance owed by or to the customer. Please allow 4 to 6 weeks for delivery. Offer available while quantities last.

Your Privacy—The Reader Service is committed to protecting your privacy. Our Privacy Policy is available online at www.ReaderService.com or upon request from the Reader Service.

We make a portion of our mailing list available to reputable third parties that offer products we believe may interest you. If you prefer that we not exchange your name with third parties, or if you wish to clarify or modify your communication preferences, please visit us at www.ReaderService.com/consumerschoice or write to us at Reader Service Preference Service, P.O. Box 9062, Buffalo, NY 14269. Include your complete name and address.

Special excerpt from Harlequin Nocturne

*In a time of war between humans and vampires,
the only hope of peace lies in the love between
mortal enemies Captain Fiona Donnelly
and the deadly vampire scout Kain....*

*Read on for a sneak peek at "Halfway to Dawn"
by* New York Times *bestselling author Susan Krinard.*

* * *

Fiona opened her eyes.

The first thing she saw was the watery sunlight filtering through the waxy leaves of the live oak above her. The first thing she remembered was the bloodsuckers roaring and staggering about, drunk on her blood.

And then the sounds of violence, followed by quiet and the murmuring of voices. A strong but gentle touch. Faces...

Nightsiders.

No more than a few feet away, she saw two men huddled under the intertwined branches of a small thicket.

Vassals. That was what they had called themselves. But they were still Nightsiders. They wouldn't try to move until sunset. She could escape. All she had to do was find enough strength to get up.

"Fiona."

The voice. The calm baritone that had urged her to be still, to let him...

Her hand flew to her neck. It was tender, but she could feel nothing but a slight scar where the ugly wounds had been.

"Fiona," the voice said again. Firm but easy, like that of a man used to command and too certain of his own masculinity to fear compassion. The man emerged from the thicket.

He was unquestionably handsome, though there were deep shadows under his eyes and cheekbones. He wore only a shirt against the cold, a shirt that revealed the breadth of his shoulders and the fitness of his body. A soldier's body.

"It's all right," the man said, raising his hand. "The ones who attacked you are dead, but you shouldn't move yet. Your body needs more time."

"Kain," she said. "Your name is Kain."

He nodded. "How much do you remember?"

Too much, now that she was fully conscious. Pain, humiliation, growing weakness as the blood had been drained from her veins.

"Why did you save me? You said you were deserters."

"We want freedom," Kain said, his face hardening. "Just as you do."

Freedom from the Bloodlord or Bloodmaster who virtually owned them. But vassals still formed the majority of the troops who fought for these evil masters.

No matter what these men had done for her, they were still her enemies.

* * *

Discover the intense conclusion to
"Halfway to Dawn"
by Susan Krinard, featured in
HOLIDAY WITH A VAMPIRE 4,
available November 13, 2012,
from Harlequin® Nocturne™.

Copyright © 2012 by Susan Krinard

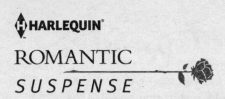

HARLEQUIN®

ROMANTIC
SUSPENSE

Get your heart racing this holiday season with double the pulse-pounding action.

Christmas Confidential

Featuring

Holiday Protector by **Marilyn Pappano**

Miri Duncan doesn't care that it's almost Christmas. She's got bigger worries on her mind. But surviving the trip to Georgia from Texas is going to be her biggest challenge. Days in a car with the man who broke her heart and helped send her to prison—private investigator Dean Montgomery.

A Chance Reunion by **Linda Conrad**

When the husband Elana Novak left behind five years ago shows up in her new California home she knows danger is coming her way. To protect the man she is quickly falling for Elana must convince private investigator Gage Chance that she is a different person. But Gage isn't about to let her walk away…even with the bad guys right on their heels.

Available December 2012 wherever books are sold!

www.Harlequin.com

HRS27801

HARLEQUIN®
Desire

ALWAYS POWERFUL, PASSIONATE AND PROVOCATIVE.

**A brand-new Westmoreland novel
from *New York Times* bestselling author**

BRENDA JACKSON

Riley Westmoreland never mixes business with pleasure—until he meets his company's gorgeous new party planner. But when he gets Alpha Blake into bed, he realizes one night will never be enough. That's when her past threatens to end their affair. So Riley does what any Westmoreland male would do…he lets the fun begin.

ONE WINTER'S NIGHT

"Jackson's characters are…hot enough to burn the pages."
—*RT Book Reviews* on *Westmoreland's Way*

Available from Harlequin® Desire December 2012!

www.Harlequin.com

HD73210BJ